Praise for the first book of
Regency-era

"Dark and passionate. Mack weave[s] . . . hood, and love. Highly sensual an[d] . . . *Times* on WILD: THE PACK OF ST. JAMES

"Encompasses passion, mystery, and magical wonder . . . a delightful read. Exactly the sort of book you can sink your 'reading teeth' into and devour each and every page and still be ready for more."
—*Romance Junkies* on WILD: THE PACK OF ST. JAMES

"This is one hot pack of wolves. The story line will hook you quickly and keep you interested until the last page. The love scenes are scorchers and the climax of the story is incredibly exciting. I cannot wait to read more."—Coffee Time Romance on WILD: THE PACK OF ST. JAMES

And more praise for her novels and novellas of erotic romance . . .

"A sexy romp on the wild side. Compelling characters and chemistry. Mack does an excellent job maintaining sensuality and fire while keeping the reader firmly engaged in the story. Location and theme make this story stand out. A true page-turner."—*Romantic Times* on NIGHTS IN BLACK SATIN, a Top Pick! (4 ½-star review)

"Original and romantic time-traveling fantasy."—*Romantic Times* on Noelle Mack's story in SEXY BEAST II

"Hot sex, humor, and great details about advertising . . . a winner. Sizzling and innovative."—*Romantic Times* on JUICY, a Top Pick! and winner of the 2007 *Romantic Times* Reviewers Choice award for Erotic Romance

"Incredibly sensual and well-done."—*Romantic Times* on Noelle Mack's novella THE HAREM

"Mack does a great job of blending sensuality, sexuality, and humor . . . memorable characters and stories that are romantically satisfying."
—*Romantic Times* on RED VELVET (4-star review)

"A truly sensual story that will titillate and captivate readers."
—*Romantic Times* on THREE (4-star review)

"The queen of seduction meets the king of rakes. Sensual, sexual, stupendous. A truly fabulous erotic romance."—Harriet Klausner Reviews on THREE

Also by Noelle Mack

WILD: THE PACK OF ST. JAMES

JUICY

NIGHTS IN BLACK SATIN

ONE WICKED NIGHT

RED VELVET

THREE

Anthologies containing novellas by Noelle Mack

THE HAREM

PERFECT KISSES

SEXY BEAST

SEXY BEAST II

Published by Kensington Publishing Corporation

WANTON

The Pack of St. James

NOELLE MACK

BRAVA

KENSINGTON BOOKS
http://www.kensingtonbooks.com

for the friendly wolf at the door . . .

1

London, 1816 . . .

Marko was sure he'd fallen in love with her almost against his will. Severin bewitched him instantly. He'd needed an escape, needed the noise and frivolity of a crowded ball. And then he'd seen her . . .

She waited demurely in a corner with downcast eyes, sitting in a chair that he supposed had been brought for her to sit in by some other admirer, who had conveniently disappeared to fetch a glass of punch. Or so he hoped.

Marko sensed she was anything but demure. Her gown was daringly low-cut, made of subtly striped velvet that fell in voluptuous folds beneath her half-bared bosom and looked from a distance like the valuable fur of some rare and dangerous cat. He looked at the hands folded in her lap, and noted that her nails were beautifully shaped and—were they touched with gold? The unusual adornment added to her exotic appearance and was sensual in the extreme. He wanted to kiss each pretty fingertip one by one, feel her gilded nails rake his back . . .

She rubbed one hand absently over the other. He could well imagine being caressed by her. Marko collected himself. He did not want to be caught staring.

"Who is she?" he whispered to Denis, grateful that the youngest man in the Pack, the one they all called the cub, had agreed to come along with him tonight. Of late Denis had cut an amorous swath through the crème de la crème of female London, dark hair pomaded, strong neck dabbed with musky cologne. He represented an extreme of male style but it worked. Denis had to stay a step ahead of a few outraged husbands, who, of course, were unfaithful themselves as a rule. Still, his cubbish interest in who was sleeping with whom, married or not, meant he kept up with the latest London gossip and his information was generally accurate. It worked to Marko's advantage, as he tended to avoid social occasions, not having the time for many.

"I am not sure," Denis said, to Marko's surprise. "She has an odd name—I don't remember it. Not married, as far as I know. And she is not upon the town."

Marko nodded, studying her. "Then what does she do?"

"I believe that she is an arbiter of fashion or something like that. She is not a dressmaker, though—far from it. A friend of mine pointed her out to me once, but I was rather drunk at the time."

"And that is why you don't recall her name."

"Exactly. But I do remember that my friend called her something odd. A mistress of illusion, I believe. Yes, that was what she said."

"How interesting." Marko's curiosity about the self-contained beauty in the corner grew sharper. If only she would look up and let him catch her eye. He needed a pretext to talk to her.

"Do excuse me," Denis was saying.

"Of course."

"Good luck, old man." Denis raised his glass.

Marko scowled at him. He could have done without the "old man." He was not that much older than Denis. But then, he thought with a sigh, Denis was still a cub, for all his sexual adventurousness.

He crossed the room to the woman in the corner. She raised her dark head and gave him a melting look from eyes the color of amber. Marko was mesmerized. There was a knowing quality in her gaze that he found instantly erotic. She was very different from the usual females who infested London balls and assemblies, foolish young things who twittered and blushed, while keeping an eye on the relatives bent on marrying them off. No, she was quite alone, as far as he could tell, not seeming to care about propriety or even the appearance of it.

Yet before he asked her name, he found her so beautiful that he thought he might be dreaming. She was about to speak to him and he watched her extraordinarily sensual lips form two very ordinary words.

"Good evening," she said.

She might as well have been asking him to kiss her. He would have too.

Marko bowed. "Good evening. I have not had the pleasure of being introduced to you. I am Marko Taruskin."

"My name is Severin."

She rose when he asked her to dance, not looking about for the admirer Marko had imagined. He had a feeling at once strange and delightful that he had fallen into a trap.

The music began and the orchestra played a minuet, orderly and precise. All he touched was her hand, but at that moment of connection, a sensation flowed between them that was powerfully sexual.

Going through the figures of the dance, Marko saw only her. Her complexion was as exotic as her gown, a creamy contrast to those dazzling amber eyes. As if to complement them, her amber pendant was nestled between her breasts.

Oh, Wolf above. How he tried not to look at it.

From the chandelier above, the pendant picked up light and cast a golden shadow upon her bosom, a little shadow that looked like a drop of honey. He thought then of how she would look with nothing on but that jewel, her nipples dark and rosy, her beautiful breasts heavy in his hand. He would bend down and apply his tongue to the drop of imaginary honey. Then her nipples. Then her neck.

He would not be satisfied until he could sweep her off her beautiful bare feet and carry her naked to his bed.

Marko realized that Severin was studying him each time her steps turned her to face him.

He managed a polite smile. He lifted his arm for her to pass under and turn again, observing the way the velvet of her gown moved sensually over her hips and legs. It caught the light and emphasized her delectable curves. How long had it been since he'd had a woman?

But Severin was not just a woman—she was closer to a divine incarnation of womanhood, someone a man might worship with his body and his soul. She had entranced him utterly in less than an hour. How she had done it, he could not say.

In his mind, she was naked, dancing just for him in a private chamber to which they had retreated. Not here, in this crowded ballroom, with others looking on, going through the motions of social intercourse, when he longed hotly for quite another kind.

The other women in the room seemed to be noting the details of her gorgeous attire, but the men knew how to see beneath. They looked at her again and again. Avidly.

He would willingly battle them all just to have her. Just for one night.

No, that would not be enough. He vowed not to let her go after this dance. He would find out more about her, where she lived, why she had come here alone—she had to have come alone. The admirer he'd imagined did not exist. No one had tapped him on the shoulder or called him out.

For now, she was his to dance with. He wanted more.

Her swirling gown brushed against his legs, ever so lightly but repeatedly, exciting intense desire. Marko gritted his teeth. He caught a glimpse of himself in the mirrors that lined the ballroom walls. His expression would pass for a half-smile. He dared not look lower.

No one else seemed to care. The glittering company moved through the steps of the dance. Other women wearing gowns in hues as light as spring flowers shone in their way, but none was as dazzling as Severin. The men partnering them shot envious glances at Marko. The patterns of the minuet intersected and separated them all upon the floor.

If everyone else had vanished at that moment, Marko would have been sublimely happy. He could ask her to come away with him without fear of being overheard, without exposing her to the censure of other women.

Ah, if they could be alone and somewhere else. A room just for them, with a fine, four-postered bed. He would bury himself between her fine thighs, hold on for dear life to the rounded cheeks of her beautiful arse while he thrust deep within her body . . . again and again . . .

"The music has stopped," she said, executing a final pirouette and looking up at him.

Marko didn't let go of her hand. "So it has." He willed his erect flesh to subside and kept her in front of him as he guided her from the dance floor. The exchange of pleasantries with other guests was an excruciating necessity.

He contrived to dance with her again, several times, and allowed no other man to get closer. He plied her with champagne—had they had one bottle or two? He did not remember that detail. At last he maneuvered her into a quiet corner and begged her to come away with him.

To his joy, she agreed, flirtatiously and tipsily. He'd told the driver, who discreetly ignored Severin, to just drive. They could decide upon their destination in time. Rolling away from the ball as the other guests departed, leaning back in the carriage that had waited for him, Severin's face was flushed and her eyes were sparkling. He told himself not to take advantage of her at that second she murmured the words he wanted most to hear.

"Kiss me, Marko."

He needed no further encouragement. He pulled her into his lap, enjoying how her backside pressed into his lap with each jounce over the cobblestones. The horse trotted briskly when the street was smoother, and the carriage swayed a little from side to side.

He held her in his arms, running his hands eagerly over every part of her body he could reach, giving her enough room to rock with the motion of the carriage while he kissed her. Her lips were hot and the inside of her mouth, silky wet. Her tongue teased his and then she nipped his lower lip.

"I love to make love in a carriage. It has been far too long since I . . . oh, never mind. I am here with you and that is all that matters."

"Have you no lover then?" Marko murmured. "It seems hardly possible that a woman like you would not."

"No."

Marko pulled up the velvet folds of her gown, pushing it back to reveal her bare thighs. "Marvelous stuff, this. As soft as your skin, I suspect."

And he very much desired to find out just how soft that was.

Severin sighed when his hand settled upon one thigh, curving around it in firm possession. His other hand gripped her waist, keeping her on his lap, her head nestled against his shoulder. "Don't stop," she breathed in his ear. "I love to be stroked on the inside of my thighs."

"Do you now." He obliged. Her skin there was unbelievably soft, far softer than the luxurious velvet that had hidden it.

Marko traced his fingertips up, feeling first one thigh and then the other, savoring the heated fragrance of an excited woman. No perfume on earth compared to it.

Severin parted her legs to allow him more room. Great Wolf, if she didn't stop squirming and rubbing all over his lap, he was likely to explode. He didn't want to touch the sweet, soft flesh between her legs just yet. No, he would save that ultimate intimacy for later.

To have her open to him this much was intensely sensual. That he did not know her added spice to the unexpected encounter. He would need every bit of what was left of his self-control not to move her off his lap and lean her back against the cushions.

"You've stopped," Severin moaned softly in his ear. "Why? I liked what you were doing."

"And so did I. You are so beautiful, Severin," he murmured. "And shameless." His exploring fingers moved just a little higher.

She slipped a hand inside his coat, touching his tight nipples under the linen of his shirt.

Marko drew in his breath. She knew what she wanted—and she knew what men liked.

Her expertise became more evident when she moved her hand over the front of his breeches, rubbing and squeezing the stiff rod trapped within.

She murmured naughty things in his ear. How much she wanted to see what she could guess at was the least of it.

Marko moved her hand to the buttons at one side. "All shall be revealed," he whispered.

One by one, she undid them, single-handed, with great dexterity. He cared not where she had learned to be so wanton—he only wanted to receive pleasure from her experienced hands.

She dragged her gold-tipped nails over the taut flesh of his groin. The stimulating effect went straight to his cock, which was still trapped beneath the flap of his breeches. She had undone only the buttons on one side.

The pressure was agonizing, although she had moved to the side to help free his eager flesh. Severin settled herself beside him and undid the other buttons.

There. He groaned. His cock rose up of its own accord. She took him in her soft fingers and gently stroked the heated shaft, searching for his mouth with her own, kissing him tenderly.

Marko scarcely knew where he was at that moment. In heaven or about to be, he thought vaguely.

He reached over to cup her breasts within the velvet bodice. Her nipples were erect and easy to feel in his cupped palms.

He squeezed both breasts as gently as she was handling him, following her lead. If, later, she wanted him to be a little rougher, pleasuring her darker needs with love bites and firmer handling, he would do that.

For now, as aroused as he was, it was best to go slowly. He thrust his tongue into her mouth, kissing her lasciviously. He broke off only to breathe. "Severin . . . I wish I could rip this damned dress to pieces."

She laughed a little. "But then we would not be able to leave the carriage."

"Must we leave it?"

"Do you not want to lie with me, Marko?"

He wanted nothing more. At last, by a stroke of luck he would never understand, he had found a woman whose talent for amorous play went beyond his wildest dreams. Consumed by lust though he was, Marko knew that there was far more to Severin than that. He would never get enough of her. In just one night—and the night was far from over—his world had been turned upside down.

Eventually, he answered her question with sensual strokes and loving murmurs. "Yes. Yes." She responded in kind. He could love her, he thought, befuddled. Surely the intensity of everything he was feeling, even its suddenness, was a sign of that celebrated emotion. They were off to a wonderful start.

Marko trusted his instinctive response. Dimly he remembered Kyril telling him that one just knew when the love of one's life appeared, because there was nothing else like it. The body echoed the joy of the soul at that moment.

The carriage began to slow and Marko groaned, stiff all over with the aching need he felt for her.

"Where are we?" she asked softly. Severin pulled down her dress and patted her hair, breathless with excitement. "I am not fit to be seen."

"I disagree."

She moved away but she shot him a sensual look. It was clear that she was as thrilled as he was by the dizzying progress of their encounter. The odd feeling of déjà vu that had followed his first look into her eyes had been a sign of sorts. Marko was almost convinced that the mysterious Severin could be his one and only.

To join completely with her would naturally come next. He was drunk with new love and just able to keep from declaring the unexpected feeling then and there. He did not really know her. He wanted to, he would, but it would not do to rush that either.

She pushed aside the curtain that covered the small window of the carriage, and looked out.

He noted how her face had changed when the carriage came to a sudden stop. Had the sudden jolt brought her to her senses? Her rosy cheeks paled and the radiance in her eyes vanished. Marko leaned over, wondering if she had seen some swaggering ne'er-do-well who frightened her. The street was empty but it was familiar, at least to him. The driver had brought them to St. James's Square and the house of the Pack, evidently tired of going in circles.

"Is this where you live?" There was a wary edge in her soft voice.

He thought nothing of her question. There were at least a thousand buildings just like it in the better neighborhoods of London, remarkable only for their anonymity. Which was precisely why the Pack had made it their headquarters—that, and its nearness to the Court of St. James. As well, its thick walls made it ideal for a lair, when they were in the mood for a Howl, the traditional celebration of the Pack, or just a wild party. "At times, Severin. Not always. The driver came here out of habit."

She only nodded, pushing the curtain back a little more to look far up at the top windows of the house.

Marko sat back and fumbled with his buttons, willing his overexcited cock to soften. In another minute, he managed it. He could hear the horse stamp upon the cobblestones. Before long he would have to decide where they would stay the night, most likely at a hotel. Not here. And they could not stay forever in the carriage and expect the unwilling horse to trot through the streets of London indefinitely.

Severin sat back from the window. "That man—who is he?"

Marko craned his neck. So she had seen someone at a window. It must have been Feodor, who was now coming down the front steps of the house—but why would he have frightened her? The man was not a full-blooded member of the Pack and did not possess the masterfulness they prided themselves on. If anything, he was ordinary, except for his odd yellow eyes. Marko had no wish to talk to him at the moment.

"A distant cousin of mine. Feodor Kulzhinsky."

Severin seemed uneasy. "And he lives here?"

"The house belongs to my family. All of us are free to come and go."

She seemed to be studying Feodor, who strolled away. Excellent. A tedious explanation would not need to be made, Marko thought. Feodor could be inquisitive and might be especially so under the circumstances. Of course, Marko had never brought a woman to the house, although he had been advised that his cousin had sneaked a few by the major d'omo, and that they were not the sort of females that required introducing or expected politesse. Feodor had low tastes.

"I cannot stay the night with you," Severin said suddenly.

"What? But we don't have to stay here, my dear—"

She smiled a little wistfully. "I am sorry, Marko. Please take me to my house."

"But—" He fought for self-control. Severin had aroused him to fever pitch and suddenly she wanted nothing to do with him. What had cooled her ardor?

She sat back. "Now."

Mystified, Marko studied her, half-wild with sexual frustration. "Very well," he said. "But you will have to tell me where that is."

She gave him the address. He hoped it was the real one.

It had been. In the ensuing weeks, he'd been permitted the liberty of calling upon her there, if nothing else. They conversed often, sexually charged but outwardly sedate sessions that drove him half-mad with desire for her.

As for the rest of it—the ridiculous emotions, overwhelming feelings that he had mistaken for love—well, she had dazzled him. To some degree, he felt he'd been played for a fool, but it could happen when a man was not on his guard.

As to who would have the upper hand in their love affair, Marko realized two could play at being mysterious. He would provide tidbits of information, mostly misleading, about the Pack if she should ask. He would never give away all.

As far as the mystery of Severin herself, his connections insisted that she was not a courtesan and never had been, only that she was employed by the best of them and aristocratic ladies as well, keeping her clients in the height of fashion. Other than that, there was very little gossip about her, good or bad.

It occurred to him that he had come too close to her somehow during the night of the ball and the carriage ride afterward. No wonder she had become suddenly skittish and refused to stay. By caressing her beautiful body with all the expertise he possessed, he had managed to storm her heart as well. Her surprise at his doing so had been genuine.

There was certainly something between them. Call it animal attraction. Her sensuality could very well be her undoing, if he had his way. Marko knew that Severin desired him. Her amber eyes glowed brightly when they merely talked—he knew what the light in them signified. Without intending to, she had given her innermost self away to some degree in the carriage.

Since then, her body—the way she leaned toward him, came a trifle too close—had seemed to promise much, but they were not progressing on that front. She would not say yes and she would not say no. Very well. He might have to help her arrive at a decision somehow where sex was concerned. He felt that she owed him, ungentlemanly and rude as it was. If love had nothing to do with her desire, then he could live with that. Lust would do.

A bribe and a bottle of good port for her manservant would smooth the way to bliss. Failing that, he could go to her house and demand that she see him—no. He would just walk in . . .

The last chord died away and Marko heard the almost noiseless click of a piano lid closing. Severin had played beautifully, soulfully, quite unaware that he listened unseen. She sighed and put the sheets of music in order before she rose, pushing back the padded bench with a faint scrape.

He heard the questioning meow of Severin's cat, following her mistress about the adjoining chamber. Silk skirts rustled over polished floors. Then Severin swept through the double doors that led to her bedroom and stopped, her lips parting with surprise. "What are you doing here?"

Her glorious eyes moved over his body in a sensual way. It was the one response she could not seem to control around him. Good. He had hoped for that.

"Waiting for you," Marko said nonchalantly. Would she shriek? Have him thrown out? He was prepared for anything.

Severin glided past the bed on which he lay, stopping in front of the looking glass on her lace-topped dresser. "But it is the end of the day and I was about to take my bath. And I do not remember inviting you."

He stayed where he was, but his heart beat faster as she began to take down her hair, looking at the reflection of him in the silvery glass, her back to him.

"No, you didn't."

"Then how did you get in?"

Marko shrugged. He was quite at his ease stretched out on her featherbed, luxuriously so, in fact. He rolled to his side, bracing himself with one arm and letting the other rest on his side. "I let myself in. Your manservant did not hear my knock and I tried the knob. The door was unlocked. I heard the music playing and decided to enjoy it from in here."

"I see." Her tone made it clear that she didn't believe one word of his explanation. "How indiscreet. Anyone could have seen you enter unannounced."

"Would you rather I used the trellis or the balcony, Severin?"

She laughed a little. "Do you wish to play a romantic hero? You are well suited for the role."

"No. Not in that way. In any case, it is raining. The front door seemed much easier."

"Oh?" Severin gave an unladylike snort. "I imagine my man was easy to bribe, too."

"I did not have to."

Her gleaming hair rippled over her bare shoulders. He longed to bury his face in its fragrant softness and forget about the world, be consumed by the heat of his passion for her. Severin's nearness sent a thrill through his body. He wanted to kiss her madly, but he stayed where he was. She turned to face him, putting her hands on her hips and looking him over.

Marko could almost feel her gaze upon him. He was nearly as aroused as if she had touched him. Since he was fully dressed, from his fitted half-coat to the breeches tucked into his high boots, the sensation was not comfortable. He drew up one leg and bent his knee to conceal his physical reaction to her hot-eyed study of his body.

"Boots in the bed?" she murmured. "How uncivilized of you."

"I could not very well strip, Severin. You might have screamed when you saw me."

She permitted herself a small smile. "I don't think so. I have seen you naked before."

"Not all the way." He remembered their first encounter in his carriage with renewed chagrin.

Her eyes glowed with amusement, much to his irritation. "Nearly. But I was not ready."

"Are you ready now?"

The question was bold, but she was bolder. Severin sat on the bed and leaned over him. He restrained himself from running his hands through her hair, even though soft tendrils brushed his face.

"Yes," she said. And then she kissed him. *That* they had done, but—

Marko could not hold back another second. His arms went around her and he rolled her over until he was on top, pressing her down.

Her lips parted and her eyes shone with desire as strong as his own. He kissed her neck, then felt something touch his cheek. It was a pendant, a drop of amber set in gold. The fine chain it hung from had come unclasped.

Marko captured the pendant before it rolled away, preventing the chain from tangling in Severin's tumbled hair. The gem was as smooth and warm as her skin.

"It is my talisman," she said softly. "Look closely. There is a flaw in it that looks like an eye."

He closed his fingers over the heavy drop of amber. "I would just as soon not be watched, if you don't mind."

Severin laughed in a low voice. "Then put it away."

Marko found a small pocket that usually held a watch and tucked the pendant and the chain in there without another thought, going back to kissing her. Severin moaned into his mouth as he caressed her breasts, arching her back, almost shoving her body into his exploring hands.

So she too had held back. The knowledge pleased him.

She was unfastening her bodice, revealing her breasts. Her nipples were dark, tightened with arousal.

No doubt she craved a good sucking on both. He fastened his lips upon one and rolled the other between his fingertips. It was exciting to make love to her when she was nearly dressed. He might want to keep her that way, at least for a little while.

Severin took hold of her skirts and lifted the rustling stuff over her knees.

She was utterly beautiful and wanton. No, he wanted her just as she was, a flower of silk with those lavish skirts pulled up and spread around her bare legs.

Marko sucked her nipples in turn, and stroked the rounded thighs that she allowed to fall open. Because they were on a bed and not in a closed carriage, she could open them very wide.

His fingertips trailed from her knee, moving several inches up from there. But as he had done then, he did not touch the juicy flesh between them. He looked forward to witnessing her complete sexual excitement.

Marko nuzzled her neck, letting her rub her bare breasts and hard-sucked nipples against his shirt. She gave little cries of pleasure and tugged at his coat.

He rose halfway and dragged it off, flinging it across the room.

Severin swiftly undid the tie at his neck, parting his shirt fronts and sliding her hand inside to touch his chest. She seemed to enjoy the light tickle of the hair upon it, and the Wolf knew how much he enjoyed feminine nails lightly scratching at his sensitive nipples.

Her hand moved down to his waist to draw his lower body closer, but her voluminous skirts got in the way. Well, he might have to undress her completely after all. But not just yet.

Her dress would be crumpled just from their kissing, but he had a feeling she would not mind in the least. He wanted to remove every article upon her with sensual thoughtfulness.

She still had on her pretty embroidered shoes and stockings that stopped at the knee. He had touched the garter of one stocking but not undone it.

He struggled away from her, eager to prolong her pleasure and his own. One might make love with one's eyes. Studying the beauty of Severin's body, even letting her tease him by taking off her clothes herself before he continued to touch and stroke and lick—it would be a very great pleasure.

"Where are you going?" she asked.

"Nowhere," he replied, sitting back on his haunches. "I only want to look at you like this."

"As on the night we met," she murmured. "I left you so frustrated—"

He patted her thigh. "Never mind that."

Marko got off the bed and shucked most of his clothes at last, keeping his drawers on. She kicked off her shoes, laughing when he caught each one, and unrolled her stockings. "You will have to help me with this dress," she said.

"Roll over."

She did and he undid the fastenings at once. She could feel his hot breath on her bare back as he pushed the sides of the gown away from her body. She wore no corset.

"Roll over again. I mean, roll off the dress." She did and he whisked it off the bed and away, tossing the crumpled silk into a heap upon the floor. "Ah. You are as beautiful as a nymph."

Severin looked at him, as if, naked, he was glorious. All it would take is one touch, he thought wantonly. Her fingers. Her mouth. I will not be able to control myself. Her gaze moved up and she looked longingly into his eyes.

"Not yet, Severin," was all he said.

She was eying him with sensual hunger. Stripped bare by him, lying upon her bed, his to take . . . ah, she was pouting. Actually pouting. Marko was delighted.

"Not yet?" she asked. "Then when?"

"I think that we should take our time."

"Bah."

Marko smiled slyly. "I believe you mentioned something about a bath. We could start with that."

She floated in the hot water, blissfully relaxed. He watched, running a hand through the water now and then and letting it dribble over her belly and breasts.

To be bathed by him was incredibly sensual. She wanted to make it last forever.

Severin tipped her head back and let her tangled hair soak in the water, closing her eyes. She felt a large male hand slide under her back and lift her gently after a minute.

The hand worked creamy liquid into her hair and separated the tangles. She kept her eyes closed, letting the water and cream run in rivulets down her back. He soaked a washcloth in the bathwater and cleaned the excess from her face so she could open her eyes.

Oh my. He was almost too beautiful to look at. His linen drawers were splashed and clung to his thighs in places.

The cream had splashed on the fine, dark hair on his muscular forearms, and one hand was still covered with it. He smoothed that one carefully over her head.

"Do I look like a wet cat?" she asked dreamily. "Bedraggled and miserable?"

"You look beautiful, Severin. And very happy."

"Liar."

Marko grinned. "Give me a spoonful of truth and then we will see if I am lying."

"Maybe later."

His creamy hand moved down her back. "Lie down again."

He supported her as she did, and Severin arched her back even more, tipping her chin to the ceiling to get her hair completely under the water. Her lips had to part in this position and she gave a little groan of satisfaction . . . and then, through the walls of the marble tub, heard an answering growl.

She had noted that animal quality in him, found it wildly attractive. Yet his ministrations were as tender as a woman's. His hand continued to comb through her hair. The strands were free of each other at last, the snarls undone by the special cream. He used his fingers to gently massage her scalp and Severin arched even more.

Her breasts rose out of the water and she felt a chill tighten the flesh of her nipples.

Then she felt Marko's mouth come down on one . . . and suck . . . and then . . . he sucked the other. Just her nipples. Clean and tight. The rest of her was soapy or creamy.

He lifted his head and she heard him heave a sigh that was pure lust. Severin let him lift her. She felt boneless. The size of the tub allowed her to float. It was fit for a harem, an unusual luxury for London.

He put both his big hands on her head and pressed out the water. "There. Your eyes look huge when your hair is back like that, Severin. And how they glow. Your wet eyelashes are so pretty."

"You can find nothing wrong with me. You are better than a mirror."

"Do you want to look in one?"

"No," she said hastily. He might think her beautiful, but feminine standards were higher.

She looked at him, feeling purified. She suspected, however, that his thoughts were anything but pure at the moment. Sitting on a low stool, his long legs folded at the knee, he could not conceal the massive erection in his knee-length drawers.

Ah. How wonderful to see him stripped down. Fine leather breeches were not made to withstand bathwater.

The drawers were made of linen that creased where he creased. They cupped his balls just so. His cock had risen well up within them, almost lying against the very inside of his thigh. She could see the dark curls all that glorious male flesh sprang from right through the linen.

Marko looked down. "I cannot help it."

Severin savored his embarrassment. It was one thing to be an angel of mercy, but it must be quite another to have to care for her with a rod that size getting in the way.

"You are forgiven," she said.

He stood up and adjusted his various parts so that he could sit comfortably.

Shamelessly, Severin watched. Her hesitancy had vanished utterly from her mind the second she'd seen him lying sprawled on her bed. And now she got to look at him in nothing but a wet shirt and drawers. Bare-legged and barefooted. His hair tousled from the heat and moisture in the air.

And he was so hard.

She wanted more. Severin took the soap and rubbed it over her breasts, although they were perfectly clean. She squeezed the bar a bit too hard and it shot out of her hand, landing on the floor.

He reached for it.

"Never mind. I have enough." She made a good lather and lavishly caressed both breasts with it. His eyes were riveted on what she was doing. She closed her eyes and purred as she lathered up more, lifting her breasts and pressing them back against herself. Then she opened her fingers over them and captured each nipple between her middle fingers and forefingers.

Again she squeezed and rubbed. She looked down at her nipples and not at him. Severin was sure he liked to think of women pleasuring themselves alone.

Her soap-tipped nipples stood out between her sliding fingers. Up and down. Then around. And again.

Marko gasped, as if the erotic sight were too much for him. Then he leaned forward and placed his hands over hers.

Her fingers kept the nipples up. His palms stimulated the tips. Together they rubbed. Severin lifted her head and he captured her lips in a kiss, thrusting his tongue deeply into her mouth. She moaned around it. A deep pulsing began low in her belly.

She was going to come. Her own skillful stimulation of her breasts, the sliding tightness of her fingers around her erect nipples, and his palms, circling, exciting the very tips she presented to him . . . ohhhh.

He knew she was experiencing orgasm. He did not alter his subtle attention to her sensitive flesh, but his kissing intensified.

Severin moaned, long and low, letting the waves of pure pleasure course through her entire body. Oh dear God . . . ohhhh . . . it felt so wonderful . . .

She let go of her breasts at last and her hands dropped into the water. He laughed, a deep, sensual, very male laugh, and splashed the soap off her breasts.

They gleamed, water dripping off the elongated nipples, and she laughed with him. Then she glanced down.

The front of his drawers was soaked with jism. He shook his head. "I came when you did."

"Without touching yourself?"

"My hands were on you, Severin. And so were my eyes. It was more than enough."

"Take them off."

He stood and gingerly peeled off his drawers.

"You might as well throw them in the tub."

"Thank you," he laughed. "I feel privileged to have such a beautiful laundress wash my dirty drawers for me."

"They are not dirty—it is only come. But I didn't say I would wash them. No, this tub is big enough for two. Climb in."

She leaned back as he lifted one big leg and set a foot down carefully in the tub. She couldn't resist what she saw and reached up to stroke his balls, heavy and round.

"Like the low-hanging fruit, do you?"

Severin sat up and gave him a nuzzle there before he could get his other leg over. "It is the sweetest," she said and pressed a kiss to his thigh for good measure. Then she let him get in.

"Ahhh," he said. Their legs tangled and their feet bumped but they figured it out. "Still hot, I see." He reached down between his legs and adjusted himself again.

"It is your turn," Severin said.

"For what? I have already come."

"I want to do what you have done for me, Marko. You need to be washed all over and scrubbed and—"

Severin almost said *loved*. She gazed at him with shimmering eyes and he returned her look without speaking. Then he handed her a washcloth.

"Have at," was all he said. "I'm yours."

Within another hour, they were in bed. She was sitting up, resting her fine bare behind on a pillow. Between her widely spread thighs was her sweet, freshly washed cunny, plump as a peach, swollen with sexual excitement.

He craved a taste of it.

Marko kneeled in front of her on the bed and nuzzled her neck, letting her rub her bare breasts and sucked nipples against his chest. She gave little cries of pleasure and tugged at his earlobes.

He muttered his appreciation into her mouth, then pulled away a little. "Spread your legs more," he said roughly.

She put her hands on her thighs and stroked them, wiggling to show herself better. Her action made a fine display of her tight cunny and her willingness excited him. It was unlike her. And then he whispered. "Touch yourself there, Severin. As if you had just come home from—from a ball and found yourself aroused by your partner. You need to be satisfied right away."

"Yes," she murmured. One of her hands moved to her cunny and he stiffened with excitement when she slipped two fingers into her slit.

"Go ahead," he whispered into her ear. "Show me how you pleasure yourself when there is no one to see."

Her eyes drifted half-closed. Almost lazily, Severin stroked in between the plump halves of her cunny, thrusting in to make her fingers slick again.

Marko took her wrist and brought her hand to his mouth, licking each fingertip just as he had wanted to do when he'd first seen her. They were not gilded now, but if anything, they were prettier.

Flushed pink. Tasting of the sweet female flesh they had touched. He sucked on her fingertips and Severin moaned. She rose slightly, then sprawled back upon the bed, completely supported and comfortable.

Marko brought the hand he was holding to one of her breasts and rested it there, then did the same with the other.

"Tease your nipples while I taste your clit," he told her huskily. "You and I both know how good it will feel."

He waited to see her begin, and slid his hands under her bottom. The abundant flesh filled his palms and he squeezed each cheek in sensual rhythm before he went down on her.

Severin tugged fiercely at her nipples. He alternated the squeezes, then did both sides of her arse at once. She was literally in his hands, wriggling with wanton pleasure.

He leaned forward and sought out her clit with a probing tongue, teasing it up from the surrounding flesh. Flicking it.

The sensation made her thrust up in tiny pushes. He touched his tongue to her clit each time and kept on squeezing her behind in his strong hands.

Severin moaned too loudly and he stopped, sliding his hands out from under her arse, then sitting up and wiping his mouth. "Not yet, Severin. You have already come once. You are a greedy one, my girl."

"Ohhhh . . ."

Severin looked at him. The massive cock that she had handled so freely before stood straight up and the heavy balls beneath it were drawn against his body.

Marko quickly encircled it with one hand, drawing down the foreskin and releasing the head. Her eyes widened at the sight of the pearly drop that trembled on it. She knew there was more, far more, where that single drop had come from, even though just looking at her had made him soak his drawers with jism. She wanted all of it, in hot jets. In her. On her.

She stayed where she was on the bed, reaching out to him.

On all fours, he moved over her, letting her rub her bare breasts with his cock. Shamelessly, she trapped the shaft between them, squeezing the soft flesh in precisely the rhythm he had employed to stimulate her buttocks.

Marko gasped. She continued to press and rub, tipping her head up. Her tongue just reached his nipples. They were too flat to suck but she could flick at them. And she did.

He reached down and cupped his hands over hers. Severin continued to excite him, knowing he wanted to savor it, knowing he loved having his big rod enfolded in a woman's full breasts.

She pushed his hands gently away as she let go. Released, his cock bobbed in midair. Severin put out her tongue and licked the hole in the tip as precisely as he had licked her clit.

Marko only pretended to be made of sterner stuff than she. He was a man like any other. He moaned with enjoyment.

"How do you want me?" she asked boldly. "On my back now? On all fours?"

He growled, "Both."

"Which one first?"

"As you are. On your back."

Severin lifted her legs and held them far apart with her hands. Letting him see everything a man might want to see. With another growl, a deeper one, he clasped an ankle and then the other, lifting the lower half of her body from the bed.

Severin clutched the sheets. What she was about to get, she didn't know, but she was ready for anything.

With one big hand, he managed to hold both her ankles. Two fingers of the other slowly penetrated her cunny. Severin cried aloud, enjoying the vigorous but gentle thrusting. He would have been too big for her otherwise and his amorous preparation would serve them both well.

Breathing hard, Marko wiped his slick fingers carelessly on

his thigh as he set her down. Severin knew exactly what she was getting next.

A beautiful man on top of her, naturally dominant. Her secret dream come true.

And he had come prepared. Marko turned to find his clothes again and retrieved a condom folded inside a paper from some hidden place. He unrolled it as she watched, handling the thin membrane carefully as he slid it over his massive rod.

"You are a gentleman."

He looked up from his sensual task. "You are worth it."

Marko slid over her in another second and Severin grasped his cock to guide him in. Their eyes met. Something in his look made her shiver. With pleasure. And also with an edge of fear.

She positioned the head at her cunny and he thrust in with a sound that was almost a roar. He was huge. She was eager—and ready. She pushed her hips to take it all.

Marko fucked her sweet and slow, reaching down to grip the condom and keep it on. That he would bother with one meant a great deal to her. She had been so aroused, she almost had not cared, and had not asked him to come outside her body.

He had been ahead of her on that. Ah, he was a man she could love . . . Severin reached around him to stroke his back, then let her hands move down to his buttocks. They clenched with every stroke and she grabbed them, holding on tight, pulling him still deeper within her until he moaned.

"No . . . not yet . . . no!"

Marko pulled out of her. Severin reached up to him but he was too tall for her to easily capture. "What is it?"

"I said I wanted you both ways," he said, his voice raw with desire. "Get on all fours."

Severin was happy to do his bidding. He positioned himself this time, taking a little time to catch his breath before the first thrust in this new position.

This time he did not move slowly. She could feel his fingers encircling the base of his cock, hanging on to the condom for dear life as he fucked her with wild abandon.

Severin put her head down and reached back, teasing her clit, stroking his slick balls. Marko's whole body was shaking. The smooth, extremely deep thrusts, the balls that touched her fingertips when she slid her fingers over her clit had her crazy with pleasure. She cried his name over and over as she came, and he was—yes—right behind her. He let go of his cock and grabbed the front of her hips with both hands, not thrusting, staying rammed all the way inside to feel her pulse around him, giving it to her all the way, almost lifting her off the bed.

Marko howled when his orgasm hit. The sound was primitive, more animal than human.

Slowly, slowly, almost sobbing, he came back to being a man again. He pulled out and collapsed on the bed. Spent. Sweating. Blissful. The condom had miraculously stayed on.

Severin marveled at him. Even when he was trembling, Marko looked powerful. She wiped the sweat from his brow and blew gently on his furry chest to cool it.

Eyes closed, he growled his thanks.

It was odd how like an animal he could seem, but he was very much a man. A glorious, incredibly sexual man.

Not her man, though. Her conscience pricked her. She had only lain with him to satisfy her physical needs, she told herself. At least at this most vulnerable of moments for both of them, she did not have to look into his eyes.

An unexpected wave of tenderness for him nearly made her cry.

Not yet, Severin, she told herself fiercely. Not yet.

2

The next day . . .

Seduction. There *was* an art to it. A woman who wished to in-
trigue a man must present herself just so, preferably seated, her
pale hands curved in a silken lap and her hair swept up with artful carelessness as if a lover's hands could easily let it down. Her
smooth neck ought to curve submissively, adorned with only a
ribbon or a thin chain. A poor beauty could forgo both and
make do with a spiraling kiss-curl, perhaps. But rich or poor,
her gaze must be demure and downcast, the brilliance of her
eyes shadowed by the gentle angle of her head . . . followed by
a raising of her pretty chin and a heated look upward, lasting no
longer than a fraction of a second, through long eyelashes.

There was no man approaching and they were not in a ballroom, but Miss Georgina Lennox managed the trick well
enough on her third try. Severin studied her pupil. At nineteen,
Georgina did not possess the porcelain-doll beauty of her
mother Mary, an actress, but she had potential, fortunately.
Mary herself had just married an elderly earl, who'd requested

that Georgina, an inconvenient reminder of his wife's wayward past, be married off as soon as possible. He'd let it be known that a handsome dowry would be settled on the girl.

The new-minted countess, grateful for her escape from the creaking, dusty boards of a Covent Garden theater and sudden elevation to ladyhood, was watching.

"Georgina, you are a gawk," she said to her daughter. She nodded at Severin. "But she is coming along. It is good of you to take her on."

Severin only inclined her head, not wishing to embarrass the girl by thanking her mother for paying in advance for instruction. The agreed-upon fee was enough for Severin to live comfortably on for the next year. And it was not the first such assignment she had undertaken.

"I congratulate you on finding an honest way to earn your bread," Mary said to Severin.

Was that a dig? Severin was not quite sure.

"You have done very well for someone who started out as a modiste, my dear."

Not a dig, perhaps, but certainly condescending. But true enough. However, Severin had moved up from there to teach the niceties of style, fine speech, and gracious manners for women of the demimonde. She was so good at it that aristocratic women now paid her to work the same magic on their behalf. "Thank you, Mary."

Her father, an eccentric Englishman, had seen to it that both of his daughters were relentlessly groomed for a worthy marriage. To that education, Severin's mother had added a knowledge of the secrets of womanly beauty from her Persian maidservant.

"You are good at what you do, Severin."

She smiled at the countess in reply. "I try my best."

"Georgina will benefit from your knowledge of London society."

"I am more of an observer than a member of it."

"You know everyone, my dear Severin, from those with a precarious first foot on a rung at the bottom of the ladder to the climbers at the very top."

"I suppose I do."

"And you are the height of fashion when you want to be."

"Sometimes I don't." Today Severin wore a flowing gown of plain linen, adorned only with a narrow sash of golden silk.

"Well, you have your pick of beautiful gowns." Mary clucked disapprovingly. "Those vain women who wear them once or never wear them at all! But it is to your advantage. You could pass for a lady any day of the week."

Severin answered her with a thin smile. She didn't care if she was taken for a lady or not.

Her singular trade conferred a curious half-invisibility that she found pleasant at times and irksome at others. At balls and assemblies, Severin was sought out by the most dashing men as a dancing partner, but she was ignored in public by most of the women. The most formidable mamas regarded her as unsuitable for their sons and competition for their daughters.

So be it. Her name had been whispered in connection with some fascinating scandals but she made it a point to ignore gossip and do as she pleased. She lived by herself and was happy that way. The one marriage proposal she'd received had come to nothing years ago. Her lovers—and she had not had many, unlike her half-sister Jehane—had been unconventional men. Adventurers. Second sons forced to seek their fortune however they could. Lone wolves, really.

Marko was an intriguing example of the last. She hadn't been able to find out much about him.

Finding out that the unpleasant man who'd once harassed her and Jehane in the street was his cousin, however distant, had unsettled her at first. Feodor Kulzhinsky—their last names were different and so were their natures. She had come to trust Marko himself in the intervening weeks, torturing him quite pleasantly with genteel conversation. Still, she suspected that Marko had known how much she wanted him all the same.

"May I get up?" Georgina asked, startling Severin out of her reverie. "I am tired of sitting and posing like this. Allow me a minute to be myself."

Severin laughed. "Certainly," she replied, but she nonetheless observed the way Georgina walked as she moved about the room. The long-legged girl naturally had a long stride. Severin would have to teach her to place her steps as carefully and as prettily as everything else the girl had been instructed to do.

"I suppose you will tell me how this is done next," Georgina said.

"You are right," Severin replied.

"And you must do exactly as she says, my darling daughter."

"Yes, Mama."

The countess gave Georgina a disbelieving look. "Are you quite well, my dear? You are too well-behaved at the moment. It is unlike you. Always so mischievous, rummaging through my costume trunks and nicking my things—you only just stopped doing that. And reciting my lines all the while."

Georgina nodded and did a pirouette. "I still love to deck myself out in tattered finery. But I suppose I will never go on the boards like you. Are those days over, Mama?"

"Indeed yes," Mary said with great satisfaction. "Thanks to Coyle. It is lovely to have an earl for a husband. We shall never have to worry about another provincial tour or where our next meal is coming from."

"The reciting did you good," Severin said to Georgina. "You have a lovely voice and that will be to your advantage." The way Georgina spoke reminded Severin very much of her half-sister Jehane, in fact. Jehane's voice was a sensual purr that men found irresistible, her light accent only making matters worse for susceptible male hearts.

Avoiding the piano but bumping into the settee, Georgina stopped at a small oil painting of an odalisque, examining the languid pose of the petal-skinned beauty wrapped up in sumptuous fabric that was not fashioned into a dress. "How lovely she is."

Severin only nodded, not inclined to reveal that her mother's servant had modeled for the painting years ago. It had been a particular favorite of her father's. To English eyes, the painting was only a fantasy, done during a vogue for such things. But the woman in it was real enough to Severin, although she had never seen her mother looking like that. She kept the painting for sentimental reasons, even if Oriental splendor was not currently in fashion in London, along with all of her mother's possessions, from perfume bottles to furniture.

At the moment, Georgina was promenading up and down the center of a Persian design meant to represent a hidden garden.

"Turn your feet out just a little," Severin said.

Georgina did, humming to herself. Her mother applauded.

"Very good," Severin said.

Later, in her own chamber, she sat at a desk inlaid with geometric designs in ebony and mother-of-pearl, writing out a bill for Georgina's coming sessions. Mary was next to her, settled in a comfortable armchair.

"Wherever did you get that desk?"

"It was shipped from Tashkent with the rest of our things. It used to be in my mother's room. She valued it highly."

"That's why I've never seen it. A mysterious female, your mother. No one caught more than a glimpse of her either, not while you and Jehane were girls, according to my sources. Not ever."

Mary had an unfortunate tendency to pry, especially when

she had a glass of whisky in her hand. She took a large swallow and coughed.

"Would you like some water?" Severin asked.

"No, thank you. What was your mother's name again?"

"Giselle."

"How very exotic. From Persia, wasn't she?"

"No. She was French, but raised in Constantinople. Her servant was Persian. There seems to be some confusion on the matter. I cannot imagine who would spread such tales."

Mary narrowed her eyes. Severin braced herself for the inevitable rude inquiry. "Oh. Aren't those women raised to do nothing but obey and be beautiful and bear children?" She gulped the last of the whisky. "And someone said that your father bought and paid for her. In gold. Is that true?"

"Who told you that?"

"Don't be cagey, Severin. Aren't we friends?"

"Of course." Severin concentrated on Mary's bill, adding an extra charge of several guineas for nothing at all.

"Then tell me everything."

Severin lay her pen down in the slot on the inkwell and blotted the bill meticulously.

"Please?"

She sighed as she handed Mary the slip of paper. "My father traveled a great deal. He was not the only Englishman who acquired a wife abroad and a servant or two into the bargain."

He'd traded in silks for several companies based in London and Samarkand, and lived like a pasha in Tashkent, to the north.

"Indeed not," Mary said eagerly. "There's a fellow who has five beautiful houris under lock and key in his Mayfair house. A factor in the East India Company, he is. And I heard that he keeps a harem in Calcutta too."

Her father had not been that ambitious. He had started out with a traditional wife, European, and kept a harem of one: Ruksana, her mother's maid, who died giving birth to another daughter, Jehane. Growing up innocent of how others lived, the two girls thought nothing of their domestic arrangements in Samarkand and, later, Tashkent, until they'd moved to England. They had not been told they were half-sisters for a very long time.

They were as close as twins, and could finish each other's thoughts before the words that expressed them were spoken. Only when they had left Tashkent to resettle in London, and were permitted the greater liberty of English girls, did they discover that their previous domestic arrangements were regarded as unusual. Even scandalous. Her father's wealth and eccentricity begged questions wherever they lived.

Severin could not deny that her mother's servant had been bought and paid for.

Her mother, Giselle, hid herself away from the outside world wherever they lived, an unhappy wife. That her maid had become her rival for her lord and master must have galled her deeply, but Severin had been a baby at the time. Her mother had never mentioned it until the last week of her life.

"The Persian servant was brave to come to London, all the same."

Dig, dig, dig. Mary was not likely to stop. Severin made no response. She didn't have to explain that Ruksana was no longer alive.

"Veiled, I expect. I had a costume like that once," Mary prattled. "Had a devil of a time trying to see out."

Severin only nodded. She did remember the long voyage over land and sea, and their arrival at the vast and gloomy warehouses of the East India docks. Her father had handled it all. Her mother had been too withdrawn and too miserable to demand much of anything from him by that point.

In some ways Giselle had not been that different from her luckless servant. She obeyed her husband in everything and followed him, accepting her lot as destiny. At least Severin's father had made over the house he bought in London into an exotic hybrid of East and West, like his wife's native city of Constantinople. From the outside the house looked like any other. Though he left Giselle well provided for before his untimely death, his daughters did not mourn him overmuch. Grieving, homesick, and loathing London, a city she found grim and ugly from the windows she peeked out of, Giselle had died a year to the day after him, attended by Severin and Jehane in her secluded bedchamber.

"Well," Mary was saying, "if you have no good gossip to pass along, I shall be on my way. No telling where Georgina has got to. I expect the friend who came for her has dragged her off to a show. That will have to stop until we marry her off, eh? Not respectable."

"You ought to know," Severin said dryly.

Mary gave a snort at that remark and patted Severin on the cheek. "You are a sly one, Severin. Ta, then."

When her friend had collected her extravagant hat and departed, Severin went upstairs.

Within the house, once past the prim and proper, very English rooms on the first floor, the décor changed utterly, as if one was moving through all the exotic worlds her family had left behind. A visitor, although none ever got very far, might pass through room after room tiled with intricate designs, filled with divans and cushions and gorgeous carpets, until the inner sanctum had been reached.

Severin had not altered one thing inside that room, and rarely went in there. On its walls was a most affecting portrait of all three of them: Giselle, Severin, and Jehane, as they had been ten years ago. Blessed with a loving heart, Giselle had never called the orphaned newborn anything but her daughter and found a wet nurse for the infant girl on the day of her birth. She, without family besides them, had often told her girls they were lucky to have each other.

Severin paused on the threshold. It was a room that her mother had seldom left. Thoroughly French and devoutly Catholic though Giselle was, she had possessed an odd gift. Her mother could see into souls, or so Severin thought. It had been impossible for her to keep secrets from the woman whose sad amber eyes followed her everywhere when she stayed indoors. Jehane had been rather better at it, a slyboots even then.

Before her death, on the day on which she'd explained everything as best she could, Giselle had given her oldest daughter the amber pendant that Severin still treasured. She'd shown Marko the flaw deep within its golden depths that looked very like an eye in the right light—an animal's eye.

"Ruksana gave me this. The eye can see," her mother had whispered in French. "It will watch over you and your sister when we cannot."

That day had come too soon. The memory of it was still painful.

Yet, despite her husband's betrayal, Giselle had believed in love, giving all of hers to her daughters. She'd loved fairy tales and romances and anything magical—they'd been spoiled that way.

London was a merchant's city, bustling, chaotic, with very little romance about it. The ever-creeping fog softened its hard edges now and then but they were still there underneath. Passionate and impetuous as he was, Marko scarcely seemed to belong here. Then again, neither did she, Severin thought with an inward smile.

3

The rising mist from the Thames drifted through the streets near the river, almost obscuring a body abandoned on a side street. A woman. Quite dead. Her head rested in a slowly spreading pool of blackness that seeped into her white gown and the delicate lace that trimmed the low bodice, thread by dark thread. In another hour, the mist cleared. The mortal wound that had severed a vein in her neck had long since ceased to pulse and the pool of black no longer widened. Its still surface reflected the rising moon, which illuminated the woman's calm face in due time. Her open eyes saw nothing.

The link-boy carrying the torch turned at Marko's touch upon his shoulder.

"Stop," Marko told him quietly. He peered down the side street, just able to see a crumpled white shape that had the unmistakable contours of a female body. He had caught the iron whiff of blood from a hundred paces away. "Stay well behind me, lad."

Marko had no wish to expose a boy to the details of murder.

He knew instinctively that the unknown woman was long past saving.

Reaching her first, looking down upon her by the light of the moon, he could see that she had been very beautiful. In a macabre way, she still was. Her dark hair flowed into the pool of blood in which she lay, stiffened by it so that the strands separated as if carved from black stone.

The link-boy came closer, disobeying Marko, compelled to see for himself what death looked like. Marko shifted his position to block the sight of the murdered woman's body as much as he could. Save for the slash upon her white neck, there was no sign of a struggle with an adversary. The moon shone straight down into her open eyes and just for a moment, Marko saw their color. The irises, beginning to dull, were blue around the black pupils, forever fixed.

He kneeled and studied her more closely, to see if there was truth in the saying that the eyes of a victim in extremis recorded the face of a killer. There was nothing. He glanced back at the boy to be sure he kept a little distance away, then back at the woman. To his surprise, he glimpsed a tiny flicker of red inside the black center of her unseeing eyes. A last pulse of life ebbing deep within the brain, perhaps.

He heard the link-boy mutter a half-remembered prayer and Marko straightened. "There is nothing we can do," he said.

The boy raised his torch and glanced past him, down to the end of the side street. "Look there!"

Down at the opposite end of the street stood another woman but not for long. The link-boy gasped and his torch wavered as she turned and fled, leaving the impression of a flash of gold and scarlet in the empty air. Her gown, mostly hidden under a dark cloak, would have seemed colorless in only the moonlight, Marko thought, which turned all bright hues into spectral shades of gray and black. But the glow of the torch had revealed, for a fraction of a second, a magnificence the gown's wearer wished no one to see.

"Who was she?"

"I don't know, lad." The fleeing woman could have been anyone—a prostitute or a noblewoman coming from a rendezvous. From what he saw, the unfortunate beauty at his feet had been killed a while ago. He could not leave the boy alone with a corpse and run after the cloaked woman.

Marko kneeled again by the dead woman, noticing for the first time the fine, broken chain that lay upon her bosom. A remnant of jewelry taken by a thief? The man had thought nothing of taking her life as well.

Marko pulled gently upon it, feeling a weight attached to the other end. It must be a pendant or a locket or some such valuable thing. So the thief had not succeeded in that at least—Marko hoped suddenly and savagely that the man would be tried for his crime and hanged on the Tyburn gallows. Pulling a little harder on the chain, he drew forth a smooth oval of hinged silver that had been trapped between her breasts. Perhaps it held some clue to the woman's identity. With luck, her entire name might be engraved inside or at least her initials. She wore no wedding ring. If it held a miniature of her lover, the man might be found.

One appalling thought after another raced through Marko's mind as he turned the locket over in his fingers without opening it just yet. If there was a little painting inside it, a love token to be worn over her heart, the man portrayed might have lured her here to kill her—and attempted to remove the one incriminating link to himself from her dying body before something startled him and forced him to leave it where it was. Had she been pregnant by her killer? If so, her slender body showed no evidence of it.

She might have asked to meet him in this deserted place to

seek redress, never thinking that her lover would become her murderer. It happened all too often.

The locket was still warm from her skin and the intimate place in which it had nestled. Marko wanted a better look at it.

"Lean the torch against the iron fence near me," he directed the boy. "And watch both ends of the street." It had occurred to him that the murderer might come back, but he did not want to tell the link-boy that. He wondered if the woman who'd dashed away had seen anything.

The lad did as he was told, while Marko held the locket under the flickering torchlight to examine it. He slipped his thumbnail under the catch and the locket opened with a faint click.

Marko drew in his breath. It held no miniature painting of a youthful gentleman with tender lips, nor anything sentimental like a lock of hair. There was nothing feminine at all about what was in it.

The right side of the locket held a wolf's head, nearly flat and no more than an inch in length, done with great skill in re-poussé silver. Thin slivers of ivory had been set into the mouth for fangs and its eyes glittered, picking up the yellow torch-light. Something about the fineness with which it had been crafted made him think that the eyes were probably diamonds, but it was impossible to tell.

Without looking, Marko knew that the lad was standing steadfast. He took another few seconds to study the locket.

On the left side of it was an engraved pattern of something that looked like a stylized flower. But Marko knew it was the print of a wolf's paw—the secret emblem of the Pack of St. James and his kinsmen. He closed it up and put it in his pocket before the curious boy could catch a glimpse.

How the dead woman had come by the locket, he had no idea.

The next day, on a street not far away . . .

The house near St. James's Square where Marko and many of

his kin resided was quiet for a change. He stood at the window and looked out upon the street. It was a blustery day and there were few passers-by, only men who clutched their coat collars against the wind and kept a hand upon the brim of their hats to save them.

He had no more information as to the murdered woman he'd found.

Last night, Marko had kept a lonely vigil by her after he'd sent the link-boy racing to find help. It had been at least an hour before a pair of drunken constables arrived with a cart to remove the corpse.

It struck him to the heart to see the woman, beautiful even in death, handled as if she deserved no consideration. He knew she would be taken to the dead-house and left upon a shelf. Notices would be posted with a description of sorts and the details of where the body was found, so that relatives or friends would come and take her away. Whether the claims were genuine or not would be of little interest to the keepers of the place.

The woman's body would have to be moved to make room for others. From suicide to murder to the forgotten souls who simply perished of want and disease, the alleyways and side streets of London produced no end of corpses in various stages of decay. The newspapers would provide or invent details of the vicious crime for their daily readers and eventually the story would fade away, if nothing could be proved or found out about the victim.

He had kept the locket. Marko understood that the rough men who handled the dead would think nothing of robbing a corpse, even if it would leave a victim of murder unidentified forever, forgotten and buried in a pauper's grave.

The locket was a clue, perhaps the best one, but it did not solve the mystery of her death.

The men of the Pack of St. James did not provide their women with such things. Indeed, no woman he had ever known would be likely to wear a bauble that showed so fierce an animal. Moving closer to the window, he took it from his pocket and opened it again, looking long and hard at the visage of the wolf.

It was indeed set with diamonds but they were not of the first water, having more the color of jaundiced eyes. Nonetheless, they caught the daylight and refracted it in minuscule sparks.

He sat down at his desk and took out several sheets of paper from the flat drawer at its front, intending to sketch the locket in all its particulars, as well as what he remembered of the dead woman's face. These he would send to his older brother along with an account of the gruesome discovery of the night before. Even via diplomatic pouch, the clan's preferred and privileged method of communication, since they served the English Crown in secret, a packet of letters would take some time to reach Kyril.

His brother had departed for a voyage over the northern seas to attend to the Russian interests and business of the Pack of St. James, accompanied by his wife Vivienne and their infant son, Alexander Lukian. Marko smiled slightly, remembering Kyril's protests on the subject of his wife and child's safety. But Vivienne was not to be gainsaid.

Marko had wished all three of them godspeed upon their departure from the Baltic docks, on a morning so dismally cold that each breath melted into the surrounding fog.

Vivienne hadn't said much, concerned with the swaddled baby she cradled in her arms. The pelisse over her shoulders was not fastened, except at the neck, and Marko could just see Alex's round little face underneath it, eyes closed in blissful slumber. The baby had every reason to be happy, as he was nestled against a beautifully round maternal bosom that filled her buttoned-up traveling dress to bursting.

"While I am away, you must lead the Pack, Marko." The look in Kyril's eyes made it clear how much he trusted his younger brother. Kyril would expect to be informed of a murder that could be linked to the Pack, though there was not much to say at this point.

Marko left the locket open and ran a finger over the worked silver, marveling again at how well it was made. One might almost expect the ivory fangs to bite—

He dropped the locket when he felt a prick to his fingertip.

Marko sucked the blood from the tiny wound and tasted a trace of bitterness, which he spat out onto a piece of paper.

As he watched in horror, he realized that the fang had delivered a drop of some unknown poison. Even mingled with spit, it was acid enough to dissolve the paper, leaving a small, foul-smelling hole in it.

The poison suffused the paper beneath it, some of its strength apparently evaporating as it did.

Marko rose and flung open a window. Then he found a metal box in which to hide the lethal thing, locking it so no one else would be taken by surprise. Not that his kinsmen were in the habit of taking items from his desk. But one never knew.

Several days later . . .

Marko called the meeting of the Pack to order. The assembled men were somber and quiet.

"Let us begin. As some of you already know, a woman was murdered. I retrieved a piece of evidence linking the crime to us when I came upon the scene by happenstance—"

"Do the authorities agree with that?" Feodor asked

As far as Marko could tell, the other man's bland tone was meant to undermine his own authority in this hidden room. He replied crisply, "They do, Feodor. I am under no suspicion." Marko wondered, as he had before, whether the decision to allow full membership to someone who was not fully blooded had been wise. But it had not been made by him.

"Excellent," someone else said. "But that doesn't leave the

rest of us in the clear. Exactly what is the piece of evidence, as you put it? And where is it?"

"I am not at liberty to answer either question." Marko ignored the few disputatious murmurs he heard. He had to maintain control as best he knew how, and tossing the locket in the middle of the conference table was not how to do it.

"But there is more," said Levshin, an older man with a deliberate manner. "Another woman with connections to our clan has been killed in exactly the same way. The news of the second crime has not yet appeared in the papers and will not for at least a week—or so we have been told by our sources—"

"Whose identity must remain secret lest we be implicated," someone interrupted wearily. "Will we ever have the rights of ordinary Englishmen?"

Feodor Kulzhinsky spoke next. "Ah, well. Perhaps never," he said flippantly. But someone must know who and what we really are. I say that someone has found a most ingenious way to get through our defenses."

"We have not been personally threatened," Marko said.

"Do you not think that is next?" Feodor asked.

Marko shook his head. "I couldn't say. It is true that our women are our weakness. There are not many who will consort with us."

"It cannot be helped that they are not as we are. Only our rite of marriage can truly bind human females to us, and they must be willing," the Pack's secretary pointed out.

A different man laughed a little bitterly at Antosha's comment. "Some of them are more than willing, no matter what. I am speaking of a certain duchess—"

"This is not the time for levity," Marko scolded him.

"I was going to say," the man went on, "for the manwolves of the Pack, who mate for life, falling in love remains risky."

There were nods and murmurs of agreement around the crowded table.

"Should we even talk of love? In this crisis—in any crisis—we must close ranks," Marko said. "After Lukian's violent death, we are not as strong as we once were."

"Indeed. Our brother Lukian died for us all against Volkodav and his henchmen," a grizzled elder named Braykbone growled. "We will not see his like again."

Marko was quiet, remembering that grim day and his cousin's transformation into full wolfhood, black-furred, enormous, and menacing. Lukian's final leap had taken down the infiltrator in their ranks, the ratlike Stasov, and the two had fallen into the Thames locked in mortal battle. But only one body had ever been found. In his heart of hearts, Marko felt that Lukian lived on, if only as a guardian spirit. He offered up a silent prayer for his true cousin's troubled soul as the others continued to talk.

"What are we to do?" said one. "With Kyril in Archangel and Semyon in Scotland—"

"We will muddle through somehow," another said. "We still have a Taruskin to lead us, do we not? Marko is next in the line of succession to Kyril and the Taruskin brothers are the best among us."

Marko scarcely felt up to the task. All his life he had looked up to his eldest brother, even hero-worshipped him. When he was a cub, he had thought there never was a braver, more brilliant manwolf on earth. He vowed silently to make Kyril proud of him now, without knowing in the least how he would go about it.

"There are still those who wish ill to the Pack," the grizzled elder said. "Our secret service on behalf of the Crown does not please everyone. Some see it as machination to advance our own interests or worse."

"Well, that is fair enough. We do want to exploit our connections," Feodor said, looking around the table as if for confirmation. "That is how the world works and how fortunes are made. Am I right?" The only reply he got was a cough or two. Then silence.

"Never mind that," someone finally said. "We must get to the bottom of these two unsolved murders. Marko has pointed out that both women were connected to the Pack, but they were not wives, of course."

"There is nothing for it," Braykbone said. "Those of us who are involved with women must forswear them for now."

There were no arguments. Braykbone was the oldest among them, and would have commanded respect at any age.

Marko only nodded. Braykbone was right and his affair with Severin must wait. He dared not contradict his grizzled elder—to do so would undermine all Kyril had worked for before his departure. How he would explain that to Severin was another matter, one that he would think on later.

He quieted his mind and called upon all his senses in a first attempt to discern the killer in their ranks. He looked at each member of the Pack in turn when they were unaware of his scrutiny, but he felt no tingle of suspicion or rising of the hair on the back of his neck. Either no one was guilty or his inexperience kept him from knowing if they were. Marko sighed inwardly and reminded himself of the difference between guilt for a crime committed and guilt by association.

He happened to glance again at Feodor and this time he registered a trace of nervousness in the man's smell. But—that damned musky cologne again. Denis, two seats away, obliterated the subtle signal.

No, Marko could find nothing to go on.

"Who knew the latest victim?" Marko asked after a while. "Speak."

A thin fellow, Pyotr, looked at him with sorrow. "Adele was my dearest love. Night and day her face haunts me, Marko." His voice grew ragged. "She cries out in my dreams, dying over and over, begging me to help her. But I cannot—" Pyotr broke off as tears of rage ran down his face. "If I could see her murderer's face and not hers," he said at last, "then I could find him and avenge her. I owe her that much."

The men considered his words in silence.

"Brother, it is our fate to see our beloved dead as if they were alive," Marko said at last. "For men like us, they remain so."

In another part of town . . .

Near the end of the day, with nothing particular to do and no plans in mind, Severin smoothed her skirts, grooming herself in a catlike way without looking into a mirror. The note the maid had brought up that morning rustled in her pocket— she'd had no interest in reading it when she realized it was not from Marko, but from her sister Jehane. Why had he not called upon her or written since their passionate interlude? She was baffled and angered by his withdrawal.

Her sister was probably feeling sociable and wanted her to come by and chat. Severin withdrew the note and read it, forgetting her concern over Marko. It was clear from the spikes and slashes of the inked words that it had been written in great agitation.

> *Something dreadful has happened—surely you know of it! I fear for my life. Come to me.*
>
> > *In haste,*
> > *Jehane*

Severin folded the note and locked it away, then ran downstairs to find her cloak and sturdy low boots. If a hackney coach could not be immediately hired, she would run the distance to her sister's house in Soho. She managed the hooks and buttons by herself, wondering all the while what could have happened to frighten her younger sister so. Her gaze fell upon the newspaper that the butler had left in the hall, noting a headline that screamed a warning. *A Murder Most Foul.* She took it with her.

Still wearing her cloak, Severin moved to the side of a luxuriously appointed bed. Jehane turned her head restlessly on the pillow and gave her older sister a troubled look as Severin bent down to kiss her cheek and smooth the dark hair away from her brow.

Then she took off her cloak, listening to Jehane's agitated recounting of the murder in the news. "I understand your fright, but you cannot stay in bed forever." Severin knew that her sister would be likely to do just that.

"But I am afraid to go out. Lucy Pritchett was—oh, Severin, you don't know her."

"I read today's newspaper on my way here. They gave no name for the victim. She was listed as unknown."

"Then we read different papers, I suppose," Jehane said.

Severin noted the evasion but chose not to comment on it. "We are different in many ways, my dear sister. But tell me more of Lucy."

"What do you want to know?"

Severin shrugged. "Who was she to you?"

"A friend."

"I see." Severin fell silent. Her sister's friends were more like comrades in arms, if one could think of such women in those terms. But courtesans and demimondaines had no great cause in common to bind them and no code of honor. No, they battled each other over the rich men who kept them and then quickly discarded them for younger and prettier rivals.

"Lucy was all the rage for a season," Jehane said, "but she had fallen into bad habits and worse company."

Severin was familiar enough with the scenario. If successful and very pretty, prostitutes might enjoy a precarious fame, but never for very long. And their life could be dangerous in a way that was unique to their calling. A few got out young and married well if they could. The older the husband, the better, by their avaricious reckoning. Others went into business of one kind or another—a prosperous madam could forestall the inevitable and not go upon the street at the end of her days.

Had Lucy been only a streetwalker? Her sister never associated with them, as far as Severin knew. The newspaper Severin had managed to read in the jolting coach that had brought her here described the victim as young and beautiful, and streetwalkers were usually neither.

"How old was Lucy?" Severin asked at last.

"Twenty-three."

Five years younger than Severin and four years younger than Jehane.

"And was she—did she do what you do, Jehane?" Severin felt compelled to be tactful.

"Did she earn her living on her back? Just say it if that's what you mean."

Severin only nodded.

"You happen to be right," Jehane said at last. She seemed sullen, perhaps fearful of her sister's disapproval. "I suppose a customer killed her. It happens, you know."

A murdered one among their number barely caused a ripple. Severin could not help but sigh. "Why do you think so?"

Jehane waved a slender hand as if the question did not need to be asked. "For one thing, Lucy played one man against another. She liked dangerous games."

"I hope you don't."

"Not usually." Jehane shrugged and wiggled her body back under the comforter. "Not unless I'm bored. I don't know why she did it. She never said."

"She was young, though," Severin mused.

"What of it?"

"I was going to say that her charms had not faded."

Severin couldn't help studying her sister's face. Jehane's flawless skin was beginning to show the first signs of age. Infinitesimal signs, to be sure. A few lines at the eyes, finer than the finest silk thread. Another little line between her brows that did not go away even when Jehane smiled. But she was not smiling now.

"It was not as if she had to settle," Severin continued, "At twenty-three, she still had a chance to do better." She did not mean "repent" and she knew her wayward sister knew it.

"She wanted to, Sev. She needed a steady income. Lucy had to keep three men on the hook to stay in style. She'd been slipping."

Severin's lips pressed together for a fraction of a second, but she made no reply.

"You needn't make that face," Jehane said.

"I was not aware that I was making a face."

"Severin, you may not approve of me and the women I know, but none of us care."

Severin rose from the bed and began to walk about the room. The air was heavy with attar of rose, Jehane's favored scent. Severin found it oppressive in these close quarters.

"Then who were the three men?" Severin asked after a while. "We might as well start with them."

"We? I am almost too frightened to think, Severin. No, you shall figure out what the best course of action is and tell me what to do."

"As if you would listen. You never have." Severin raised an elegantly arched eyebrow. "Besides, I am not among your inner circle and I have no expertise in murder."

Jehane shot her a glare. "You must help me."

"I am trying to, Jehane." Severin strove for patience. She and her sister had once been so close to each other and to their mother, sticking together no matter what, to their father's annoyance. He was never inside their charmed circle of three.

Severin had taken one path in life and her sister another, but their paths were not so very far apart when all was said and done. Luck was not always on the side of a woman's virtue. Her bond with Jehane, forged in the silent loneliness of their difference from others around them, had remained unshakably strong.

Jehane gave a heartfelt sigh. "Severin, you are not innocent. You know well enough that men sometimes want to control what they have bought, especially those with a taste for cruelty. If they cannot beat and hurt their wives or their women, they will hire a whore."

What Jehane was saying sank in. But it was difficult for Severin to think of her younger sister in such terms. "Do you call yourself that?" she asked at last.

"There are nicer words," Jehane said. "But I am what I am. And I cannot ignore that one of our inner circle, as you call it, was brutally murdered in the street, as if she had been a common draggletail."

Severin tried to concentrate on facts and not fear. Not that facts were necessarily safer. She changed the subject. "I suppose the newspapers are full of theories about the culprit."

"Yes, at least a dozen. They hasten to assure their readers that it had to be a peer in the highest circles of the court. Or that the guilty party is without a doubt a physician to the queen. Apparently the fatal wound was inflicted with precision. Lucy's beauty was not marred."

Severin shook her head. Her sister's tone was ironic, but Jehane had made an interesting point, however unintentional.

"No one has been named or charged, Severin, but rumors are flying all over London as to who might have done it. But it doesn't matter. I may be next—any of us may be next."

"Who found her, Jehane?"

Her sister shrugged. "The constables. A link-boy led them to the body."

Severin thought it over. She had read as much in the paper. "But link-boys do not roam through the streets alone with torches. They wait for customers at the theaters and the inns."

"What are you saying?"

"That the boy was not alone when he found the body. Who was with him?"

Jehane gave her a puzzled look. "No mention of that. How should I know?" her sister snapped. She pushed back the comforter and raised herself up halfway.

"Would it be a betrayal of confidence if you told me who the three men were?" Severin asked. If at all possible, she wanted to keep her sister out of the courts, if it came to an investigation. Given the right information, and the help of friends in high places, she might be able to.

"I suppose not," Jehane said.

"Have you ever met any of them? Or do you know them only because of what Lucy told you?"

Without answering either question, Jehane got out of bed, her fine figure visible underneath a sensual, loose-fitting gown of the sheerest imaginable silk.

"Damnation! Where is my robe?"

Severin stayed where she was but looked about the room. Jehane's clothes were strewn everywhere in wanton disarray.

"The maid puts nothing away, I see," Severin said dryly.

"She is forbidden to enter here until I go downstairs to tell her to."

"Really? Then who brought you the breakfast upon the tray?"

Severin inclined her head toward the raisin-studded bun and mug of tea on the table beside the bed that Jehane had just knocked into. Underneath it was a newspaper—the headline that Severin had seen before she left her own house was just visible. So they had read the same account. But Severin knew that Lucy Pritchett's name had not been mentioned in it.

"Charlie brought all that with him. He talked the stall-woman into letting him take away the mug. Nice of him, I suppose, but too disgusting to drink."

Severin looked more closely at it. The mug was chipped and heavy, its inner surface showing a ring left by the untouched tea after it had slopped out onto the tray.

"Charlie," she mused. "Is he the young soldier you mentioned once? The fellow you said looks so handsome in his regimentals?"

"Yes. He is a complete waste of my time, as he is penniless and far too young—he is only twenty, Severin! But he makes me happy when I let him."

Now that Severin could see the tangled sheets that had been under the comforter, she suspected that Charlie's vigor certainly satisfied the hard-to-please Jehane. It was unusual for her sister to take on a lover that could not pay her handsomely for the privilege.

"How nice for you both," she said calmly. Every once in a great while she almost envied her sister's never-ending supply of men, but there were compromises Severin would never make for love. In fact, she'd elected to do without that unreliable and troublesome emotion—indeed, do without all masculine company for the past twelvemonth—and then came Marko. She had kept him at a little distance since their first encounter, not wanting to get too used to such attention. He was the most passionate lover she'd ever had and the most skilled. So much for her solitude.

She wasn't the only sinner. Under the heavy scent of roses, Jehane's bedroom smelled of lust, and the dresses and underthings tossed on the carpet were unmistakable evidence of what happened when their owner stepped free of them.

Jehane only sniffed at that reply, finding her robe at last and thrusting her bare arms into the padded silk as she got it over her shoulders. She tied the sash with a jerk and went to the bell-pull that hung on the wall, summoning the maid at last.

"We can talk over a better breakfast than Charlie brought, Severin," she said, turning to her sister after a distant bell sounded a few floors below.

"Very well. Where shall I sit?"

Jehane swept clothes off the furniture in the bedroom and kicked aside the here-and-there heaps of costly gowns and delicate chemises as if they were so many rags. "Anywhere you like."

She headed into an adjoining room, and Severin heard a splash. Her sister must be testing the water in her bronze tub, she thought. Probably with no more than her hand.

"Fie!" Jehane called. "I should have bathed last night when the water was hot—it is far too cold now."

"That is to be expected," Severin said.

"Charlie hardly seemed worth the effort last night and I was feeling lazy even before he arrived," Jehane explained from the next room. "I meant to bathe after he left, but I fell asleep. Sometimes day turns into night for me, you know."

Her sister's louche ways usually set Severin on edge, but not today. "It does not matter," she began. "I—"

A brisk knock on the door interrupted what she was going to say next. Jehane came back into the room and opened the door to let in the maid, who deposited a laden breakfast tray draped with napkins on the nearest clean surface, a low table by a sofa, and scurried out.

"I should be grateful to Charlie, I suppose. He told me it was Lucy who had died," Jehane said with a sigh, "and he vowed to do in the murderer with one mighty blow if he could. He had heard of it at the tavern on his way to my house. When he gave me the details, I could not stop shaking. He held me for the longest time, Severin."

"Lucky you." The wistfulness in her own voice made Severin wince. Had not Marko pursued and won her, at least for now, she would not have minded such a lover for a little while. A gallant young soldier with a good heart, capable of boundless affection and protectiveness—ah, Charlie would be off to war somewhere soon enough. She hoped the affair would do Jehane good while it lasted.

"He can be so kind sometimes. I feel foolish, though, for turning to you the second he had gone. But Lucy was someone I knew, although not well. Still, there is a murderer at large and my morbid imagination got the better of me."

"You must be careful whom you see, Jehane."

Jehane shrugged as if she was beginning to not care, beginning to harden herself against the ugly possibility that something just as dreadful could happen to her. "I will try to be. I wrote to you and sent my maid to your house straightaway. An older sister always knows exactly what to do."

Severin felt a flash of guilt for not opening it sooner, but there had been no name or return address on the outside. She shook her head. "Do I? Mama made me swear to take care of you, but I sometimes think that I have failed her."

"No, Severin, you have not," her sister said, a little more politely. "My sins are my own. And when I commit them, I hurt no one besides myself."

Severin began to protest, but Jehane cut her off. "Besides, they are very little sins by London standards."

"I suppose so."

"Come, let us have a bit of bread and butter and jam. And tea, of course."

Jehane's appetite for food was as strong as all her others. She made short work of the prodigious breakfast on the tray and drank most of the tea. Severin watched her as she sipped at a cup of her own.

Inwardly she wondered how long her sister could keep up

the life she led. Although it was impossible for a courtesan to believe whole-heartedly in romantic love—and Severin was certain that Jehane thought that was nonsense—she had hoped that her sister would someday allow one of her men to make her a comfortable settlement. Or even accept an offer of marriage. What had happened to Lucy might motivate her to do so sooner rather than later.

Severin shook her head.

Despite Jehane's casual demeanor, her sister still did seem extremely nervous. It was as if her friend's death had opened a window through which Jehane could see her own possible fate.

Well and good, if that was so. Anything to keep Jehane from a downward slide in the life she had chosen, anything to keep her from the fate that had lain in wait for poor Lucy. As Jehane had pointed out, though not in those exact words, murder at a man's hands was not an uncommon ending to a whore's life.

But Severin knew her half-sister might never marry, and if she did, she might not marry well. Wary and strong-willed, Jehane had a feral quality about her that men found dangerously attractive. And she was most attracted to men who were not in the least domesticated.

Character traits that Severin shared but not to the same degree. And she kept them well-hidden and safely under control. All the same, her amber-colored eyes had been likened to those of a wild cat more than once. By her father, first. And then by the men in her life. Severin wondered why she thought of marriage as a safe haven for herself or her sister. None of the men she'd thought she loved had stayed. In truth, she had not wanted them to.

Jehane wiped her mouth and tossed the napkin down. "There. I am done. Now we can talk."

Severin put down her cup. "Where did we leave off?"

"Lucy's three men. You wanted to know more about them."

"Yes. It might put your mind at ease if we can puzzle this out."

Jehane frowned, as if she was trying to remember. "One was

an officer, a Yorkshireman with a thick accent. She used to imitate it—Lucy was an excellent mimic." Her eyes filled with tears. "She amused us all, Severin. She even shared her men if she was tired of them."

"With you?" Severin could not keep the question to herself. Was Jehane afraid for reasons she was not willing to explain?

Jehane looked at her narrowly and Severin had a feeling she had hit her mark.

"No," Jehane said a little too quickly. "The fellow is no longer in London. She'd told me that he went back to his wife."

"Then let us discount the Yorkshireman for now."

"Very well."

Severin realized there was a question she had forgotten to ask. "When did you last see Lucy alive, Jehane?"

"A month ago, maybe more."

Severin nodded. "Go on then. Who were the other two?"

"One was a foreigner, I believe, attached to the king's court. A Russian."

Severin stiffened. "What was his name?"

"Feodor Kulzhinsky."

How odd that Lucy's lover would be Marko's distant cousin, the man who had once harassed her and Jehane upon the street, although Jehane had not mentioned knowing him then. Severin had not thought of him since seeing him by chance outside the building that Marko said was sometimes his home.

"And the third man?" she asked Jehane.

"He was a jeweler. An Englishman, she said. Paul Clavell. He gave Lucy the prettiest necklaces and things, Severin—"

"Is it possible that one of the other two—no, we have decided to consider only Feodor for now—saw some such trinket he had not given her and grew jealous?"

"Yes, I suppose. Feodor liked to think of himself as passionate. It might have happened that way."

Jehane seemed to know quite a lot about Feodor. But Severin knew well how wary her sister could be. Asking pointed questions would be likely to elicit no answers at all. "Then we must find out more about him." Severin said quietly.

"Ah," Jehane said. "That may be difficult. Besides being received at court, Feodor is a member of the so-called Pack of St. James or so Lucy said. It is like a club, I believe."

"London is full of men's clubs."

"This one is different."

Severin studied her sister, again sensing that there was information Jehane was holding back. "Where do they meet, then?"

"In their own house." Jehane named a street that led into the square proper.

"I have seen it." Severin picked up the newspaper that had fallen to the floor and perused the article on the murder. "Just as I thought. That street is not far from where Lucy was killed," she said.

"Is it? I don't read every word as you do," Jehane said, gesturing in a careless way at the newspaper in her sister's hand. "Lucy told me that Feodor took her there once."

Severin looked thoughtfully at her sister. She had a feeling that Jehane had some connection to this Pack, as she herself had, without knowing it. How very strange. As so often happened, they had come to the same point via different directions.

"But I have never been to the house myself," Jehane added.

That was an answer to a question that had not been asked. A sisterly sense told Severin that Jehane was lying. But why?

As if she sensed her sister's unease, Jehane paid no further heed to Severin for the moment, sauntering into the adjoining room and going back to getting ready for her day or what was left of it.

Severin rose and went to the window. Outside was a row of crooked-looking houses that seemed to lean on one another. She stared at them without really seeing them as Jehane's voice faded away.

A vision of the house they had been discussing, entirely

imaginary as far as Severin knew, suddenly loomed in her troubled mind. She could not dispel it, not even by closing her eyes.

The house that had appeared to her was unremarkable but distinguished in its way, plain and solid-seeming. The blinds in every window were drawn. No light came from it and no light entered. She shook her head, trying to make it disappear, wondering for a second if she, Severin, had come all of a sudden into her mother's odd gift for seeing things. Had it been triggered by her fear for her wayward sister? It seemed possible.

It was the lair, if that fanciful word was correct, of the Pack of St. James. The vision shimmered as she sought to penetrate its dark windows with her mind's eye. For the moment, that was all she could do. The amber pendant with its mysterious flaw was locked away safely in her desk at home—no. Marko must still have it.

Severin reminded herself that she had sometimes seen patterns like fracturing prisms during the course of her severe headaches. Perhaps this vision was nothing more than that.

But this house was somehow there and quite real . . . and not there at all, not real at all, at exactly the same time. Severin took a deep breath and held it. If she concentrated even harder, she could see through the St. James house to the crooked ones across the street.

A frightening thought echoed in her brain: that someone—a man—within the Pack's house was looking at her, even though she could not see him. She felt a chill go down her spine and looked about for her cloak, flinging it over her shoulders when she found it. She closed her eyes and let its warmth comfort her. The unknown house appeared again.

Distantly aware that Jehane was still safely occupied in the adjoining room, Severin concentrated next on a single part of the vision: a window near the top where a gleam appeared, as if the blinds had gone up and there was a fire lit in the unseen room behind the dark glass.

She looked harder at the gleam. It was red—light danced upon a glass of ruby-colored wine in—in a man's hand. Severin looked up to gaze in wonder at his spectral face. He came forward to touch the glass with his other hand.

Marko. Vision though he was, something about him was far more real than the house. He was exactly as she remembered him, with thick hair the color of wheat and eyes that held the glow of animal health.

His sensual mouth formed the syllables of her name. *Severin?*

"Are you real?" she whispered.

It doesn't matter. Where are you?

"Never mind." She could barely draw breath.

I cannot see you for a while. Will you wait for me?

"Marko—"

The vision of the house and the man inside it disappeared when Jehane shouted from the next room. "Why are you talking to yourself, sister?"

"I was not aware that I was," Severin called back, shaken to the core by what she'd seen and the voice she'd heard.

"You were, though. What are you doing?" Jehane came into the bedroom, clad only in a large Turkish towel.

"Looking out of the window."

Jehane edged close enough to peek outside without revealing herself. "There is nothing to see. Oh, Severin, I should not have asked you to come to me. I see that I have upset you. It is one thing to read of a shocking murder in the newspapers—"

"And quite another to find out that one's sister knew the victim and thinks she may be next," Severin murmured. "I cannot help but worry, Jehane. I will do whatever I can to find out more and try to protect you."

Even if you are lying to me. She did not say the words out loud.

4

In the Russian port of Archangel...

Marko's packet of letters concerning the murder of a young woman had reached Kyril at last. He pored over them, then handed them, along with Marko's drawings of the locket and his sketch of the woman's face to his wife Vivienne.

She cast a glance at the plump baby boy who slept peacefully beside her in the cradle, then took them from Kyril's outstretched hand without saying anything.

"Would you read these for me, Vivienne? I mean in the way that you read things, of course. Rather more than between the lines, my darling."

Vivienne nodded. "I will try." Her supernatural ability changed colored illustrations in a book or drawings into living images that spoke and loved and, sadly, suffered and died before her wondering eyes. It was not something Kyril could do and he marveled at her talent to do so.

It had happened first with his book of folktales, and a few times since. Her ability to read in that way was strongest when she was among the Pack. She had not done it for a while. The weeks at sea had made her unwell and her only thought was to stay strong enough for her son. She was curious to find out if the knack had left her.

Married as she was to Kyril, their leader, and the mother of his child, living for a while in the land where he'd been born, she thought her readings might be stronger still.

The second she looked at the drawing of the locket, which was on top of the other papers he had handed to her, Vivienne knew it was so. The wolf face in the depiction of the locket radiated an evil so strong that it shocked her. She got up from her chair and moved across the room from her sleeping son.

Vivienne went over to the window to study the image more closely. Marko had done the eyes in yellow watercolor, adding a note about their powers of refraction and that they were undoubtedly diamonds.

As Vivienne looked at the wolf's eyes, she fought the feeling that the wolf was looking at *her.*

"This is very odd, Kyril," she said at last. "The locket shows a wolf's head, to be sure, but I do not feel that I am looking into a wolf's eyes."

"What do you mean?"

"They are the eyes of a man. Who he might be, I cannot say."

Kyril rose from his desk and looked over her shoulder at the paper. "That is the emblem of the Pack on the other side."

"Yes," she said absently. "The pawprint. I can read nothing in that. It is what it is."

"But the wolf's eyes disturb you."

"Yes." She took a letter from the bottom of the sheaf and covered it up. "If I look too long, I might create a connection from the man to here."

Vivienne set those two sheets of paper aside before she looked at the others.

The room they were in was vast but the flickering fire in the hearth made it seem somewhat cozy. A dacha in the country had been lent to them to stay in while Kyril got through the business of the Pack in this forgotten corner of Russia.

She glanced at the paper she had set aside. "I feel almost as if I should feed it to the fire."

"Is it that evil, my love?"

"Yes."

Kyril hesitated. "The locket in Marko's drawing was found around the neck of a murdered woman."

She grew pale. Dim as the room was, he could see it. "You did not tell me there had been a murder."

"You may read of it in the other letters. He found the victim."

"Dear God."

"By chance," Kyril added hastily. "He happened to look down the street where her killer had left her."

She put a finger to his lips. "No more. It seems wrong to speak of such things with an infant in the room."

"Alexander does not understand."

"But I do. And I must nurse him—do you understand?"

Kyril took her in his arms. "I think so. Being a mother is not easy for one so sensitive."

"It is my greatest joy, Kyril," she murmured. "Next to being held like this."

He stroked her hair, chuckling. "And why is that?"

"Your heartbeat. Your warmth. When I am in your arms, nothing can harm me."

Kyril set her a little distance away from him and placed a husband's kiss on her forehead. "I am sure that little Alex feels the same way when he is in your arms, Vivienne. Come, we shall burn the letter with the wolf's head. Nothing will trouble you."

His hand came down over it and the paper that covered it,

and he crumpled them both together. Then he threw them into the fire.

The flames sprang up and devoured them. Vivienne nodded. "There. I feel better, Kyril. Thank you."

He only laughed. "You make it easy to be a hero."

"Did I say you were one?" she asked indignantly.

"Man and wolf, I hope to be."

She slipped her arm around his waist. "My dear Kyril, I was only teasing. You are everything to me, you know."

They walked across the vast room to stand at the side of their son's cradle.

Alex slumbered on, curling his chubby fingers into tighter fists.

"Do you think he is cold?" Vivienne asked anxiously.

"He is dressed in wool and wrapped in wool and blanketed in wool. Yes, he is warm enough, woman."

"We are in Russia," she said reprovingly. "It's wise to be careful."

"Of course."

They looked down. Alex was making a juicy little sound in his sleep. His lips moved in and out. He was suckling an invisible nipple.

"Aha. He dreams of his mother," Kyril said mischievously.

Vivienne pressed a hand to her breast. "It is not quite time for that. A mother's love may be infinite, but mother's milk is not."

"He takes all you can give, I know." Kyril put his arm around her shoulders. "He is growing fast."

"So are my hips and my bottom," she said ruefully. "When is the extra weight going to go away?"

"I like you exactly as you are, Vivienne. If I, your husband, have no complaints, then you must be happy with your bottom."

He gave it a friendly slap that she could feel even through her own layers of wool.

"Hmph. I suppose I must be satisfied with that."

Kyril clasped her hand in his own. "Silly one. Now, are you sure you are up to reading the letters from Marko?"

Vivienne nodded. "So long as I am not doing it near my boy, yes. I know you want to write back as soon as you can."

"Our letters will cross but that can't be helped."

"How is he doing in your absence, Kyril? He only ever followed the leader."

"The role is new to him. He will adjust, I suppose."

"Oh, dear. That sounds almost too tactful."

Kyril snorted. "You are difficult to reassure, my dear."

"But I don't know what you mean. Are the members of the Pack running wild in London? Has the exchequer been emptied to buy vodka?"

"Marko did not say, so I assume that neither is true."

Vivienne squeezed his hand as they walked away from the cradle that held their sleeping child and back to Kyril's desk. "No wonder only I can read between the lines," she said. "The ability must be female."

"I am sure you are right, my dear wife." He pulled out a chair for her and went over to where she had set down the other letters.

"Thank you," Vivienne said, taking them from his hand. She glanced at them all, pausing to peer at odd bits of handwriting. Marko had written in haste.

"What do you think?"

"That he is right. The murder could be linked to the Pack. Someone at the house had something to do with it."

"He could not imagine who. Can you?"

Vivienne sighed. "Now I wish we had not burned the paper with the wolf's head. It might have been him—"

"Who?"

"The man who hid behind the wolf. His evil nature shone in its eyes."

"But you saw only the wolf otherwise, not the features of a man."

"That is correct. But even so . . ." She hesitated. "Sometimes a longer look will reveal more."

Kyril frowned. "What's done is done. Your maternal instincts were correct."

"I suppose so."

"Whoever the woman was, she will never come back to life. We cannot help her."

"But what if the killer strikes again in our absence?"

"He already may have," Kyril said soberly. "Correspondence between here and England takes an infernally long time. And if the Archangel harbor is icebound soon, we will know nothing for months."

"Yes, you are right," Vivienne said. "We will have to help Marko with the matter upon our return to London."

He patted her hand. "Still, it would help if you could give the letters a careful reading for me now. I am not sure of what to say to my younger brother."

"Then I will do it."

She bent her head over the letters again, absently touching her fingers to them now and then.

Kyril watched his thoughtful wife in silence. Alex kept her up at nights often enough, but even his infant demands had not diminished her beauty.

Vivienne came to one she had not looked at: the drawing of the young woman. Marko had included the wound on her throat, but not the blood. There had to have been a great deal of blood.

"She died in great fear," she said with a catch in her voice. "And I am sure she saw her killer."

"He did not strike from behind, you mean."

"Exactly. She saw him. The knife he held was flashed in front of her."

"You are sure it was a man?"

Vivienne looked into the staring blue eyes of the drawing. "Yes." She touched a fingertip to the woman's cheek. "But I sense female jealousy played a part in her death. She worked with women in some way. Some of them must have hated her."

"Can you read anything more? Who she was, perhaps?"

"She was English, without a doubt," Vivienne said. "Her features are not in the least Russian."

"Is it possible for you to read her name somehow?"

"No." Vivienne stopped to think. "That may have to do with how she died."

"What do you mean?"

"Whoever cut her throat left her alive to bleed to death alone. No one knew her name when she passed from this world to the next."

"I see."

"Which is not to say that she was nameless. Only that I cannot pick it up from this."

Kyril nodded and sat forward, covering the dead woman's face with Marko's letters concerning the matter. "Then what shall I say to my brother?"

"That we will come home as soon as we can. Kyril—" Vivienne put a hand on his arm. "We must book passage on the first ship crossing the White Sea. Tomorrow, if possible."

"I will see what I can do." He turned at the sound of a lusty wail that came suddenly from the cradle. "And you must see to our son."

Far away in London . . .

Marko was reading a letter as well. It had come in the afternoon post and was brought upstairs by Will, the boy who blacked everyone's boots and did other dirty jobs that no one else wanted. Marko frowned when he realized why this particular dirty job had been handed off—Will did not complain, as a rule. He kept his head down and he did whatever he was told to do as best he could. But Marko intended to have a word with whoever had entrusted the letter to him. It reeked. The strange smell was one that Marko recognized instantly. Like an invisible cloud, the reek emanated from it even as it lay on the silver tray that the boy held out.

"Thank you, Will." He took the letter, tray and all, from the lad's outstretched hand. He did not expect a response. Will, a deaf-mute, could make none. The boy nodded and clattered back down the stairs.

Marko put the tray to one side until he could find gloves and build a fire in the hearth. The day was warm for it but that could not be helped. The evil-smelling letter had to be impregnated with the poison from the locket that he had accidentally tasted. That he had spat out instantly onto a piece of paper and seen a hole eat right through it. The letter would have to be burned as soon as he was done reading it.

It wouldn't take long. The envelope was quite thin. It most likely held only one sheet of paper, folded in half. He would have to handle it with great care or risk a blast of powdered poison in his face, perhaps. This lethal communication had to be linked to the two mysterious murders.

To be on the safe side, Marko opened the window and sat near it with the tray. Then, gloves on, he opened the letter a little awkwardly with a blade he would consign to the flames to purify.

He used it to flip open the folded note and scanned the crooked handwriting.

Two dead whores. There will be a third. And soon the murders will be linked to you, Marko. What will you do?

It was unsigned. The handwriting struck him as male—it was angular and to the point, as was the message. But poison was certainly considered a woman's weapon by many.

He looked at the message with a feeling of blank horror. There was no telling who would be next. He had not known the first two women, though Adele's connection to the Pack had been made clear enough. She'd had a sister, apparently, who had been duly notified but never responded and never claimed the body for burial. Marko had paid for a plot for Adele and flowers out of his own pocket. He had not returned to the dead-house in time to rescue the first victim from burial in a potter's field, of which there were several in London alone.

A strange thought entered his mind and lodged there. Should he ask Severin for help? No, he could not do it, although she had friends in places high and low, and lived independently, indifferent to social censure and not caring about scandal. Nonetheless, he was sure she would end their relationship at once if she thought he or his kinsmen were connected in any way to this ominous matter.

He threw the letter, the tray, and the knife into the fire he'd made, and then pulled off his gloves. All of that nearly smothered the flames. He took the poker and moved the metal items underneath the coals and kept the paper above it, holding his breath until the letter curled into ash.

His gloves lay there, smoldering. He used the poker to push them apart and spread the fingers away from each other. The gloves caught fire eventually and their edges glowed red. The fingers curled and seemed to be clutching the very coals. Marko straightened, feeling as if he was looking at the hands of Satan himself. He shut the door of the grate with a vicious bang and gave the devil his due.

5

"I did the best I could, Jehane!"

Severin's younger sister put her hands on her hips and glared. "I don't think so. You were supposed to find out more about the Pack of St. James and Feodor, and you haven't come up with a thing. Obviously you were distracted."

"What do you mean?"

"You let the oh-so-virile Marko Taruskin make love to you."

"How do you know he did?" Severin shot her sister a worried look.

"I can see it on your face. You have an unmistakable glow," Jehane said with a note of contempt. "The sort that lasts."

"That is rouge," Severin said.

"Bah. You have never used it."

Sometimes the closeness of sisterhood was oppressive, Severin thought. She and Jehane knew absolutely everything about each other.

"I kept him at arm's length at Almack's." Which had not been easy—everyone who mattered among the ton was there and the press of the crowd had forced them together. She'd wanted to dismiss him altogether, baffled by his polite conversation and seeming remoteness. It hadn't lasted, but the subsequent encounter had been unsatisfying.

"Not for long. You left together. Denis told Anny and she told me."

Severin raised an eyebrow. "Who is Denis? Or Anny for that matter? I did not know you had sent spies to watch me."

Jehane only shrugged. "There is more going on than you know. I have received letters."

"I assume they are not love letters," Severin said tartly. She was hurt that Jehane saw fit to spy on her. And embarrassed to seem naïve, as she must, in the eyes of her younger sister for not being able to resist the charms of Marko. His sensuality was irresistible. She could not keep her distance and extract information from him simultaneously. As it turned out, she had not succeeded at either. It had been too long, far too long since she had been with a man—and she had never in her life been with one like Marko.

"No. The threatening kind."

"Jehane, you must tell me the entire truth. I feel that you have not."

Jehane sighed and rolled over onto her back. "You know what I do for a living. What is there to tell? I have survived worse in the past."

"You have received threatening letters before?"

"Yes, two years ago. Then they stopped."

"Why?"

"The man who was threatening me was hanged for another crime and I went on my merry way."

Severin did not know what to say. Her sister liked to live on the razor's edge. Sooner or later it was going to catch up with her. Perhaps it had. "Jehane, I cannot shake the feeling that you are mixed up in something and you will not say what it is."

"True enough."

"Fie! You beg me to aid you and say you fear for your life. Yet Marko cannot be involved in this—"

It could not be him. So warm-hearted and gentlemanly. Still, she was racked with guilt that she hadn't found out anything that might protect Jehane.

But coming to Jehane's rescue could be a thankless task. Her younger sister could be her own worst enemy.

Jehane snorted. "Is he not the leader of the Pack of St. James?"

"I don't actually know. He could be. He is masterful enough."

Jehane didn't seem to believe it. "They are dirty dogs, nothing more. So what do they do to amuse themselves? Drink themselves blind or hold wicked orgies like the Hell-Fire Club?"

Severin considered how best to answer that. For all that Marko had made passionate love to her, the cat-and-mouse game she was playing with him now was going nowhere, and she was ashamed to admit that she knew nothing.

"I never entered his house the first time I was alone with Marko and I never went back. He has visited mine. We have met elsewhere—"

"Why didn't you go in his house?"

Her sister's imperious question irked her, but Severin felt compelled to answer honestly. "I saw Feodor come out and it stopped me cold. Speaking of him—why did you not tell me you knew him when he bothered us on the street weeks ago?"

"I wanted to get away."

It was Severin's turn to sigh. "Yes, well, he exudes an odd sort of evil. As if he could kill someone with his bare hands, clean his nails thoroughly afterward, and sit down to dinner."

"An astute observation, Severin. He is evil in exactly that way."

Severin threw up her hands. "Then why have you set me at Marko?"

"He is rather easier to get around, I suspect," Jehane said

thoughtfully. "Feodor is much cleverer. And he likes foolish women. Marko, I have heard, does not."

That at least was flattering, Severin thought. But she was thoroughly baffled as to what her sister expected of her. "I cannot continue until you tell me everything you know, Jehane."

Jehane sat up on the bed and then slid off it. "Never mind that for now. Let me show you the letters."

She rummaged in a drawer and took out several folded sheets of paper, which she handed to Severin.

Severin read them in shocked silence. Her flesh crawled. There were seven in all, of no more than a few lines, which repeated in random order.

Tell-tale tit, your tongue shall be slit. Mind who you lift your skirts for, you dirty girl. You filthy whore. And so on.

"Jehane, these are truly frightening."

"They arrive like clockwork. I have received one a day for the last week."

"Are you not afraid that something is about to happen? I would be." Severin thrust the letters back at her.

"What can I do?" Jehane snapped. "Show them to my customers? Ask young Charlie to stand at my door and wave his sword at each man who passes by?"

Severin thought for a minute. "It would be better than nothing."

Jehane shook her head. "I don't want to involve Charlie. You are the only one who knows anything about the letters."

"Are you so sure that they are from a man?"

"Severin, I have no idea. But I suppose there are women who have it in for me. I have helped myself to a husband or two."

"Jehane!"

Her sister looked at her calmly. "I didn't make the world and I can't change it. Men are what they are."

"Still. For shame."

Jehane looked at her narrowly. "I hadn't known you were such an ardent champion of marriage, sister."

"Ah—"

"You seem to have dodged it successfully so far."

Severin raised her chin. "I prefer to live alone. I haven't dodged it."

"Do you mean that no one has asked?"

Her sister's sharp question cut Severin to the quick. There was nothing for it but to answer honestly. "If you must know, someone did ask for my hand a long time ago. Then a friend of his told him what you did."

Jehane flashed her a contemptuous look. "And he said he would rather not have a whore for a sister-in-law."

"How did you know that?"

Jehane tossed her hair. "What else would he say once he knew the truth? I am sure he visited many on the sly. Men are hypocrites."

Severin knew the truth of that. But a romantic part of her soul clung to the passé notion that a marriage vow ought to mean something. No doubt that was why she had avoided the matter—she would not use the word *dodge*—and stuck to less involving love affairs for a while, then given it up altogether. Jehane was not entirely wrong. Still, she hated the self-righteousness that had colored her brief answer . . . but she did not hate Jehane. Her younger sister's trade had coarsened her. She saw only the worst in the men who wanted one thing from her.

For which they paid dearly. And Jehane paid too, in a different coin.

"Come now," she said, softening her tone. "You asked me to alter a gown for you. Go try it on—let's get it done."

*   *   *

The argument with her sister had upset Severin and she left as soon as she could. She retrieved her cloak and her bag from a housemaid, and rushed away.

Severin drew the hood of her cloak over her head. Night was falling and the air was cool. The hood got in the way when she turned her head, but she was on a well-lit street where the shops stayed open late. She wouldn't trip.

She would go slowly and look in every window and pretend she could afford it all. Window-shopping always soothed her soul.

Severin stopped at each one—the bookstore, the china shop, the place that sold landscapes painted in oil—and inspected the goods. A notions-seller came out to talk to her.

"Good evening, miss. Lovely ribbons inside."

"No thank you," she murmured politely, moving on.

There were fewer shops as she went further along and her footsteps echoed. She pushed back the hood to see if she was being followed.

No one was there. The street behind her was empty, except for the notions-seller, who had come out again to smoke a cheroot.

She went on. Again she heard footsteps nearly identical to her own. Nearly.

Severin felt a prickle of alarm. She pushed through a shop door without seeing what was inside.

"We were just closing," said an old man politely, coming forward to meet her.

He must have been working at his craft somewhere unseen—he still had a jeweler's small hammer in his hand. She saw it shake slightly, until he clutched the handle. The shop sold silver items: tea and coffee services, tableware, and some jewelry.

"Please . . . if I could stay for a little while. I think someone was following me."

"Are you quite sure?"

Severin looked at the old man's untroubled face. She saw no guile in his rheumy eyes. "Yes."

"Very well. I would not turn out a lady onto the street."

"Thank you."

He locked the door after her. From the inside. "If you don't mind. As I said, we were closing."

Severin felt a prickle of unease. "Not at all."

The old man indicated a chair for her to sit in and went back to his bench. She heard the tap-tap-tap of his hammer and relaxed a little.

Then she leaned forward to look at the jewelry in the glass case. There were pieces done in engraved silver and repoussé silver. Hearts and roses. Lockets and chains. Nothing that interested her.

Wondering how soon she could leave, she stood up and went to the window. The street, what she could see of it, was empty again.

She tried the knob and then remembered that the old man had locked it. She looked up and realized that he was now standing, watching her silently over a barrier that was as high as his shoulders.

Severin felt as if she was caught.

"Do you want to go now?" the old man asked mildly.

"Yes, if you don't mind. I've rested. Perhaps my nerves are bothering me. I probably need a tonic."

"In just a moment, then. I must finish a tricky bit of work. It won't take long."

Her eyes darted toward the street. Why was he stalling her? The key must be in his pocket.

She looked at his reflection in the glass. The old man was at his workbench again.

If he had left the key on it, she could grab it, let herself out, and run back to the better-lit part of the street where there were more shops.

She walked very quietly to the back, going around the barrier that shielded the area from the main part of the shop, looking over his shoulder as she approached him. He gave no sign that he heard her coming.

Emboldened, Severin moved closer. She could see what he was working on—a silver piece that he was hammering out from behind.

It looked like a tiny mask, wrong side out, but whether it was human or animal was hard to say.

There were bits and pieces of ivory and small colored gems on the top of the workbench. The old man picked up a yellow stone with a tweezers and turned the silver thing over.

He dropped the stone into its setting. She came another step closer and craned her neck. He used the tweezers to pick up another little stone and dropped it a fraction of an inch further away from the first one.

The stones were eyes, set in sockets on either side of . . . an animal's nose. Severin realized that what she had taken for a mask was the face of a wolf.

It seemed malevolent somehow, for all its small size.

No woman would wear such a thing, despite its delicate workmanship. She ran her gaze over the top of the workbench and noticed a blank locket, left open, which seemed to be exactly the right size for the wolf face to fit into.

A silver oval lay next to it, with an embossed pattern that might have been a flower. Humming, the old man set the wolf face next to it. And Severin made the connection between the two things in an instant. The embossed pattern was not a flower but the print of a paw.

The old man turned around all of a sudden, startling her. "Oh dear. You had wanted to leave and here I still am, working away." He got up. "Forgive me."

"Y-yes, yes," Severin said, backing away. "But please let me out."

"Of course." He went ahead of her to the door.

Severin dashed out the second it swung open and ran the opposite way. She never saw the sign above the shop. *Paul Clavell, Silversmith.*

The old man looked after her. He left the door unlocked and went back to his work.

Feodor entered in a little while, closing and locking the door behind him and going to the back.

"So. She dashed in here, of all places. I should not have followed her so closely. But I wanted to find out where she went after she saw Jehane."

The old man only nodded. The tiny hammer tapped away.

"Did she see our trinkets, Mr. Clavell?"

"Only this one. And only for a moment, over my shoulder while I was working. I couldn't very well jump up and bellow at her for surprising me, could I?" He fitted the silver face of the wolf into the locket. "There. That will do nicely. Do you have the payment for it?"

Feodor gave a curt laugh that was almost a bark. "You may have to wait another week. I think that Marko Taruskin has told our resident moneybags to keep a close watch on the exchequer. Levshin seems to be getting the idea that things don't add up. But he hasn't noticed that Marko's signature on the bills is a forgery."

"I see. But I want my money."

"You shall have it as soon as I steal it. Marko is sure to be distracted. He is by no means as capable as his brother Kyril."

"Ah. Who is far away.'"

"Yes. Time for crime." Feodor laughed rudely at his own joke.

The old man turned at the sound of it. "If you haven't got money, a girl will do."

"Any girl? A blonde, a brunette? You pick."

"I would take Jehane."

Feodor shook his head. "You don't want that one. She is too willful and she talks too much."

"I like to hear dirty talk." Clavell protested in a mild voice.

"No," Feodor said firmly.

Paul Clavell sighed and set aside his work. He wrote out another bill and impaled it on the iron spike. "Then you owe me. You paid me for the first."

"Lucy's. Yes."

"And how did she like her locket?"

"Very much. She said it marked her as a female of the Pack."

"The women want to be marked, do they?" Clavell picked up the wolf face and turned it this way and that. "A wolf has power. And animal magnetism. And strength."

"A she-wolf is nearly equal to her mate, when it comes to that." Feodor's lips stretched in an unpleasant smile. "I had been teaching Lucy how we kill. She wasn't much of a one for blood, though. Too squeamish about tearing out throats. That's why she liked the poisoned fangs you added. Said they might come in handy for eliminating rivals. Good for business."

The old man shook his head. "Shame about how she died. I wouldn't have minded a personal thank-you from a pretty little thing like Lucy."

"It is a shame."

"Who did it, Feodor? Do you know?"

Feodor clapped the silversmith on the back. "Not a clue."

"A shame," the old man repeated. "Do you think it could have been Jehane?"

"That did occur to me. But no. She is a finicky one, careful about who she lifts her skirts for. She wants no trouble. She would not have murdered a rival. I don't think she's capable of it."

Paul Clavell grunted. "Anyone is capable of murder."

"No, not her. Jehane doesn't like blood either. And she may leave the life someday and marry up. You know how whores will do."

"Useful for blackmail purposes, I must say. They never want new husbands finding out things like that. Unless the new husbands are old like me. In which case, a nice case of apoplexy means the grieving widows come into their cash right away. I have a poison for that too."

"Clavell, you are a genius. That could be a lucrative sideline."

The silversmith nodded. "Do you know, Feodor, I forgot to ask you what happened to Lucy's wolf locket. You didn't let her wear it when she wasn't with you, did you?"

"Er—no," Feodor said. "I followed your instructions on that."

"Good, good." The silversmith fitted the pawprint and the wolf face in and tested the locket to make sure it would close. It did, with a quiet snick. "Then where is it?"

"Ah—at my apartments in the Pack's house."

"Bring it in. I can polish it up, replenish the poison, and you can give it to another girl."

"An excellent idea." Feodor scowled at Clavell behind his back.

"No reason to waste it just because Lucy's dead."

"No."

The silversmith set aside the locket he was working on and the tools. "But I do think it's time to close up shop."

"Yes, it is late," Feodor said. Then he caught the old man's narrow-eyed look. An uneasy silence fell between them, charged with the mutual wariness of partners in crime. Paul was the one to break it.

"Not just for tonight. We can't attract attention and it may not have been by chance that Jehane's sister came in here."

"I doubt that but—"

Paul Clavell shook his head. "No, I shall take the sign down and pay off the rest of my lease and close up permanently. No sense taking unnecessary chances, is there?"

"No. Blackmail is a good business and growing nicely."

"We could use a respectable front and a clerk to manage for us."

Feodor laughed. "You may be right. In the meantime, I have to manage these women."

"I don't envy you that, my boy. Now, at my age, a nice docile woman does you good. But the spirited ones like Jehane—well, they make your heart beat faster."

"She is good at that."

Paul Clavell rose a bit creakily from his bench. "Do you have her on the side?"

Feodor made a rude noise. "Jehane has so many sides I have no idea which one I'm on. Just so long as I can get between her legs now and then. She says I'm ugly but she lets me. So long as I stay behind her."

"Indeed. I can imagine it."

6

Her sister was not at home the next day. Nor the next. On the third day, Severin stormed past Jehane's slatternly maid and went up the stairs to bang on her bedroom door.

"Jehane! It's me!"

She heard a groan. A female one, for which she was thankful. She hoped her sister was alone.

"What is it, Severin?"

"It's about—" she lowered her voice—"about the Pack of St. James."

Jehane got out of bed and came to the door. "What about it?"

"I may have found a clue. It is not easy to explain. First of all, I thought I was being followed two nights ago—no, three—"

Jehane looked out to see if any servants were listening and pulled her sister inside her bedroom. Severin looked around. As before, the room looked like a volcano of clothes had erupted. But at least there was no man hastily tugging on his breeches and putting his coat on over his inside-out shirt. It had happened.

"You are a little pig, Jehane," she said with a smile, and kissed her sister on the cheek. "But I am glad you are all right."

"A pig, you say?" Jehane pointed to the chandelier. "I washed out my stockings and hung them up."

Water dripped from the toes but they were clean. "Good for you."

"So what is it, Severin? What have you found out?" She patted the bed. "Come and sit down."

Severin settled herself and caught her breath.

"All right—it has been a few days. Let me think it through."

"Do."

Severin took a deep breath. "I was upset when I last left you and decided to walk. No particular destination—"

"And?"

"I stepped into a silversmith's because I thought someone was following me. I lingered a while and then went to the back, where the man did his work—and there I saw something odd."

Jehane gave her a puzzled look. "What was it?"

"A little wolf's head set into a locket, done in silver. Surely it was meant for a woman of the Pack."

"Perhaps."

Severin tried to compose her rushing thoughts. "I am thinking in several directions at once. Did your friend have a locket like that? Something with a design of a pawprint or a wolf's head?"

"Not that I knew. But Lucy and I were not so very close and I have no idea what was in her jewelry box or around her neck. The thing sounds hideous. Who would wear it?"

"It was ugly," Severin said. "And cruel-looking. Like something worn by a woman in prison or a roaring girl upon the street."

"Lucy never went to gaol. And she stayed off the streets. For what it is worth."

Imprisonment. Murder. Severin pushed away the thought that both could happen to her sister.

"Anyway, do you think it is worth pursuing?"

"I don't know, Severin. Who was the silversmith? Paul Clavell was Lucy's admirer, but he made lovely things for her. I don't know what he looked like, though."

"I don't remember the proprietor's name," Severin said, abashed. "If there was a sign, I didn't see it. But I could go back and find out. I am not afraid."

Jehane rose from the bed and squeezed the remaining water out of the toes of her stockings. "You should be, at least a little. I still think I should not have involved you in this."

Severin was silent for a little while. "Jehane," she said at last, "I must confess that I enjoy aspects of it. The element of danger does me good. My life has grown too safe of late—"

"Lucky you."

Sisters forever, Severin thought ruefully. Would they never stop wanting what the other had?

"A man like Marko is exhilarating to pursue," Severin said. That was far from what she was feeling, but she had no wish to discuss her mixed emotions on the subject of her lover with her little sister. Her vision of him had been prophetic—he had not made amends for their unsatisfying encounter. What had he said? *I cannot see you . . .*

"Oho. So you like being a huntress."

"Not that much. I have no taste for blood."

"Severin, tell me the truth. Were you not jealous when you saw a bill for women's jewelry with his name? Not that a man would dare to give you something ugly. You are renowned for your perfect taste."

"A little silver wolf? I don't know, Severin. It is not much of a clue, if it is a clue at all."

"Is there another reason you wish to investigate? Do you need a reason to go poking around in St. James's Street? And I do mean that tall Taruskin."

"Marko?" Severin realized that it was ridiculous to even try to sound innocent where he was concerned.

"Yes, Marko. You must be curious as to where he goes and who he sees."

"Not that much."

"Liar. Tell the truth."

"I—I am having a fling with him. You know that. I am not in love."

Jehane sighed. "He is magnificent, though."

It occurred to Severin of a sudden to wonder whether her sister had slept with him too.

"No, Severin."

"I beg your pardon?"

"Don't even think that I lured him into my bed, Severin. Not ever. I have seen him at social occasions—the few I am invited to."

"I was not thinking any such thing."

Jehane patted her cheek. "Good."

Severin took a deep breath and let it out with relief when someone knocked on the door.

"Come in," said Jehane, looking toward the door.

Another maid entered, balancing a tray that held a china teapot, a dinner of sorts, and an evening newspaper. She set it down by the sisters, looked at Severin, bobbed a curtsey, and left.

"She never does that for me," Jehane complained. "But then she doesn't think I'm a lady."

She picked up a slice of meat and nibbled at it, glancing at the newspaper she'd moved out of the way. Severin saw her stop chewing.

"What is it?"

"There has been another murder. A young woman, found in—" She scanned the long column of fine print. "It is something like Lucy's case."

Severin reached for the paper but Jehane wouldn't give it to her.

"Then read it aloud, Jehane."

"In a minute. This goes on and on."

Severin looked at her sister's downcast eyes. The thin line between her finely shaped brows deepened as she read.

"*Miss Adele Darrieux, a respectable female of tender years, becomes the second victim of the brutal killer who struck another near St. James's Square not long ago. The hallmarks of the vicious crime are much the same. The pure white throat of an innocent slashed*—and so on." Jehane continued to read silently for half a minute, then went back to reading aloud for her sister's benefit. "*A locket was found around the neck of Miss Darrieux, which opened to reveal the head of a wolf in repoussé silver. Its fangs held poison. A constable is recovering in the hospital*—there's more, but that is the gist of it."

"Dear God."

The sisters stared at each other.

"You did stumble upon a clue, Severin."

"We will have to go to the authorities at once—"

Jehane shook her head. "Severin, you don't understand. Lucy and Adele were anything but respectable. Adele wanted to leave the life." She folded the newspaper tightly and moved it away from her. "She never got her chance."

Severin gave her an astonished look. "You knew her too?"

"Not well. But . . ." Jehane hesitated for a few seconds, studying Severin. "Keep this to yourself, but Adele and Lucy were sisters. Not in the way we are. Different fathers. But they were as close."

"Why can't we tell someone?"

"It is useless to do so. Half the men in London breathe easier when a whore is murdered. And the other half leave town. No one would be prosecuted for such a crime in any case."

"You are appallingly cynical, Jehane."

Jehane rolled her eyes. "Am I wrong?"

"I could not say. But you and I are sisters no matter what."

"Thank you for that, Severin." Jehane grew more thoughtful. "I should not hide behind your skirts, though, even if you are older."

"What are you saying?"

Jehane put her hands on her curvy hips. The action pulled her nightgown down and it slipped over her shoulders. Something about her stance reminded Severin of a warrior goddess.

"That I will do the dirty work from now on, Severin."

"Oh no."

Jehane threw her a fierce look. "Did you ever succeed at telling me what to do?"

"Occasionally. If I pulled your hair at the same time."

Jehane touched a hand to her flowing locks. "I seem to remember you doing that. But no—you have taken a few too many risks already."

"Please, Jehane. I want to help. What if you are next? Ah, that I should have to ask such a question!"

Jehane folded her arms over her breasts. "If you must, then return and look at the silversmith's shop. Find out his name. If it is Paul Clavell, then that is something to go on. But stay on the opposite side of the street and wear different clothes and a large hat."

"The hat will be conspicuous."

"I do not want anyone remembering your amber eyes."

"Very well."

* * *

Severin retraced her steps the next day. Several times. But she could not find the place.

Yes, it had been night when she happened upon it and yes, she had been frightened by her follower. The inside of the shop had been well-lit—she ought to be able to remember it. But she peered in window after window and saw no glass cases, or silver items or the chair she remembered.

The shops on the busy end were exactly as she remembered them, down to the items in their bowfront windows. Severin walked very slowly toward the other end, not willing to believe that an entire shop could have vanished overnight.

Of course, it had been too dark to see the color of the outside and the sign—if there was one, she had not noticed—could have been removed.

If the shop front had been repainted to disguise it, the boards and shingles would still be wet. Nothing she saw was. There were two places that were empty, but neither seemed familiar in the least. She could see all the way to the back of both. There was no wall within either.

The silversmith and his stock in trade had vanished.

Marko was walking along the Thames, on the south side, near the Baltic docks, where he had last seen his brother. If a ship from the north was docked, there might be a reply to his letters to Archangel. Weeks had gone by. Weeks without Severin, he thought wearily. Their unexpected meeting at Almack's had led to an unsatisfying tryst afterwards. Far too rushed, in his opinion—he liked to take his time to arouse a woman and she had been disinclined to tarry long. Fair enough. He could not blame her for being angry with him. Unfortunately, he could not explain why. He had to hope that her feelings for him were of the enduring kind. But he could not expect saintly patience from so passionate a woman—ah, if only he could ask Kyril for advice.

He sorely missed his elder brother and his wife Vivienne and their newborn. It seemed unfair that babies grew as fast as they did. He had been enjoying unclehood. Dandling a baby on his knee was excellent practice for one of his own. Marko thought of his first, powerfully instinctive response to Severin and how convinced he'd been that she was his mate. How distant that wild rush of emotion seemed now, only weeks later. Still, his feelings for her had not cooled. It was more that he was . . . willing to wait. Love at first sight was a dangerous business. But he had other things to worry about.

He liked being by the river. Twenty-five or so miles inland, he could still pick up a whiff of the open sea. The winding Thames was dangerous too, subject to freak floods and high tides. Today it simply flowed, crowded with small ships and watercraft and all the commerce of London.

He had been walking for a very long time but his feet were not sore. The men of the Pack had remarkable calluses, not unlike their wolfish ancestors. If those warrior wolves had made it across uncounted miles of snow, ice, and barren steppes, Marko thought nothing of going all the way across London and crossing a bridge or two.

The seagulls wheeling and screaming overhead against the gray sky cheered him up. They at least were free to fly away from the troubles of the world.

He was in luck—there was more than one ship in at the Baltic docks. He could see the slender masts rising high above the squatty houses of Rotherhithe. Marko walked on.

He hailed a dockmaster and asked after the post, and was directed to the small station where letters could be claimed.

Bulging canvas sacks blocked the door. A lethargic old sailor seemed to be in charge of sorting them. But he had a good sense of humor. When Marko asked if he might look through the bags himself, the sailor simply opened their necks and upended them, resting a seadog's boot upon the pile.

Marko found Kyril's distinctive colored envelope in about a half an hour, tossed a coin to the old sailor, who bit it first and then thanked him gruffly.

It was a good thing the Pack went in for niceties like colored stationery. Not the sort of thing that was easy to find in an isolated northern port like Archangel—his brother must have brought it away with him.

He tucked the thick letter into his overcoat pocket and headed back along a different route. He needed the distraction.

Once home and safely in his apartments at the top of the house, Marko opened the letter. Half, it seemed, had been written by Kyril and half by Vivienne. He scanned their news, such as it was, of Pack business interests, mostly having to do with English guns traded for Russian lumber, and smiled at Kyril's fond account of his infant son.

It was good to know, Marko thought, that his nephew was a genius. According to his proud papa, there had never been a smarter cub born into the Pack. He would soon be going about on all fours, Kyril informed Marko, warning the new uncle to watch out for ankle bites.

He sighed with fondness and unfolded Vivienne's half. He knew of her supernatural ability to read deeply, and he was very curious to know what she had perceived in his sketches of the locket and of the dead woman's face. It was odd, though, that no one had ever claimed the victim's body.

He had not looked at the poisoned locket since he'd put it into the metal box. He was loath to handle the thing—there was no telling if one of the other fangs held poison as well. Taking it to the authorities might land him in Newgate, in a cell reserved for those who would swing on the gallows.

He could not imagine explaining that he had simply found a murdered woman to someone other than two drunken constables. An inquiry conducted by bewigged men of the law would draw public attention to him, a nominal leader in his older brother's absence, and to his kinsmen. He would have to field a slew of questions as to who he was, where he lived, what the nature of his business was, and would he care to add a few words about the mysterious Pack of St. James?

The answers would be scribbled down by a clerk or two, and carefully scrutinized by still more men, who might interpret it all in the worst possible way.

The members of the Pack had friends in high places, but in cases of unexplained murder, their friends were likely to stay well-hidden. However, there were too many threads that connected high and low levels of society for anyone to want to pull too much on one or another. A little whore might well be acquainted with a chancellor. Everyone had something to hide.

So . . . he would keep his mouth shut and continue to investigate. If one of their own had something to do with the unfortunate woman's death, retribution would be meted out according to the ancient law of the Pack, and it would not be pretty.

Marko turned his preoccupied mind to Vivienne's letter.

My dear Marko,

Kyril has related the family news, so I will come to the point. I tried several times to read your sketches on different levels but the task proved difficult.

I hope that you have found the young woman's family.

They would grieve her loss deeply, but it must be said that if she has none, then so much the better.

She died in terrible fear, as you might have guessed, simply by the nature of her wound. And she saw her killer, whose eyes looked into hers when her life was taken. She was alive when she fell to the street but not for long. I am sure a man did the deed.

As for the locket, it is a curious thing. By my reading, the face of the wolf on it is nothing like the Great Wolves that befriended the Roemi, your warrior ancestors. There is nothing noble in its mien, and the eyes are small and shortsighted. Of course, a locket is an inanimate object but something about that little silver face tells me that it was done from life. It is more of a man than a wolf, and both were evil to begin with.

That is all that I could read.

But I sense that more terrible things are about to happen, and that the best of the Pack will stand alone by the end of the fight. Precisely where and how that will happen, I cannot say. You must be very careful, Marko! We tried to book passage on a ship but could not—Kyril asks me to add his apologies. But he says you are the right man to lead us all at this time, and he knows that right itself will prevail. He hopes to join with you in a welcoming Howl upon our return to London, and so do I.

With fond love from your sister-in-wolf,
Vivienne

Marko folded the letter with a sigh and locked it up in a niche in his desk. He was no farther along than he had been, but he valued her reading. His brother and Vivienne were too far away to help much at all. He was indeed on his own.

He found no comfort downstairs in the Pack's house when

he quitted his study, restless. His wolf brethren were lounging about the great hall in various stages of inertia or intoxication.

There seemed to be no end to the cares of a leader. He understood why Kyril, the eldest brother, had taken to it naturally, but Marko had little taste for ordering other fellows about and making sure they did not run wild.

There was no one to talk to and nothing to do. He would go out, he decided, by himself. To a music-hall.

Low entertainment and raucous laughter might take him out of his gloomy mood.

7

The Adelphi Theater placard was long and crowded with acts. The Two-headed Pig and Dancing Dog had top billing and six exclamation points, beating out the Buxom Damsels All In A Row, who were down at the bottom with only two exclamation points. Never a good sign.

Marko bought his ticket and edged through the chattering crowd to a seat that was not worth what he'd paid for it.

Orange peels and nutshells flew by occasionally. The distinguished patrons seemed more inclined to bicker, and complain about fleas in the seat cushions than they were to watch the show, which was abysmally bad.

He endured it in silence, glad enough for the distraction. At least he was not expected to talk to his fellow theater lovers, who were quite content to shout at the musicians in the pit when they were not shouting at each other.

For some strange reason, the clamor and the anonymity of the crowd helped him concentrate on the problem at hand.

He reviewed the facts in his mind, not even seeing the stage below. Two women had been murdered. He did not know the name of the first, nor even where she was buried. He had not returned to the dead-house in time and he assumed she lay in a lonely potter's field in an unmarked grave. It was a tragic fate for her.

Had her body been claimed, he might have been able to investigate from what they would have told him about her. But he would have dreaded telling his side of the story to respectable and loving relatives. He was half-convinced she had some.

Perhaps not.

Still, if she had been connected to London's teeming underworld, it was surprising that no one from it had come forward with information. For sale, of course. That was how it worked. The more money, the better the information tended to be.

Not a whisper from that quarter.

The second woman was a different matter. She had a name: Adele Darrieux. She had been the consort, for want of a better word, of a down-at-heel manwolf of the Pack, who was happy to settle for a female who had seen better days.

But apparently Pyotr had loved her.

No family came forward for Adele—he had paid for her burial, though. At least there had been a name to put on a tombstone and a duly recorded ceremony, should anyone need to know of it someday.

As far as he knew, Adele had not possessed a wolf's-head locket, but then he had not found her. No, a gang of louts reeling home from the tavern had stumbled over her body.

There was no getting around the still unexplained connection to the Pack for both murders. The most probable hypotheses was that someone very high up indeed sought to break their code of secrecy and self-sufficiency by enmeshing them in a scandal from which they could not escape. They might be expelled from England forever, despite their work on behalf of the royal family and Parliament and ministries that operated out of the public eye. The thought was deeply troubling.

Marko was roused from his reverie by a seller of postcards who squeezed by, flashing his wares. Engraved images of naked women with buttocks and bosoms tinted a lurid pink were shoved under his nose. He shot the postcard seller a disgusted look and waved him away. The man cursed and moved on.

Marko leaned forward, looking at the crowd in the cheaper seats below. He thought for a moment that he recognized a face—yes, it was Feodor, sitting by an old man whom Marko did not know.

He leaned back. He had no wish to halloo down and start a raucous conversation of his own.

Marko pressed his fingers to his temples. He was not sure how much more of this dreadful entertainment he could take, but the prospect of going back to St. James's Square was not attractive in the least. It was a dull place late at night—the royals set the tone for the area and the royals weren't what they used to be. Restive, he leaned back and looked up.

Into Severin's amber eyes. She was seated in the front row of the balcony tier above him, and did not seem pleased to see him.

Why should she be? He had hardly been as attentive as a lover ought to be. No flowers, no billet-doux, no serenades below her window—he noticed how her eyes narrowed and it occurred to him that she might well throw a pail of cold water over him if he tried that.

But she gave him a polite nod and turned her gaze back to the very young woman who sat with her, a chit whom he remembered seeing at a few social gatherings, paraded around by her mama. Her name escaped him. Marko thought harder, staring at the stage now as if the answer was written upon the closed curtain. Yes—he did know it. Miss Georgina Lennox.

She was undoubtedly one of Severin's clients. He looked up at the two of them again, noting how gracefully Georgina wielded her fan and how smoothly the girl avoided his gaze. She seemed considerably more polished than when Marko had seen her last at Almack's, galloping around the dance floor in a way that was unseemly, but amusing to watch. Watching her then, Marko had wished he'd had a younger sister like her. She'd seemed to be full of fun and not in the least interested in the serious business of making a match.

He vowed to find a way to speak to them both during the interval and returned his attention to the stage. The heavy curtains had been dragged apart and the dancing dog was beginning a waltz of sorts.

"Do you know him?" Georgina whispered as Marko approached.

"Yes, but only slightly." Severin was not about to share the details of her amorous acquaintance with Marko with someone as fundamentally innocent as Georgina.

The younger woman bobbed a curtsey when Marko reached them and introduced himself, nodding once more to Severin, who in turn introduced him to Georgina.

"Good evening, Severin. It is a pleasure to make your acquaintance at last, Miss Lennox. Although I have seen you a few times in the last months, no one took the trouble to introduce us. But I did overhear your name."

He gave Severin a look that nettled her. A thank-you-very-much look. She moved closer to her protégé. "Of course not," she said sweetly. "A lamb like Georgina cannot wander among the wolves."

Georgina gave him a wide-eyed look. She seemed thrilled to be able to talk to him, much to Severin's further annoyance.

Still, since they were at the theater, he could not ask Georgina to dance.

"Would either of you like an ice? Allow me."

Severin was not sure if Marko's request was addressed to her or to Georgina, who was simpering. She made a mental note to tell the girl not to do it.

"Oh yes. A fruit ice would be lovely. Raspberry for me."

Severin frowned. Georgina would go home with a red tongue and stains on her light-colored gown, and her mama would not be at all pleased.

"No, lemon," Severin said. "Two, please. I myself prefer lemon."

Marko nodded and withdrew to purchase the ices at the nearby counter. Men stood three or four deep, waiting to be served, loudly ordering stronger refreshment and jostling each other.

"I hate lemon," Georgina said. "Am I not old enough to choose?"

"Your natural exuberance does not go well with raspberries, my dear."

The girl giggled. "I suppose not."

"Lemon will leave no spot if it spills and your mother won't cluck over a ruined gown."

Georgina groaned. "I am not allowed the smallest sin, Severin. I thought I would have some respite from all that if I came here with you. The theater is so much fun. Not like a dance. It's wonderful not to endure bowing and scraping and being eyed by eligible young men."

"When you are married you can have all the fun you like."

"Really?" Georgina asked.

Severin realized that her remark was easy to misinterpret. "I meant that you will have a husband to squire you around town and your reputation will be safe."

"Wanting raspberry ice instead of lemon will not ruin my reputation."

Severin had to laugh. "Well, you are right about that. But your mother trusts me. Let us not give her a reason she shouldn't."

"Oh, Severin," Georgina sighed. "Mama and I do nothing but quarrel these days. She wants to know everything I do or she doesn't want to see me at all. She thinks the worst of me no matter what."

"She wants you to be happy," was Severin's temperate reply.

"But not to have fun." Georgina looked at Marko, who was waiting to be served. "He is very handsome."

Severin stiffened, feeling a flash of jealousy that she knew was irrational.

"Do you know if he is married, Severin?"

"I don't think so."

The bland answer seemed to satisfy Georgina, who looked up eagerly when Marko returned bearing two lemon ices. "Thank you, Mr. Taruskin."

"My pleasure, Miss Lennox." He handed one to her and one to Severin. "The proprietor of the refreshment stand advised me that the glasses are to be returned."

"We did not plan to take them to our seats," Severin said dryly.

He only nodded and made small talk with Georgina, who spooned up her ice while she surveyed the mingling crowd before the bell would be sounded for the next act. Severin finished her ice, feeling like a governess. Ignored. Of no consequence.

But when she heard Georgina's spoon clatter into the empty glass and the girl's squeal of pleasure at sighting an acquaintance, she realized she would soon be alone with Marko.

"May I go off with Ellen for a bit?" Georgina asked. The other girl came over, and begged for the privilege of a private talk with Miss Lennox.

"I don't see why not. Don't leave the theater, though."

Both girls looked aghast at the dangerous prospect. Ellen went so far as to flutter her fan. Marko smiled and collected the glass that Georgina held out to him.

"You must meet me back in the balcony in fifteen minutes," Severin said.

"Thank you, Severin," Georgina cooed and gave her a kiss on the cheek before walking off arm in arm with Ellen to converse among the potted palms in the lobby.

Marko held out a hand for Severin's glass of lemon ice as well, which she had barely eaten. "Not to your liking?" He put both glasses onto the tray of a passing waiter and nodded in the direction of the refreshment stand.

"I could not very well allow you to purchase an ice just for Georgina," Severin said. "I don't see anyone I know here, but you know how gossip can start over just such a trifle."

"And how did you come to be the guardian of that young lady's virtue?"

Severin took a deep breath, not wanting to answer that irksome question. But she couldn't just ignore it. "Her mother is a friend of mine, that is all."

"I see." Marko looked at her as if he found the whole idea amusing.

"Georgina is a sweet girl, but innocence can be exhausting," Severin said at last.

Marko grinned. "I don't doubt it. I much prefer a woman of experience."

The remark soothed her ruffled feelings a little. "Hmm. I don't know what to say to that." Severin tilted her chin up and gazed at Marko.

This was not the place to bring up the matter of the unsolved murders. Marko had told Severin nothing of use, and she in turn had been less than forthcoming. So that was that.

Then Severin turned slightly, as if compelled to do so by some unseen force. She could feel eyes upon her and the sensation was uncomfortable.

Marko looked over her shoulder at whoever was standing in back of her, and frowned. "There is someone I know. Ah—hello."

A tall man brushed by her and twisted his head to look down her bodice, and then looked at her face. Severin flinched when she looked into his eyes, which were on the small side, their irises tinged with a yellow that wasn't warm.

"Severin, as I remember, you saw Feodor once," Marko said. "But I shall proceed with the introductions. Feodor Kulzhinsky, this is my friend Severin."

"You have only one name?" Feodor inquired.

Severin nodded. She kept her gloved hands folded together, not wanting to extend the slightest gesture of friendship to him, even if he was Marko's relative.

"Why? Is that the latest fashion or do you have something to conceal?" He didn't seem to be joking.

"Shut up, Feodor," Marko said.

Feodor only lifted a shoulder in a gentlemanly shrug. "I thought I would ask. I meant no harm by it."

Severin could not shake the feeling that he wished her ill. His manner and his bearing reminded her of a weasel standing on its back legs and looking watchfully about, as it hunted some plump little bird. As it happened, Georgina and her friend Ellen sauntered back at that moment. Make that two plump little birds, she thought.

"Well, well," Feodor murmured. "Who have we here?" The girls were not close enough to hear him, but Severin wanted to tell them to go back under the potted palms for their own safety.

His gaze traveled over their light, clinging gowns and Severin half-expected to see a soiled mark where it touched on their youthful thighs and bosoms. The girls were still a little distance away, chattering happily.

Marko was looking at his cousin with ill-disguised contempt. "Come away, Feodor," he said. "Allow me to buy you a glass of whisky. The people next to me said the show goes downhill after the dancing dog."

"Excellent," Feodor said, not taking his eyes off the girls.

The bell for the beginning of the next act sounded loudly, and Marko smiled. "Too late. We shall have to remain sober and return to our seats. You were in the orchestra seats, were you not, Feodor?"

"No. I was talking to a friend there." Feodor did not name the man. "I am in the highest tier. Not the best for seeing the stage, but ideal for spying." He laughed in an unpleasant way.

Severin frowned. Feodor was above her and Georgina. No doubt he had been watching them both. There was something predatory about the man. She would do anything to keep Georgina away from him and nodded her thanks at Marko when he led his cousin a step or two away.

But they were stopped by a third man, younger than they both were and very handsome. Severin was sure she had seen him before but for the life of her, she could not remember where.

"Denis!" Feodor said jovially. "Imagine meeting you here."

The two shook hands, but Marko only nodded to the newcomer. Severin felt a slender arm slide through hers on both sides, as Georgina and Ellen reached her at last.

"Goodness me," Georgina said. "Who is he?"

She meant Denis, it seemed. The rapid rise and fall of her bosom when she looked at him and the sparkle in her eyes were obvious.

The crowd shoved and shouted around them all, and Ellen lifted her fan so she could whisper behind it to Georgina. But Severin heard her perfectly. "I believe that is Denis Somov—he is Russian, I think. And rich, although no one seems to know how he makes his money. But money is money, is it not? He is quite a ladykiller, from what I understand."

"Oh." Georgina said the one word very softly.

Severin led the two of them off at that moment, not wanting either girl to venture a come-hither look at such unsuitable men, angry that Denis and Feodor were smiling when she turned Ellen and Georgina away from them. The trio, arms linked as if they hadn't a care in the world, headed to the staircase that led to their tier, where Ellen had sat unseen before their meeting in the lobby, on the other side, with her chaperone.

"Must we stay for the rest of the show?" Georgina asked. "I am feeling a bit sleepy."

"Are you?" Severin asked. "I suppose we could go home." It would be a good thing if the impressionable young women saw no more of Feodor or Denis tonight. If she could get Georgina home before midnight, and offer a ride to Ellen and her chaperone, Severin would be quite content. "Ellen, what about you?"

Ellen shook her head. "I will stay for the next act with Mrs. Gryche."

The girls said their good-byes, but Severin was sure some unspoken communication had passed between them. She had not been sister to Jehane for a lifetime not to be aware of such things.

She didn't doubt that Ellen would elude her chaperone somehow and talk to both men again. If only she could get to Marko somehow and ask him to keep an eye out for the girl. She peered down into the next tier, trying not to be conspicuous. He had settled back into his seat. The light from the sconces that adorned the curving walls of the tiers and balconies gleamed on his wheat-colored hair. She watched him run a hand through it absently, looking about and looking at nothing.

Severin wished she could be sitting with him, without a care in the world, just enjoying herself, the trying and dangerous matter of the unsolved crimes set aside for one night.

"And how was the show?"

"Not very interesting," Georgina told her mother.

"I see. Well, it is probably for the best if you didn't go to the theater or music-halls at all."

Georgina swung her stockinged foot. The other was tucked underneath her on the sofa. Her loose dressing-gown fell open in front, revealing her nightgown and some of the uncorseted figure beneath, which was very fine.

Her mother looked at her and frowned. "Did you stay with Severin the entire time?"

"Yes, I did," Georgina replied. "Except for when I was talking to Ellen. I was so happy to see her—I haven't seen any of my friends since you decided to marry me off."

"There will be plenty of time for chitchat and idleness once you are," was her mother's taut reply.

"Yes, Mama," Georgina said. Her tone was taunting. "I have noticed that the earl leaves you alone in the evenings. So do your former friends."

"He goes to his club. And do not be so impertinent."

"I was only saying," Georgina began.

Her mother interrupted her. "I don't want to hear what you have to say. My dear husband is doing everything he can so that you can make a good match."

"He is very kind."

Her mother didn't miss the acid note in Georgina's tone. "Would you rather he didn't bother, Georgina? It isn't as if your real father would give you a dowry or social entrée or anything worth having."

"Where is he?"

Her mother only shrugged. "No one knows. Not even the

bailiff. Once Jacky Lennox got out of debtor's prison, he was never seen again."

As if she knew what was coming next, Georgina made a face, but not so her mother could see it.

"And that's only one reason you're not free to do as you please, my girl. You are not going to go upon the boards, or be ruined, or lose your heart to a worthless fellow with no fortune and no prospects—"

"I almost forgot. I met a rich man tonight, Mama."

"There is something alarming in the way you say that." Her mother gave her a suspicious stare. "Mark my words, I won't have you throwing yourself at strangers. Whatever could Severin have been thinking?"

"She watched over me like an older sister," Georgina said, "the way she always does."

"Good," her mother said. "She is handsomely paid to do so."

Georgina looked hurt.

"Did you not know that?"

"No, because you never told me."

"I did not think I was quite up to the task of civilizing you, Georgina," her mother said, "and although I know Severin, we are not quite what I would call bosom friends. However, she is an expert on the social graces."

"How lucky I am."

"More than you know," her mother sniffed. "So how did you make the acquaintance of this 'rich man' if Severin was watching you? And find out about his fortune, while you were about it?"

"I didn't really. It was Ellen who said that. She whispered about him behind her fan."

"Do I know Ellen's mother?"

"You wouldn't want to," was Georgina's quick answer.

"And why is that?"

"She owns a tavern."

Mary Lennox gave her an appalled look. "I must insist that you find yourself a better class of friend, Georgina."

"Oh, what airs you put on!"

"It is all for your own good." She studied her daughter for a long moment, noting again her deshabille and the nubile flesh revealed by her careless pose on the sofa. "You are becoming very attractive, Georgina. It seems to have happened overnight."

Georgina pouted. "Then you have Severin to thank."

"Do I?" Her mother thought that over for a minute or two. "It is a good thing I trust her, then. But don't you go getting any ideas about running off with a soldier or a dancing-master or any nonsense like that."

Her daughter groaned in a put-upon way. "I won't. I promise. What do you take me for?"

"You are nineteen. It is a dangerous age."

The next week found Georgina wandering along High Holborn Street, doing a little shopping. Her mother deemed it unladylike to stop in at the greengrocer's or the bakery, lest her daughter be seen eating on the street, so Georgina was limiting herself to booksellers and the like.

She paused in front of a jeweler's shop, admiring the delicate creations in the window. Georgina fingered the fine chain around her throat, feeling for the little link that was bent—she had been meaning to have it fixed.

Surely there was no harm in going in and seeing to that. It was not as if she could afford diamond shoebuckles or a pearl necklace. But she had enough for the repair.

Georgina entered, making the shop bell chime.

A male clerk, soberly dressed, his chin sunk into a stiff white collar, came over. "Good day, miss. May I assist you in some way?"

She fingered the chain again, finding the bent link. "I need to have this fixed, if it's possible. One link is about to break."

He peered at the place for a second. "Oh dear."

It occurred to Georgina from his immaculate attire that he did not work at a jeweler's bench, only assisted customers. "Do you have someone here who could do it?"

The clerk nodded. "We do, but he is not in yet. He should be here shortly. If you would like to examine the stock while you wait . . . please feel free to do so."

Georgina didn't know whether to believe that or not. No doubt the clerk had been instructed to keep customers in the shop however he could. The jewelry in the glass cases sparkled and shone, and she told herself that there was no harm in looking at it.

He stood at attention while she studied the different pieces, imagining what they might look like on her neck or her ears.

Another customer came in, and then a second one followed. Both were men. The clerk helped one and asked someone to come out of the back room to see to the other. She could study the jewelry to her heart's content.

Georgina thought a pair of emerald ear-drops were magnificent and certainly costly. She would not even ask to try those on. But there was a coral necklace that she fancied—she might ask to see that, just to hold the smooth beads in her hand and enjoy their brilliant color for a few moments. And, oh, a finely carved cameo pin . . . she was lost in thought over the array of small treasures when she realized the soberly dressed clerk was standing on the other side of the case.

"Mr. Clavell is here if you would like him to look at your chain," he said.

"Of course." She straightened and glanced up at the clerk and the man who was standing by him.

Mr. Clavell had mild blue eyes, a bit rheumy, and a face that was unexceptional. She would describe him as old and let it go at that.

"Allow me," he said, reaching out with hands that were wrinkled and veined, but quite steady.

Something in the sureness of his gesture made her lift her chin with equal confidence, presenting her throat to him. She caught a glimpse of herself in the mirror behind him, realizing with a start how vulnerable she seemed in that position. But he scarcely touched her skin as he slid the chain around to find the clasp and open it.

The fine chain slid into his palm and he poured it out on top of the glass case, handling it with care.

Georgina wondered why she had ever prized it. It seemed pitifully thin and cheap next to what lay underneath it.

But Mr. Clavell made no comment on that. He pulled the chain into a straight line and pointed to the bent link with a small, sharp tool. "I can fix that for you, but it will take several minutes."

"I can wait."

"Very well, Miss—?" The clerk waited for her to tell him her name.

"Miss Lennox. Miss Georgina Lennox."

"Would you like to sit down?"

She nodded and took a chair. He seemed to understand that she would rather not succumb to the temptation of trying on beautiful things she could not afford.

"My name is Tait, by the way, should you require any further assistance."

"Thank you."

The first customer who'd come in after her had left, but the second one was still there. He looked at her curiously and rather boldly. Georgina felt uncomfortable and looked mostly at the floor.

She ignored the low murmurs that passed between the clerk and the customer, who was clearly buying something for his mistress.

"I don't want the wife to know. You do understand, Tait."

"Yes, sir." The clerk's voice was bland and unjudgmental.

"Let me look at the pearl ear-bobs. Those big ones. Molly would like 'em."

"They are very fine." Georgina heard a click as Tait lifted the lid of the case and took them out, putting them into the customer's palm.

"Yes, they would get her noticed. But I wonder—"

Georgina felt the man's gaze upon her. She refused to look up.

"Perhaps the young lady sitting there would like to try them on."

"I could not say, sir."

Georgina's cheeks flamed. She actually wanted to. But if anyone she knew should pass by . . . and see her trying on ear-bobs with a strange man at her side . . . no, she couldn't.

The customer laughed under his breath. "Well, I will ask her if you won't." He came down the aisle in the center of the shop and stopped by Georgina. "Forgive me if I seem forward, but would you mind—I assume you heard what we were saying—"

"Yes, I did." She looked up.

"Then if I may introduce myself . . ."

In for a penny, in for a pound. Perhaps there was no harm in any of this. "Please do."

"Jeremiah Cooke, at your service."

"How do you do, Mr. Cooke."

He wasn't bad-looking, just rather brash, with ruddy cheeks and a thatch of reddish hair. In his late thirties and probably a brewer or a prosperous man of business. Not someone she was likely to run off with.

Georgina felt her usual confidence return. This was a lark,

nothing more. She could try on the ear-bobs and make him happy, then be on her way.

When the chain was fixed, of course. She put a hand to her neck where it normally lay.

The ruddy-faced man grinned at her and Georgina wondered why. There had been nothing suggestive about the gesture. She straightened from the chair and went to the glass case, where the clerk was setting up a mirror.

Georgina fastened the ear-bobs to her lobes and admired herself for a moment before turning back to Mr. Cooke.

"They will look good on Molly. But they look even better on you."

She only nodded, not wanting to dignify the comment with a thank-you.

She took them off and dangled them over Jeremiah Cooke's outstretched palm before she let them drop. At that moment, Mr. Clavell returned with her chain.

"I have fixed the link. Here it is, good as new and pretty as ever." He let it swing, holding one end of it in his fingers.

"Oho. Now who gave you that, my girl?" asked Cooke.

"My mother," said Georgina with a guilty start. She had not thought of her until that second—but then, she told herself, at nineteen she didn't have to.

"I see."

Her inadvertent mention of a mother didn't seem to diminish his flirtatious mood at all. She looked from him to Tait, just in case she would need rescuing.

"There will be a small charge for the repair, Miss Lennox." The clerk raised one eyebrow a quarter of an inch, and Georgina realized that he was more concerned with collecting a few shillings at the moment.

"Waive it," the old man said. "It took me no time at all. I am happy to be of service to such a pretty young customer."

"But Mr. Clavell," the clerk began to say.

"I won't hear of you charging her. Just give her our card in case the chain breaks or bends again, eh?" Clavell gave Tait's upper arm a squeeze that made the younger man wince.

"As you wish." He gave Georgina a pasteboard card from a holder on the glass case.

"Well done," Jeremiah said. "You ought to get her address in return, of course." He winked at Georgina.

"I would rather not," she said quickly. "Thank you, Mr. Clavell. I would certainly come back if something else needs fixing."

"Our Mr. Clavell is highly skilled," Tait said. "He does engraving and silver work, as well as miniature paintings for lockets and such."

"Now a lady does like a nice miniature for a keepsake," Mr. Cooke said jovially. "Especially in a locket. To have the face of her beloved tucked right between her—"

Tait shot him a killing glare.

"My apologies, Miss Lennox," Cooke said.

She made no reply, but thanked the clerk and Clavell again, and left the shop.

8

Jeremiah Cooke left a half hour later, after a matching necklace in a presentation velvet box was wrapped up with the ear-bobs and a card for Molly.

Another man had come in. Tait looked up from setting the shop to rights. "Good afternoon, Mr. Kulzhinsky."

"Call me Feodor. Let us not be so formal."

Tait nodded toward the back. "Clavell is hard at work."

"Good." Feodor went that way, pushing aside a heavy velvet curtain that divided the front of the jeweler's shop from the back. "Hello, Paul."

The old man sitting at the workbench didn't get up. He was using a pointed knife to carve a small piece of ivory, handling the blade in a skillful way.

"You seem happy enough," Feodor observed.

"I am. This place does nicely for a temporary location. We do need more girls. Got a lovely one in today—you just missed her."

"I am sorry," Feodor said.

"Some lout of a customer scared her off, Tait said. A Mr. Cooke. Jeremiah Cooke."

"Oh, him. Yes, I have procured several girls for him," Feodor mused. "He seems to like Molly the best. Well, what was the lovely one's name?"

"Georgina Lennox."

"Ah. I have been introduced to her. But she is well-guarded."

"By whom?"

"Severin. The amber-eyed beauty who dodged into the old shop."

The silversmith looked up. "Oh her. Ought we to leave Miss Lennox alone then?"

"I don't see why."

"Because the girl seems genuinely innocent."

"Then we can charge more for her." Feodor said recklessly. "Do we know her address?"

Clavell shook his head. "Ask Tait. He might have it. I expect she'll be back. Pretty things love pretty things. Georgina didn't look rich."

"Then she can be bribed."

"Perhaps, Feodor. Her eyes did light up when she was look-ing into the cases." Clavell snickered. "I don't think she knew that most of the jewelry was imitation."

"We don't have to use jewelry as bait," Feodor said.

"What do you mean?"

"There is always Denis."

"Oh, right." The jeweler set aside the piece he had been ex-amining and looked up at Feodor at last. "Your dissolute cousin."

"Yes, indeed. Denis is young, but he is a master of the art of seduction."

Clavell shook his head and managed to look sad. "Miss Lennox seemed genuinely naïve. He will not have to work very hard to ensnare her."

"Naïve, eh? Then why was she in here? Innocent young girls don't purchase expensive jewelry. Their papas give it to them."

"She didn't say. The only parent she mentioned was her mother."

"Why?"

Clavell glanced his way. "Because her mother had given her the chain she wore, which I fixed for her. A cheap thing of no consequence. I wondered at first why she wanted it repaired. It is sure to break again."

"Perhaps it had sentimental value."

"No doubt."

Feodor settled himself on a chair to the side of the jeweler's bench and picked up the small blade Clavell had been using and cleaned his nails with it.

"Do you mind?" Clavell plucked it out of his hand. "I use that for delicate jobs."

"Sorry, old man."

Clavell flashed him a rheumy-eyed glare.

"I seem to have struck a nerve," Feodor said dryly. "Were you lusting after Miss Lennox?"

"The young ones don't even see me," the jeweler muttered.

"It wouldn't do if they were interested. We can't blackmail evil earls and lascivious lords and dastardly dukes if you insist on sampling the merchandise first."

"It's all a game to you, isn't it? You Russians are quite mad."

"Are we?"

"Yes," the old man said. "Calling yourselves the Pack of St. James and all that, as if you really were wolves. What do you do then? Howl at the moon every third Wednesday of the month?"

"Only if it's full," Feodor said lightly.

"Bah."

"Come, come. Let us remember that there is a good deal of money yet to be made. We have only just begun. It is unfortunate that two women have died at the outset, but it couldn't be helped. They are easily replaced in any case."

"You never did tell me why you killed the second."

"Who said I killed the first, Clavell?" Feodor's light tone had acquired a sharp edge.

"I merely assumed you had. Someone must be breathing down your neck if you're saying you didn't."

"No, no one is. But we're in this together, Paul." Feodor rose and clapped him on the back. "You and me and Denis."

"And a stable of headstrong women." The older man licked his dry lips,

Feodor seemed irritated by the sound. "A stable . . . hmm. Yes, it will do as a metaphor. But hacks must make way for the younger stallions, Mr. Clavell. About time you were put out to pasture, eh?"

"I think you have beaten the metaphor to death." The older man tested the sharpness of the blade he held against his finger. Then, suddenly, he pressed it against Feodor's throat. The gesture was not a joke but he drew no blood, even though his hand shook. The thin mark on Feodor's neck vanished in an instant.

He pushed Paul's hand away with ease. "You don't have the strength to kill a kitten, you old bastard," Feodor scoffed and rubbed his neck. "But you should not play such games."

Mary Lennox set down her half-finished glass of brandy and watched her daughter enter the house. Georgina's hair was down, as if she had been running.

The little hoyden. Then it crossed Mary's mind that her daughter might not have been running at all. Hair came down for many reasons. The one that came to her mind involved manly fingers who wanted to play with a pretty girl's long tresses.

"Georgina!" she barked.

Her daughter whirled around. "Yes—what is it, Mama? I have come home—I was not gone long."

"You are breathless."

"I was running."

Mary folded her arms across her chest and just looked at her daughter, her foot tapping. "I hope so."

"I am telling the truth." Walking more slowly, Georgina proceeded past her mother and up the stairs.

"No, I don't think so."

"Mama, please!"

Mary Lennox decided to ignore the odd note of emotion in her daughter's voice. A point needed to be made. She would make it. "Where have you been?"

Georgina touched the chain at her neck. "I had this fixed. A link was bent."

Her mother only sniffed. "That didn't take two hours."

"I—I was looking at the things in the shop. And talking to—" Georgina hesitated a little too long.

"Do let me guess. You were chatting with the clerk? Somehow I don't think so."

Georgina was silent for a few seconds. Then an argument exploded that would have put the quarrelsome devils of hell to shame. On both sides, frustration and anger took over and terrible things were said.

Forty-five minutes later, at a high pitch of self-righteous fury, Mary reached for the fine chain around her daughter's neck. "There was nothing wrong with this! You don't deserve a gift of gold!"

"Stop it! Leave me alone!" Georgina's sudden motion snapped the chain. She tried to grab it from her mother's hand without success.

"Damn you, Georgina!" Mary cried. "Can you not see what will happen? I have tried so hard to protect you—"

"I don't want to be protected," Georgina snarled.

"And to advance you socially—"

"I am far from sure I want that!"

"Then get out of my house!"

Still clutching the chain, Georgina came closer to her mother, who shrank back. "Your house, is it? I don't think it is, Mama. You are allowed to live here, that is all. And so am I."

Mary stood like a statue. "Get out," she repeated.

"Where will I go?" Georgina's lower lip was quivering. She bit into it hard enough to draw a tiny drop of blood.

"Wherever you like. Go to whoever it was you were talking to at the jewelry store. If it was a jewelry store."

The two women stared fiercely at each other.

"I will go to Severin," Georgina said at last.

"If she will have you," her mother countered.

As it turned out, Severin was not at home. Georgina was invited into her parlor to wait, as the servants knew her, and forgotten about. By the sofa was a basket that held the clothes she had flung into it and expensive jewelry taken from her mother's case that she intended to pawn. Fidgeting, she was glad enough to go to the window when she heard a carriage stop in the street outside.

She peeped out from behind the curtain. A man got out—Marko Taruskin. Oh no. With her luck he would be shown into the same parlor and left to wait with her. The thought made her more melancholy than she already was.

"Is Severin in?" she heard him ask the maid who'd come to the door.

"No, sir. She isn't expected back for some time."

That answer seemed to disappoint him, because he sighed. "I will go, then. Tell her I called."

"Very well."

A minute later Georgina watched him swing himself up into the carriage and depart. She felt more miserable than ever. The world outside seemed overwhelming and its freedoms more nerve-wracking than not. But she could not simply stay here for hours until Severin's eventual return—she felt she would go mad.

She collected her basket and her things, and made her way out a side door without anyone seeing her.

9

Mary Lennox sobbed as if her heart would break. "I do not know where she is, Severin. We had a fight—I think it was the worst we have ever had."

"And neither of you apologized?"

"N-no. I wanted to make amends, but when I went up to her room, Georgina was gone."

Severin shook her head sadly. "It will be difficult to find her in London unless she wants to be found. What did she take with her?"

"Only some clothes. Not many. I checked her closet."

Severin nodded. "Then she might have gone to her friend Ellen's."

"Would you—" Mary hesitated. "Would you mind if I looked through your house?"

"She is not here," Severin said with surprise. "Do you think I would hide her from you?"

"No, of course not. But she is good at hiding and this house is big. She might have concealed herself here, thinking she would slip out later and return home. When I was good and scared," Mary added peevishly.

"The maid said Georgina did not stay long," Severin said, "And that she went out a side entrance because she seemed to think no one was looking."

"She could very well have come back in that same door in another minute. And then there is the matter of Marko Taruskin. You mentioned that he was here, Severin. A fascinating man. Those Taruskin brothers are the talk of London and some of it is very salacious talk—"

"It is only talk, Mary. And my servant was quite sure that he came and went before Georgina made her escape . . . though I could not call it that."

"What do you mean?"

"She escaped from your house, not mine, Mary."

"I could not really say that she escaped. I told her to get out."

Severin's eyebrows went up. "I see. You did not tell me that."

"What would it have mattered if I did?" Mary burst out. "She is gone, that's all I know, and she came to you first."

"And now she has gone somewhere else," Severin said firmly.

"Please allow me to look. You said you have not been at home all day."

"True, Mary. Well, I suppose we could look together." The idea of opening doors all the way up to the attic and rummaging through the cellar seemed pointless. Jehane had once run away at a younger age than Georgina and had been found in the house of an admirer. Severin did not care to inform Mary of that.

She rose from the settee and extended a hand to help Mary. The countess waved it away and heaved herself up, inelegantly, from her comfortable chair and stood, wiping away her tears.

"I almost forgot to ask if you had told Coyle."

"My lord knows nothing of it."

My lord indeed. How different Mary had become since her marriage. Severin had known that the earl wanted the girl gone, but not in this way, she was sure.

"He would be alarmed to know that Georgina is not to be found."

Severin only nodded.

"There are so many dangers, Severin—"

"Which begs the question of why you ordered her to leave your house."

Mary stepped back. "I am her mother. I have every right to tell her what to do."

"But think of the consequences! London is full of traps for unwary girls who think they are sophisticated."

"If she sees herself that way, Severin, it is because you taught her to."

Severin shot her a meaningful look. "I watched over her as if she were my own sister."

"And we all know what happened to her," Mary blurted out. "But I at least have left that world far behind."

Severin was deeply offended but she reminded herself of what was at stake. It would be difficult to return Georgina to her mother and the only home the girl knew if Severin and Mary quarreled. Still, her voice had a noticeable edge. "I see."

"May I mention the company you keep, Severin?"

"What do you mean?"

"Everyone knows that you and Marko have had—well, you know exactly what I mean. And what about all the other mysterious Taruskin men? Foreigners. One never knows what to expect."

"Don't be ridiculous."

"I am merely speculating. It may be that your Marko gained

your confidence and wormed his way into your affections so that one of the other Taruskins could take my daughter."

Severin began to pace upon the carpet herself. It was not as if she trusted Feodor—but until Georgina's disappearance, she had been more concerned for her sister Jehane. She was surprised that Mary had not mentioned the recent murders, but it would not help matters to encourage her penchant for hysteria. "The Taruskins keep to themselves, but they are good men, I believe. I have heard it said that they are in service to the Crown in some secret way."

Information Severin had gleaned from the scandal sheets. Marko had not told her that. And it wasn't enough for Mary.

"Exactly my point," she said. "No one really knows what they do."

"What are you suggesting, Mary?" Righteous indignation flashed in Severin's amber eyes. "Have you proof of anything? Will it help us find Georgina?"

"Temper, temper," Mary said. "People are always wickeder than they seem, you know. Marko may know something and you could get it out of him."

Severin turned to face the older woman. "Shall I tell him what you said?"

"I don't care if you do. I want my girl back." Mary Lennox folded her arms across her bosom and scowled at Severin. "Coyle is in a position to stir up trouble for the lot of them."

"Is he? Will it bring your daughter out of hiding if he does? This is a delicate matter, Mary, as you well know. And time is of the essence."

Severin was not going to tell Mary one word of her sisterly conversations with Jehane on Feodor's possible connection to at least one of the unsolved murders.

Severin wondered desperately why she did trust Marko. She supposed it was the physical connection between them. She had always thought it was difficult for a naked person to lie, and she had lain with him skin to skin, and heart to heart more than once. Even when she discounted the power of sensual satisfaction, she could not deny that he seemed to mean the affectionate words he murmured afterward and what he'd said about desiring only to please her and make her happy.

That alone had frightened her a little. But not for the reasons on Mary's mind.

10

Jehane had holed up again in her Soho apartments. Severin looked around as she entered her sister's bedchamber, not seeing a place to put her hat and gloves. Then she looked at the bed and realized that there was a man in it, sleeping peacefully with his back to them.

The maid hadn't mentioned it, but then the girl might not have known someone was with her mistress.

Severin pointed at him, wordlessly. Jehane shrugged. "Charlie had too much to drink. I can't rouse him."

"We cannot talk with him here."

"He won't hear a thing."

Charlie gave the lie to that when he rolled over. He didn't open his eyes when he murmured to Jehane, though. "Leaving me, luv?"

"No, Charlie." Jehane ran her hand over his bare chest, shamelessly caressing him as though her sister weren't there at all.

Her drowsy lover arched and stretched, taking pleasure in

her touch. Severin wanted to look away, but she didn't. He was gloriously male, if too young for her sister. She glanced at his regimental coat, flung over a chair, and amended her thought. He wasn't too young to die for king and country.

"Go back to sleep," Jehane whispered to him.

Charlie yawned and rolled back over. Jehane pulled the blankets up over his bare shoulders and stroked his hair.

Despite her annoyance, Severin smiled. Her sister's tenderness toward the young fellow touched her, and it was clear that they were happy together. Jehane eased out of the bed, wearing a shift, and padded toward the adjoining room.

"I must wash. Just push all that on the floor and make yourself comfortable." She gestured to an armchair brimming over with discarded clothing.

Severin did as she was told, listening to the clink of a porcelain pitcher and the slosh of water in a large bowl as she sat down. Jehane hummed as she made her ablutions and got dressed.

She reentered her boudoir with a very fine robe sashed around her waist, and her hair swept up. Like this, face scrubbed clean, her ears and neck unadorned with jewelry, she was still beautiful in the morning light.

But Severin could not help noticing more subtle changes in her sister's face.

Jehane's eyes had faint dark circles under them and her cheeks seemed a little drawn. Too many late nights, perhaps. Severin had a feeling that Charlie did not much care how his mistress made her living.

"Come, let us go downstairs, sister," Jehane said.

Severin rose, cast a last look at Charlie, who was snoring blissfully, and followed Jehane from the bedchamber.

They barely noticed the tea and food that a housemaid brought to them in the drawing room. Severin explained what little she knew of Georgina's disappearance.

"She could be anywhere," Jehane said.

"Do you think that some of the women you know would help us find her?"

Jehane only shrugged and sat back with her cup of tea. "I suppose so."

"Would they expect payment?"

"Some might."

Severin gave her sister a considering look. "I have most of the fee for Georgina's instruction safely hidden away at home. I would be happy to draw upon it."

"Shouldn't her mother pay for that? Or her stepfather? What is the earl's name?"

"Coyle. Mary hasn't told him, apparently."

"I imagine she doesn't want to jeopardize her position with him. She is a new bride, after all," Jehane said. "Rather mature for the role, but Mary would play any role well."

"Even that of a mother."

Jehane eyed her sister over the rim of the teacup. "I detect an edge in your voice."

"I cannot help it."

"Have you and Mary quarreled over this?"

"Not exactly," she told Jehane. "It is just that Mary is so different now. Both pretentious and anxious to climb up the social ladder. She was pushing her daughter to make a good match and I suspect the girl rebelled."

"More's the pity," Jehane said.

Severin gave her sister a curious look but said nothing.

"I often wish that I had not," Jehane said.

"But I thought—"

"What?"

"That you loved your independence."

"Pah. I have very little of it now. The life I lead imprisons me. I am beset by fear and nervousness—the murders only made it worse. Speaking of that," Jehane finished her tea and set down the cup, "does Georgina's mother know of them?"

"Mary reads the papers like anyone else. We did not discuss it, though."

"That seems odd, under the circumstances."

Severin could not answer for her friend. But Jehane had a point. "I think that Mary thinks more of herself than her daughter," she said. "Georgina's disappearance is likely to erupt in a scandal and the whole thing will make her look bad."

"How unfortunate," Jehane said dryly. "The scenario is right out of one of those melodramas Mary used to do. A reckless daughter, a budding beauty, breaks the heart of her devoted mama, a fading beauty."

"Not quite," Severin murmured, mindful of the signs of middle age on her sister's own beautiful face if Jehane herself was not.

Jehane rose and tightened the sash on her gorgeous robe. Then she went to the looking-glass to study herself. "I am fading myself, I think."

"Not at all," Severin said loyally. So her sister was aware of it. How could she not be? Beauty was her business.

"It is true. And I am only a year younger than you." Jehane stroked her throat as if encouraging the blood to move up into her pale cheeks. "I don't have too much longer," she said grimly.

"Whatever do you mean, Jehane? Are you ill?"

"No." She turned to her sister. "I meant in my trade. What shall I do next?"

"You could open an agency to reunite wayward girls with their families," Severin snapped.

Jehane ceased to study herself and moved back to where Severin was sitting. "You will find that they often do not want to be."

"That cannot always be true. Many a girl has gone astray and then found that she is no longer welcome at home. Pimps and panderers take advantage of that sad fact. They are on every corner in some neighborhoods."

"So they are," Jehane said. "And they have no want of customers for their goods."

Severin rose, agitated. "Jehane, you must help me. Georgina has to be somewhere and we have to find her as soon as possible."

"It would be for the best," Jehane said calmly.

Severin sighed. The task would be daunting.

"Where shall we begin, then? You still have not penetrated, so to speak, the inner chambers of the Pack."

"No, Jehane, I have not."

Jehane ran a look over her sister. "And is the wildly handsome Mr. Taruskin still your lover?"

The blunt question surprised Severin. "I have not seen him for a while. I am not sure why."

She could not bring herself to say how much she missed him. How could she admit to her craving for Marko's passionate skill or the beauty of his naked body? Her sister was far too jaded to care about such things and remained suspicious of all things Packish in any case. Then Severin thought again of the sleeping young soldier upstairs and Jehane's tenderness toward him. Her sister had a weak spot too, like most women.

"I am sure he will help if I ask. He is like Charlie," Severin said tentatively. "Gallant and protective—"

"Yes, Charlie is sometimes," Jehane said. "It is too bad about Marko, though. Will you take another lover?"

"Our affair is by no means over," Severin said hastily. "Just because a man does not bother a woman incessantly doesn't mean that—" Her sister looked at her with pity. "I will ask him."

All she had to do was swallow her pride. She would have to. They might not have much time.

In another part of London . . .

Georgina set her basket down inside a doorway and rested. She could not sit down like a vagrant, but oh, how she wanted to.

A man passing by made some lewd comment but she ignored him, pretending to be waiting for a friend. He went on and Georgina sighed with tiredness.

Where exactly was she? The street she had come down seemed familiar but she was not sure why. In a little while she picked up her basket and walked on.

Then she saw it. The sign for the jeweler's shop where she'd had the chain around her neck fixed. She might find refuge there.

Her mother's clutch at it had broken it past the point of repair, and Georgina was sure her mother had flung it into the fire when she'd found out that her daughter was gone. She had left no note.

She edged closer, examining the goods in the window without standing directly in front of it. A row of miniatures had been set out in a padded velvet case with niches for each little oval. The portraits were of women and one man, conventional images meant to show the skill of the painter and invite new customers to purchase more. A hand set out a sign next to the case. *Miniatures To Order.*

Georgina realized that the hand belonged to Tait, the clerk, and shrank back so that he would not see her.

Then it occurred to her that he might know where her mother's jewelry could be pawned. She would redeem it, she promised herself. But for now she needed money to buy food and find a little place to live and get on her feet. She had come away with none.

And she would not go back. Never.

Exactly what she would do, Georgina didn't know. The

harsh quarrel had left her reeling and she felt as if she could not think. And she was hungry. She hadn't had a drop to drink or a crumb to eat since sneaking out of her mother's house.

Georgina summoned up her courage and moved in front of the shop window. Tait was still there. If he was surprised to see her, he didn't show it.

She gave him a tentative wave, then held up the basket as if to explain why she was there.

He gave a stiff little bow. Georgina took a few steps more and opened the door of the shop. Then she went in.

"Good morning, Miss Lennox. Out shopping, I see."

"Yes."

She looked about, desperate for a topic of conversation. The miniatures. They would do. "I saw the paintings in the window. They are very fine."

"Indeed they are."

"I was wondering..." She hesitated and set her basket down on the floor at her feet.

"Would you like to sit down? You seem fatigued. I can take the case out of the window if you would like to look at it."

"That would be very kind. Yes. I will sit down."

Georgina selected the softest of the chairs as Tait went to the window and reached in with one long arm. He picked up the case of miniatures and handed it to Georgina.

She took her time in looking over the little paintings, not aware that she was being watched in turn from behind the heavy velvet curtain some distance away that separated the back from the front.

"She did come back," Feodor murmured almost inaudibly. "Well, well, well."

"I am not that surprised."

"And why not, Clavell?"

"As I said, she does not seem rich. And she must have some idea that this shop is a meeting-place of sorts."

Feodor squinted through the slit in the curtain. His keen sight helped him see that she held one of a woman. When the sun hit the ivory oval just right, he even knew which woman.

"Hm. Does she know that she is looking at Lucy Pritchett's face?"

"How would she?" Clavell asked.

"Well, it is very lifelike," Feodor answered. "Forgive my joke."

Paul Clavell shrugged it off.

Feodor kept watching her. "Lucy was pretty. But Georgina is prettier."

She raised her head but it was only to look at Tait, who was making some comment about the miniatures.

"Hush. She might be able to hear us," Feodor murmured. The two men were quiet.

"No, I have no sweetheart at the moment, Mr. Tait," Georgina said. "But when I do, I will have a miniature like this done of him." She had turned to the clerk and the men behind the curtain could not see that her eyes were brimming with tears as she unclasped her basket.

"Very well," Tait said calmly.

"I came in about another matter."

"Did the chain break again? Forgive me for being forward but I noticed that you were not wearing it today."

"No, I am not."

Tait blinked. "Then what is it, Miss Lennox? I would be happy to help you with anything."

She searched in her basket and drew out a roll of silk cloth. "These are jewels that I wish to pawn. Do you know where I might do that?"

His expression changed to one of faint disdain and then interest as she unrolled the cloth. "These are very fine. I am sure you know their worth."

"Oh, yes," she hastened to assure him.

"As to a pawnbroker—Miss Lennox, I am not sure you would be safe to walk in the neighborhoods where they are found."

"Whatever do you mean?"

"That your basket might be stolen and you yourself molested in some way. It would not be wise."

Georgina's look of expectancy disappeared. "I see. Well, then, I have little choice but to sell one or two pieces."

"May I ask, Miss Lennox, if you are experiencing some personal difficulty that would lead you to pawn them?"

The question was politely phrased but to the point.

"In a manner of speaking, yes. You could say that."

He hemmed and hawed and rocked on his feet. "I could advance you a small sum and pawn them myself on your behalf."

"Oh . . ." She hesitated.

"Or you could work here behind the counter and earn a bit of money until you got on your feet. We would keep the gems in our safe for you. No one would know."

By the expression on Georgina's face, she was utterly relieved that he had somehow divined her predicament—and offered her an honorable way out. Of sorts.

"That would—I think that would do for now," she said, more crestfallen than happy.

Tait pressed a button on the floor without her seeing it and she turned her head at the faint chime. "Mr. Clavell would know of a respectable rooming-house for you, Miss Lennox. He is in today."

The old man appeared from behind the curtain. "My dear, I would be happy to help. I do know of such a place."

Georgina hesitated again. Things seemed to be moving

rather fast. But her hunger and thirst had turned into dizziness. Surely the proprietors of a fine jewelry shop did not mistreat gently bred young girls.

She reminded herself bitterly that she was not a gently bred girl, merely tutored to give the appearance of being one. No, her real father had ended up in debtor's prison and her mother had only escaped Covent Garden by great good fortune.

And her rash actions had put her in the position of seeking her own.

She turned to the jeweler, seeing nothing but kindness in his rheumy eyes. "Thank you, Mr. Clavell. I would be happy to look at it if you would accompany me." She was clinging to the last shreds of her dignity.

Tait smiled. "I once roomed there. The company is most congenial. I think you will like it."

She clutched the handle of her basket. "I hope so. I suppose I should put the jewels in your safe now. They would not be safe in my apartments—my room, I mean—if I was here working. I am glad, though, that I can look at them when I want."

"Of course," Tait said. "Every day. And you may wear whatever you like from the cases each day, so long as it goes back into the safe at the end of the day."

She glanced down at the necklace of coral beads. It seemed a trumpery thing today, but perhaps it would not on the morrow. Georgina sighed and handed Tait the roll of silk. He slipped it into the inside pocket of his black half coat and she felt a pang.

Georgina lowered her eyes and sighed. She missed entirely the look that passed between Clavell and the clerk. Tait turned to the high counter under which the cash box was hidden and unlocked it ceremonially with a large key. He withdrew some money and wrapped it in light paper before handing it to her, as if to remove the taint of commerce from the transaction.

"Here you are. Please get something to eat, you look as if you need it. And you may start today, if you like."

"Today?" she asked.

"Why not? That way you can see me put the jewels away and know that they are safe. Then you can establish yourself in the rooming house."

"Very well. Then I will do just that."

That day and the next were not unpleasant. She liked dealing with the customers and told herself that it was only a game of sorts. Her ill-will toward her mother and fear of her had lessened but not enough that she would attempt to return home.

And some of the male customers were decidedly attractive and flirted with her shamelessly. Georgina enjoyed their attentions and turned her training from Severin to her advantage.

One in particular, Denis Somov, singled her out toward the end of the second day. He did not seem to remember that he had met her at the theater with Ellen. Of course, the two of them had been simpering behind their fans.

How long ago it seemed.

She allowed Denis to talk to her for quite a while. Tait was preoccupied with Mr. Clavell in the back of the store and there were no other customers. He obviously thought the world of Denis, though, and even brought out a bottle of sweet wine that was reserved, or so Tait told her, for very special customers. He had even offered Georgina a small glass.

She had showed Denis everything in the cases, thinking of herself as playacting a shopgirl without being one. Surely selling jewels was a step up from selling oranges at a theater. But she might very well end up in one, she mused. Georgina did not think it was a worse fate than this—merely different.

Their animated conversation and sweet wine and the warm afternoon sunshine pouring in through the shop window had made her giddy. Tait hadn't seemed to mind that the wine was nearly gone, and both he and Mr. Clavell encouraged her to have dinner with Denis when he'd asked. Tait seemed brotherly and Mr. Clavell almost fatherly as they joshed Denis, telling him to be mindful of her tender years and all that rot.

Several hours later, after more wine, she found herself naked in front of a man for the very first time.

Georgina trembled when Denis reached out and caressed her shoulder. Her breasts tingled with anticipation but his hand did not drift down. No, only his smoldering look did that, moving over her quickly.

He was still half-clad in breeches and boots, his erection visible beneath the fine leather.

She swayed when he stopped what he was doing and just stood there with his hands fisted on his lean hips. Georgina was quite drunk and unsteady on her feet.

Denis didn't seem to be, she thought vaguely, but then she was no judge of that in her present condition.

"You are quite perfect," he said with a smile.

"Am I?" Georgina wanted to sit down. Or lie down. But something in his eyes kept her where she was.

He stepped closer to her and took her hand, leading her to the bed.

Georgina knew she was about to lose what her mother had guarded so carefully. Oddly, she didn't care.

Denis was without a doubt the most handsome man she had ever seen. That he wanted her, in her inebriated state, was nothing short of wonderful to her. He stopped by the side of the bed and drew her close to him.

But not so close he couldn't caress her freely.

He began with her back, running his warm hands up and down, stopping at her waist at first.

Georgina relaxed and leaned back, loving the reassuring feeling of being held, even though his hands were moving.

Denis stopped at her waist, gripping her tightly as he pressed a kiss to her lips. His tongue invaded her mouth. Georgina's bare breasts rose as she arched back, and her nipples brushed his chest.

"Ahhh," she moaned into his mouth. Denis swallowed the sound of pleasure and kissed her more thoroughly.

Georgina had no wish whatsoever to fend him off.

His hands moved down, stroking and circling over the roundness of her bottom. He stopped kissing her for a moment to whisper sweet nothings in her ear. And some things that were not so sweet but they excited her all the same.

"Your bum is so soft. You like to have a man fondle it, don't you?"

"Yes," she whispered.

"And no one ever has?"

"No."

"Ah," he breathed. "I am honored to be the first."

He continued to play with her bottom, squeezing it softly sometimes and then harder, almost lifting her by her cheeks when he wanted to kiss her.

Still, he kept his body ever so slightly apart from hers. It frustrated her. Georgina pushed her hips forward. His hands came around and gripped her tightly as if he didn't want her to rub against the front of his breeches.

Looking down, she could see why. His cock was straining against them and the heavy head of it was visible at the very top of the buttoned flap.

"Please let me touch you," she said. "I want to play with you as you play with me, Denis."

"No." He laughed a little. "Do you like our game then?"

"Yes, very much. You know I do." She wriggled in the grip of his strong hands, to no avail.

"I want you to be very still," Denis said. "And let me be the master, if you will."

"What?"

"I will not hurt you. All you will feel is intense pleasure. Your first."

His words were far more intoxicating than the wine she had unwisely consumed. She passionately wanted whatever he was about to offer her.

Denis's hands moved up to her breasts and once again he told her to stay still. Lost in purely physical sensation, Georgina agreed. She felt curiously unafraid. He was commanding but quite gentle.

"I must leave no mark upon you," he murmured. He moved his hands sensually over her breasts, appreciating their softness.

He took particular care with her nipples. She had not known they were so sensitive but then she had never known a man's touch. A few fumbled kisses from youths when her mother was elsewhere, a grab or two at her flesh, but nothing like this.

Denis stroked her arms. He closed the distance between them but only made two points of contact: he allowed her erect nipples to just touch the heated skin of his chest. The fine dark hair upon it tickled in a deliciously sensual way.

Georgina wanted to rub herself against him all over like a wanton little cat. But she was mindful of his instructions not to do so.

Denis moved one hand to caress her body again, keeping her steady with his other hand upon her shoulder. The tip of one thick finger made lazy half-circles below her belly, above the nest of springy curls. Back and forth. As if he were drawing a crescent moon.

The feeling he caused thrilled her. Georgina's thighs were slick at the very top from the unfamiliar stimulation. She had explored that bit of herself often enough—she wished he would.

But Denis did not.

From underneath her lashes, she looked at his body. He was

not much older than her, in his early twenties, if she had to guess.

His belly hollowed beneath the ribs of a fine chest that had not yet developed into manliness. Still, his muscles were sharply defined and she longed to caress him, every inch of him. The dark hair that spread across the top of his chest narrowed into a twisted, alluring trail that went straight down into his breeches. There was the head of his cock as before, as if it wanted to spring forth and possess her most intimate flesh.

The thought of being penetrated by it, given how gently he was making love to her now, was overwhelmingly erotic.

His long body over hers, his big hands parting her thighs, his own first look downward at the heaven he would find between her legs, and the swollen, juicy flesh . . . ohhh. Georgina felt faint.

Denis stopped what he was doing and tipped her chin up to his. "Look into my eyes," he said softly.

She did, swept away but standing utterly still.

He held her gaze—and his hand moved off her shoulder. Pinning her with just his eyes, he took her nipples into his fingers and began to excite her more deeply with subtle tugs and pinches.

Georgina's breaths came in rapid gasps. She could not look away.

Knowing that her sexual frustration and desire for him had to be showing in her eyes, knowing that he could read it there, was profoundly stimulating.

What he was doing was sweet torment for both of them. She saw him bite his lip and hold back a sigh of pleasure.

So she had a measure of power over him too. The thought was troubling. All she wanted right now was to surrender utterly to her masterful lover. Allow him to do whatever he wished to her body.

She felt uninhibited, free of every constraint that had ever held her back. She wanted to reveal everything to him, to lie back upon the anonymous bed and spread fully, open herself to more . . .

"Lie down." He let go of her teased nipples at last.

Had he read her mind? Georgina wondered.

She half-turned, putting a bent knee upon the bed as he watched.

Did he not need to relieve the pressure of his own excitement? He did not handle himself or stroke the rod that his tight breeches held back. He made no move to take off his boots.

"Do you not want to be naked too, Denis?"

Her soft question made him smile. "Yes, very much. But it's best if I am not."

"Why?"

He pushed her tumbled hair away from her face. "Because you are an untried girl. I think I am too big for you."

"But I want—"

"What you want, you will have. Pleasure beyond your wildest dreams."

"I want you," she said, reaching up to him.

He pushed her arm away. "And you shall have me. But not all of me."

Her downward, hungry look at the immense cock inside his breeches made him sigh. "Ah, I wish it could be different."

"Please, Denis," she begged. Then she thought to tempt him and bounded on the bed. On all fours. Looking impertinently at him over her shoulder.

He stared at what he saw.

Georgina cocked her arse up and began to undulate her hips. She saw his eyes widen and heard his gasp.

He stilled her with a hand on each arse cheek.

"Am I not what you want?" she murmured.

"Oh God." His voice was ragged with desire. "Yes, you are."

"Well, then . . . I want you to penetrate me. Easily and slowly."

"I—I cannot, Goergina!"

She threw him a pouting look and rose halfway, staying on her knees upon the bed. In this position, her breasts showed to advantage—she had once glimpsed herself in her own cheval mirror at home like this.

Now she had a man to see what she was doing. Georgina took hold of her nipples, and rolled them between her fingers. She tugged and cried out, making little moans.

Denis's entire body was taut with lust, his muscles standing out and his small male nipples hard.

She would force him to grab himself, tease him until he undid his breeches, and showed her all of that cock. "I want to see you," she murmured. "I have never seen a man's cock before. I am so curious, Denis . . ."

He groaned and seized hold of his shaft, but kept it where it was, bound back by leather soft as a glove. "No, Georgina!"

"I have heard," she whispered, "that men like to be licked there. Do you?"

"Yes."

The curt reply excited her with its roughness. "Then let me."

"No," he growled, dropping to his knees and pushing her back onto all fours. "But let us see how you like it, my wanton little miss."

Georgina did not fight the hands that held her bottom steady but she moaned with surprise and pleasure when he suddenly applied his tongue to her most intimate flesh from behind.

The pleasure was intense. His tongue ran inside the tightly folded, swollen inner lips, teasing them open but only by a little. She was simply too excited for him to do otherwise.

Georgina's hands clutched the sheets and her arms stiffened.

Denis pulled back from her behind for just a moment and pushed her knees farther apart. "I need to go deeper," was all he said.

At last. He would penetrate her, she wanted him to so badly that it almost made her cry.

But she heard no soft pop of buttons being undone, no boots being pulled off, no breeches flung onto a chair. She heard nothing at all except his raw, ragged breathing.

Then the heat of his breath warmed her intimate flesh as he applied his tongue to it once again. This time he held her ankles and not her bottom. His probing tongue did indeed go deeper, touching the delicate hymen hidden inside her cunny with light pressure but not straining against it. Certainly not breaking it.

Georgina was enormously excited by his tenderness toward her. She wanted to push back, be fucked by his tongue if not his cock. Just to begin.

Denis was moaning as he buried his face in her juicy cunny, but still, he was careful. So careful.

He pulled back again and she heard him swipe a hand across his face. "You are intact," he muttered.

"I want you to be the one," Georgina moaned. "My first one."

He wasted not a second longer but he kept his tongue from going into the inside of her cunny.

Georgina didn't care, imagining he would get there soon enough or risk exploding. Surely a man of his skill knew of the hot bud above all that, the source of a woman's ultimate pleasure—

Yes. He did know.

She wanted to rear up from the pleasure of it, but she stayed down. His flicking tongue teased her clitoris with gentle strokes, lashing her finally into an orgasm so intense she saw little stars.

Georgina cried his name, over and over.

At last she heard him undo his breeches. She waited for the thrust she craved so desperately, feeling her own extraordinary pleasure echo through her. It would be all the stronger the second time if she felt rather than saw what he was doing. As if she were being taken by some nameless god of erotic desire and not just a man.

Then hot spurts of cum hit her bottom and she knew without him saying so that he had been surprised by his own sudden release. It must have been too much for him to handle his engorged flesh at last. He had been so assiduous in his lovemaking, making sure that she reached climax first.

There would be a second time tonight and a third.

Georgina looked over her shoulder with heavy-lidded eyes, playing the part of a seductress. She was enjoying herself.

Denis had found a cloth and was about to wipe off his come. His expression was sated but—dare she say it?—rather matter of fact. Had she disappointed him? He did not seem to have experienced the transports of desire that had shaken her so.

She turned around and watched him, settling her overstimulated bottom on the cool sheets. Those would be scorching hot and tangled before midnight, she thought absently.

"What is it, Denis?"

"Nothing, my dear."

"Did I not please you?" She looked at him anxiously, feeling the effects of the wine ebbing away at last.

"Indeed you did. As I said, you are intact. And that is something that goes for a very high price."

She just stared at him, not comprehending what he was saying in the least.

11

"Severin, I will do what I can."

Marko was still not sure why she had come to him. But Georgina's disappearance was a serious matter. He would have to disobey Braykbone's command to keep away from women for the time being, but he could not refuse Severin. He had missed her terribly. He was half-tempted to tell her of the tantalizing reverie in which she had appeared to him—but that had been weeks ago and he had been drinking wine at the time. She would dismiss such a tale as romantic nonsense.

He was well aware how a clever woman could conceal far more than she would reveal, but it was clear she cared very much for the missing girl. That she had not yet found a trace of Georgina despite her cleverness didn't surprise him. He and the other members of the Pack lived somewhat outside the law of the realm, and he knew what could happen to a runaway.

But there were other considerations. If anything had happened to Georgina, he might even be considered a suspect for that reason. He would have to have a word with his contact at court, Alfred Endicott, who looked after legal matters for the Pack.

Her sweet voice interrupted his anxious thoughts. "Thank you, Marko," she said gravely. He could read a question in her eyes that he knew she was too proud to ask. *Why have you not come to me?* Severin looked about the great hall of the Pack in which they sat and heaved a sigh.

"Are there no clues? Did she not leave a letter?"

"Nothing. Georgina quarreled bitterly with her mother and ran away. That is all anyone knows."

"It doesn't bode well, given the recent—events. Never mind." He did not want to say *murders* and there was no reason for anyone to assume that Georgina would meet a violent end.

"I cannot sleep for worrying."

Marko studied her. Severin's agitation was betrayed by the rapid rise and fall of her bosom, though she was modestly dressed. Still, her neat costume and its subdued hue made him feel more desire for her than ever. And compassion.

Georgina had been only her pupil, but Severin seemed to think of her as a sister somehow. A younger, wayward sibling—when it came to that, Marko supposed that Kyril might regard him in the same way. But Marko had been too preoccupied with pleasure when he was younger to have learned much about running the Pack now.

At the moment they seemed to be going from bad to worse. Kyril and Levshin had seen to the Pack's finances before Kyril's departure for Russia. They were on solid ground there. But the murders and their unexplained link to the Pack remained unresolved

The rot that Marko sensed, if belatedly, was not the sort that could be smelled. Nonetheless, it was as dangerous. He had no idea who was responsible for it—nor why any of his kinsmen might betray the high ideals of their clan.

It was not as if wrongdoers were likely to step forward, hang their heads, and confess, of course. But he was convinced there was a rogue within their ranks. A murderous rogue.

He hated to inform her of that and he would not. She was intent on solving a difficult matter of her own and that was the only reason why she was here . . . no, perhaps not. Her air of mystery surrounded her like a cloud that he could see through but not dispel.

Her very beauty was dangerous. Surely he was not the only man who thought so. Looking at her as she absently studied her surroundings, he thought that even dressed plainly and not in the velvet that had reminded him so much of a cat upon their first meeting, there was still something quite wild about Severin. Her mien was demure and her manners were impeccable. It was her eyes, he supposed.

Their curious amber color held him in thrall. No, he amended the thought. The soul that the eyes revealed despite her composure did that.

Dear Wolf, he would do anything for her.

He waited patiently to hear what she would ask of him.

"Marko," she began. "I have asked my sister to investigate certain houses."

"I beg your pardon?"

"Houses of ill-repute."

"Ah." He was astonished. "I did not know you had a sister. Let alone that she or you would be familiar with such places."

"She is," Severin said calmly. "I am not."

"I see." Marko sought to still his racing thoughts. He had understood that Severin's connection to the demimonde was superficial, involving her expertise in feminine dress and adornment, nothing more.

Apparently it went further.

"If Georgina was wandering the streets, she may have been lured into one."

Marko nodded. "It does happen."

"It happens every damned day," Severin said. "And her mother seems to have lost interest. I find it appalling."

"Tell me more of her," Marko asked. "Is Georgina's mother a friend of yours?"

"I advised her upon dress and deportment in her first leading role. She played the part of a great lady."

"And her name is?"

"She was Mary Lennox. But she just married an earl."

Marko tapped his fingers upon the table. "That also happens every day, or so it seems. The English aristocracy is full of former actresses."

Severin snorted. "She did well for herself. But not, alas, for Georgina, whom she wished to be rid of."

Marko studied her for a long moment, picking up on a shadow of uncertainty in her tone.

"Are you sure of that?"

Severin answered with a shrug and a slight toss of her head. "It is certainly possible."

"It is true that some mothers are remarkably indifferent," he sighed. "My own was a model of devotion."

"As was mine." Her soft voice held affection that ran deep.

"Then we may both count ourselves lucky," Marko said when she added nothing more to her sudden declaration.

"Getting back to Georgina . . ."

"Yes, of course." Marko frowned as he pondered the matter. "It seems wrong to ask a woman to investigate such places."

"You would not be admitted through the door," Severin said wryly. "Except as a customer."

He could feel his face turn red. Blushing seemed unmanly. Assuredly it was a trait that wolves and humans did not have in common, and he was annoyed with himself for possessing it.

"Have you ever been in a brothel?" she asked.

Marko looked at her wide-eyed. So bold a question in so

calm a voice—was she trying to unsettle him? If so, it was working.

"No," he answered at last. She would have to be satisfied with that whether or not she believed it to be true. "Why do you ask?"

"I wanted to be sure that you had not ever encountered my sister Jehane."

He shook his head. "I don't believe I have. But then I don't know what she looks like."

"You will."

Marko shot her a look. "Kindly explain yourself."

"I have invited her here to speak with you as well."

"Good God!"

Severin pursed her lips, rather primly, he thought, considering what her sister did for a living. If Kyril should ever find out that such a woman had crossed the threshold of the Pack, there would be hell to pay.

But some already had, unless Marko missed his guess. He suspected Feodor, who bought his fun cheaply, but he had no proof. Adele's lover, the forlorn Pyotr, had whispered of Denis's possible involvement as well, but Marko paid him little heed.

Denis, however, was devastatingly handsome, virile, in the first flush of young manhood, and the lover of many. Women threw themselves at him. He didn't have to pay for pleasure and he had no reason to invite his paramours to the house by St. James's Square.

Marko collected himself. "Forgive me, Severin. You caught me by surprise."

"I meant to," she said flatly.

"Oh? And why is that?"

"So you would not have an opportunity to say no. You are too much of a gentleman to slam the door in my sister's face."

"I should hope so," he said quietly.

The clock in the front of the house struck the hour in deep notes, tuned to the baying of wolves, without the natural cacophony of a full-Pack howl. One, two, three, four . . . the sound died away.

"I told her to come at quarter after the hour."

Marko nodded. "Then we have a little while."

"Yes." She seemed uneasy, shifting in her chair across from him. As if to give herself something to do, Severin placed her bag on the table and began to look through it.

"Searching for your spectacles?"

"No. I don't wear any."

That did not surprise him. He would have been readily convinced that her eyes could see into a man's very soul.

His, certainly.

"I was looking for my little notebook—I did a sketch of Georgina."

"But I have met her. I know what she looks like."

"Yes, well—ah, here is a chain that belonged to Georgina. Her mother gave it to me in this box." Severin set a tiny box on the table. "They had a tug-of-war over it and Mary ultimately won."

"It is broken, I assume."

"Yes, it snapped in two. You can look at it if you like. There isn't much to see."

"Why do you have it?"

"I don't know. I wanted something of hers. Her mother gave me a scarf Georgina had worn also."

"Now that might prove more useful—" He stopped himself, not wanting to reveal his ability to sniff through a mystery.

"Why?" Her tone was suspiciously innocent.

"I don't know—I was thinking of another case, I believe."

Severin's eyes held him motionless for a moment. He had the oddest feeling that he was in competition with a huntress of remarkable skill. He knew instinctively that Severin had no wolf in her family, but the hair on the back of his neck stood up all the same.

It was possible that there was a wild cat in her family tree. Marko smiled at his little joke, not caring to share it with her.

"Why are you smiling?"

"It was inadvertent." He almost wished Severin's sister would show up early so he would not have to endure her scrutiny.

But something about it excited him.

Marko shifted in his chair just as she had done, but for a very different reason. His cock had begun to lengthen in his close-fitting breeches and that was one part of him that had a mind of its own. A little mind, sad to say, that thought only of one thing.

Sexual satisfaction.

Severin had given him that—the memory was almost painful. With her so near, he could not help remembering her wild embraces and how she had clawed at his buttocks and his back. She knew just how to bite while she kissed too. He had been thrilled to find a woman whose sexuality was as powerful as his own. He considered himself honored to have pleasured her. Ah, he should not think of that now . . .

Severin pushed the scarf and the little box that held the chain over to him. He opened the box. There was nothing in it but a fine gold chain, which he lifted out. The broken end dangled in midair.

Marko began to sense that it held a message of some kind. Discreetly, he sniffed at it by pretending to examine it closely. There was the faintest trace of a scent he recognized—had a kinsman of his touched it?

The thought was disturbing. But he had more senses available to him than his excellent nose. Marko held the chain in the palm of his hand and tried to read it, in the way that Kyril's beloved wife could read books and letters for the deeper meaning they held.

Severin watched him without saying a word. She must have an idea of what he was doing, he thought. She might even have some ability for perception that was out of the ordinary herself.

He looked at the chain, coiled in his palm.

No wonder it affected him so much, he realized suddenly. It had brought to mind the chain upon Lucy's neck, although they were differently made.

Lucy's had been heavier, made to hold the locket with the wolf's head, and this one was very fine, almost weightless.

But it was as if he could sense that the same unknown man had touched both chains. Not a member of the Pack—Marko racked his brains—but someone close to the Pack. A man who was older than them all.

He had no way of analyzing what his mind picked up. The warmth of his palm warmed the tiny links of gold and the vision just outside his ability to see it grew stronger.

Marko saw a hand reach out to unfasten the chain from around a woman's youthful neck.

"Was this chain broken previously?" he asked Severin. "I am talking about before Georgina and her mother argued."

She looked at him, startled. "Mary mentioned that Georgina claimed to have been to a jewelry store to have it fixed. She didn't believe it, or so she told me."

"She should have," Marko said. "Someone took it from Georgina's neck." He waited for more impressions to arise from the warmed links. He could barely feel the weight of the chain in the center of his palm, but its emanations troubled his brain.

"Who?"

"A man."

Severin frowned. "That is to be expected. Someone told her it was pretty, as pretty as she was, no doubt. She is very young and easy to flatter."

Marko received no further impressions and he tipped his palm to pour the chain back into the little box.

Severin reached to take it back from him.

"I would like to keep it, if you don't mind."

She gazed at him curiously. "I suppose there is no harm in it. Mary thinks I have it, though."

"I will be sure to return it." He wrapped it in the scarf and shoved both into his pocket before she asked for that back too.

They heard a knock upon the door and the major d'omo going to answer it. Severin brightened when she heard her sister's voice. Marko had to assume it was Jehane.

He rose when she was ushered into the room.

Jehane eyed him and he felt immediately nonplussed.

Well-dressed and fresh from a hairdresser, Severin's sister seemed rather more wild than her just the same. The word for her, in fact, was feral. He definitely preferred the older of the two.

Still, Jehane was a beauty. But for all that she was younger, she still seemed harder than Severin and far more calculating. Her gaze swept over the furnishings as if she quickly noted their cost and fashionableness.

The décor was lacking on both counts, he thought with chagrin. The Pack could not afford new wallpaper at the moment. He comforted himself with the thought that many members of the nobility also lived in decaying splendor, owing to ruinous taxes on their estates. Perhaps it was démodé to be a bit poor.

He suspected she would not agree with that bit of reverse snobbery. Jehane swept past him and went straight to her sister, kissing her on the cheek. "Hello, Severin. I came as soon as I could."

Severin nodded. "Then we can begin."

Marko took his place again and looked at both sisters in turn. Then together.

"I am sure you see the likeness," Jehane said candidly. "Do you mind if I smoke, by the way?"

That was something Marko had never seen a woman do. Having Severin in the room had softened his brain, perhaps. He was feeling more and more like a wet-behind-the-ears cub. If he got lucky, these lovely ladies might scratch his ears for him. And something else.

Shut up, he told himself fiercely. But all he said to Jehane was, "Not in the least."

Severin shot him a disgusted look. "I will leave you to that strange pleasure, Jehane. I find that it gives me a sore throat even if I am not the one doing the smoking."

Jehane gave her a bored look.

"The men of the pa—our club—often smoke in here." He rose to go to the sideboard and find Jehane a receptacle for the ashes and a flint-knap.

"I am going to the library. Call me back in when the air clears." Severin left. He watched in amazement as she lit a small, thin cigar and took a deep draw on it. The fragrant smoke wafted upward.

"Ahh," she said. "That's better. Helps me to think."

Marko fought the strange sensation that it was doing exactly the same thing for him.

"It is not just a cigar," she said. Sitting wreathed in its smoke, she looked like a depiction of an oracle.

"Then what is it?" he asked.

"Sometimes I see things in the smoke as it drifts away."

Even in the short time she had been at the table, Marko found himself attracted to Jehane. This will not *do*, he told himself strongly. He coughed.

"And what do you see? Anything related to Georgina?"

"No. Only animals—running. I'm not sure what they are. Dogs, perhaps. Large dogs."

He got up and turned a painting of a wolf Pack in full cry behind her to the wall. Jehane looked behind her to see what he was doing. "I expect you got a glimpse of that when you came in."

Jehane grinned at him. So she had been trying to get him to blurt out something about the Pack. Unlike her sister, she didn't give a man a fair chance to trip himself up on his own. No, Jehane went right for the jugular.

He suspected somehow that she had known more than her sister from the very beginning. She smelled a bit . . . guilty. But not as if she was consumed by it.

He was grateful when Severin came back in the room, waving away the smoke that was hanging in the still air.

"Are you done, Jehane? Can the discussion proceed?"

"In a minute." Her younger sister treated herself to a few more puffs, and Marko began to be convinced that there was something in the smoke.

Not deadly and not particularly dangerous.

He considered a few possibilities. One, that she was reading him through it somehow, the way a fortuneteller might read tea leaves or the lines on one's palms.

Or . . . the second thought was far worse. Perhaps she knew what he was—knew what all the men of the Pack were. She was smoking to blunt his keen sense of smell and throw him off her scent, should he want to follow her.

Jehane had crushed her little cigar out. She looked up at him, the picture of engaging innocence.

Far from it, he told himself.

He would show her all the respect due to Severin's sister, but Marko was very definitely on his guard.

Severin seated herself again.

"I brought Jehane here so that we might share our knowledge. I hope to find Georgina as fast as possible, and you," she nodded at Marko, "move in the highest circles, I am told."

He inclined his head without responding in a specific way. How had she known that, he wondered.

"And you," she was looking at her sister, "move in—ah—"

Jehane finished the sentence for her. "The lowest."

Marko cleared his throat. Despite his awkwardness, the younger of the sisters didn't seem insulted at all. In fact, she seemed on the verge of laughing. Severin and Jehane were obviously fond of each other.

"Yes, well. We each have different strengths and we all want to help Georgina," he said quickly. "What is it that you expect from me, Severin?"

"That you will make discreet inquiries about Georgina among your friends and acquaintances. She is headstrong and a blooming beauty all of a sudden—it is possible she ended up in the bed of Lord So-and-so and has no idea how she would go about coming home."

"If I were her, I would stay in the bed of Lord So-and-so," Jehane said.

Severin held up a hand. "She would have to return eventually. And I would hope that you could hush up the inevitable scandal, Marko."

"I could try."

Severin continued. "After all, it is not as if Georgina is well-known. She only just came out in London society, attended a ball or two. Nothing more."

"And the theater."

"Yes, well, that hardly counts," she said.

"As I said, I will try. And what will you do, Severin?" He was consumed with curiosity.

"Nothing out of the ordinary. I will ask among my circle if Georgina has been spotted in the city or the country. And I will check the respectable shops. And I was thinking about placing an advertisement, a discreet one, in the papers. That is one reason why I did the sketch—"

She shoved it over toward Jehane, who glanced at it without much interest.

"Other than that I suppose we could ask the constabulary," Severin went on, "although—"

"They are on the take and useless even when bribed," Jehane said tartly. "And it is not as if you can check every shop in London, my dear sister. There must be thousands. And I doubt an intelligent girl, as you say Georgina is, would sink so low that she would be selling ribbons by the yard at a notions counter or doling out cough drops at a chemist."

Severin gave a troubled sigh. "There are worse fates, Jehane."

"Of course there are. I am being sarcastic."

"What good does it do?"

"We cannot place an advertisement, Severin. Georgina's reputation will be ruined forever if we mention her name or describe her accurately."

Severin shot a look at her sister. "You have never cared much for reputations, good or bad."

Jehane shrugged. "It is a respectable woman's stock in trade. If she is young, she can add her virginity to her list of qualifications."

"Oh, Jehane—"

"What? Am I wrong? Do you not want to find the girl?"

"You know that I do! We all do." Severin looked to Marko for help, but he raised his hands in an empty gesture, not being able to offer any.

He had watched the back-and-forth with fascination. Marko hadn't grown up with sisters and these two were like no others.

Jehane was talking again. "You said the girl's mother seemed to have mixed feelings."

"Oh, I suppose Mary will come around. I half think she was

jealous of her daughter, though. She was so used to having all the attention."

"Self-pity from the brand-new wife of an earl? Intolerable," Jehane said.

Marko glanced her way. Her wit had a fine edge and he was very glad it was not directed at him. He thought of the title of that play as he looked at Jehane—what was it?

'Tis a Pity She's A Whore. Something like that.

He smiled at Severin when she looked at him intently. She would not like it if she knew he thought of her sister in those terms. But it couldn't be helped. Jehane was who she was.

"I don't think an advertisement is such a bad idea," Marko said.

Jehane snorted. "Please come home, darling girl, all is forgiven? My friends and I used to laugh over those."

"Why?" Marko asked.

"Darling girls do not get kicked down the stairs and out the door. A bad girl does. And no one wants to hear the baby she got stuck with squalling in the night."

"You are cynical," Marko said.

"Give me a reason not to be," Jehane said.

"Then what will you do to help?" he said to her.

Jehane sat up very straight. "I can knock on the door of every bawdy house by the river and visit the high-class brothels as well. A few whores can be persuaded to do right if it's to help a lost girl. They were all lost girls once."

Her tone was not in the least wistful. It was as if Jehane was stating a fact that was as old as time.

Marko found it hard to look at her for very long. She had almost none of Severin's inner softness.

"What if we find her beaten or worse?" Severin asked.

"Not likely," Jehane said. "The customers don't generally want damaged goods. A healthy-looking female fetches the best price. And besides . . ." She hesitated, looking from her sister to Marko.

"What? Just say it," Severin insisted.

Marko was sure that Jehane hadn't hesitated on his account. She seemed to regard him with something in between indifference and faint contempt.

"It is more effective to break a girl's will with gentle treatment. It takes longer but the end result is a whore who is something like a willing slave."

Severin shuddered. "I can't bear to think of it."

"You must, whether you want to or not," Jehane said in a level voice. "Consider it a part of your education. Unpleasant but necessary."

"Oh, go ahead then."

Jehane waved her hand airily. "Imagine a girl fresh from the country. She meets a nice fellow who promises to help her find employment as a ladies' maid, if she is pretty. But first she is wined and dined and given little trinkets and royally pleasured in bed. Then, when she cannot do without her man, she can be put to work on his behalf."

"I can imagine what happens when her man, as you put it, grows tired of her," Severin said.

"Nothing good," Jehane said baldly. "The girls turn to drink and laudanum to numb their misery."

"Then we must begin at once," Severin said. "I fear we have already waited a little too long. There has been no sign of her whatsoever. It is as if Georgina Lennox has been made to disappear."

"We must inquire within certain circles that you will not like, my dear sister."

Marko broke the silence that followed that remark by going to a cabinet and taking out a folded map of London. He spread it out on the table.

"What is that for?" Jehane asked.

"There are circles within circles," he said. "Let us each take a pencil and outline our working area."

A few hours later, in Hyde Park . . .

The day was drawing to a close when a carriage rumbled down one of the lanes in Hyde Park. Its curtains were closed. Inside sat Jehane and Feodor.

"So. Your sister's student has gone missing, has she?"

"Yes, Feodor. Do you know anything?"

He grinned at her in an ugly way. "Lift your skirts and I will show you what I know."

"Don't be disgusting. I have never let you touch me and I never will."

He sighed in a grumbling way and sat back. "More's the pity. We could do a good business together, you and I."

"I am in business only for myself."

He looked at her slyly. "You sent me a few girls once."

"That was before I knew what you were up to, Feodor."

The hired carriage was stirring up a good deal of dust on the Hyde Park lanes and some of it drifted in through the cracks around the window. Feodor coughed. "I see nothing wrong with my enterprise. In any case, I don't know the girl you're looking for."

Jehane shot him a look. "Her name is Georgina."

"And how old is she?"

"Nineteen."

"Born during the reign of George III, was she? Then she has thousands of sisters, all named Georgina."

"I suppose that is true," Jehane said. "But you still might know of her."

"Tell me what she looks like."

Jehane waved a hand. "They are all pretty at nineteen. But

Georgina Lennox is more striking than she is pretty. Her hair is wavy and dark, and her eyes are green."

"Nothing more distinguishing than that? I could think of many girls who would fit that description."

"No, Feodor."

He looked at her curiously. "And how is it, my dear Jehane, that you are so interested in this young woman?"

"She has run away from her mother."

"Hmm," he said. "Hardly out of the ordinary. Country girls do it all the time."

"She is not a country girl."

Feodor chucked her under the chin, and Jehane jerked away from his touch. "Come, come. Who is she and why are you being so cagey?"

"There is need for discretion."

"Oho," he said, leaning back or trying to as the coach jolted along the lanes. "Is Miss Georgina Lennox trying to elope? Who is the lucky soldier?"

"No, she is not, and there is no soldier. As I said, she is innocent."

"And where was she last seen, Jehane?"

Jehane gave a shrug that made her shawl fall off her shoulder. Feodor eyed the bare skin inadvertently presented to him as if he would like to bite it. She pulled the shawl up and glared at him. "I myself last saw her at the theater. She was there with Severin."

"Ah, yes. Your beautiful and mysterious sister."

"Do not talk of my sister in such familiar terms."

"Very well, Jehane," Feodor replied. "But it may well be that she has gone into business also. A business like yours and mine." He pushed away the feminine hand that was about to strike him. "Are you insulted? Too bad."

"One of these days," Jehane muttered, "someone will do you in. And there will be no one to mourn you, Feodor."

"I shan't care if I'm dead. What will it matter?" His tone was light, almost teasing.

"While we are on that subject," Jehane said. "What of the two girls who have died?"

Feodor shook his head sorrowfully. "Most unfortunate. It seems that no woman is safe these days."

Jehane edged away on the seat as far as she could.

"Are you afraid of me?" he asked blandly.

Jehane swore. "No. But I wish there was a way to get the information I need from you. You are not forthcoming."

"But I have nothing to say that will help you, Jehane. I don't know the young lady you seek. You would not want me to lead you down blind alleys, would you?"

"Feodor, you are fast becoming one of the most notorious pimps in London. You must know something!"

"Notorious? I prefer the word exclusive."

Jehane pushed aside the little curtain over the window. "Never mind. Where are we?"

Feodor gave her an assessing look. "You said you wanted to talk in a private place, so I told the driver to keep going until I gave him the signal to stop. I have no idea where we are."

He leaned over Jehane to peer out the window on her side but she pushed him violently away. "Get off me!"

He grabbed her wrist. "I was only trying to figure out where we were," he chided her in a soft voice.

Jehane could not free herself from his grip. "There is a window on your side as well."

"Yes," he said smoothly. "But the view is not as good." His gaze dropped for a fraction of a second to her bosom, then moved up to her face. His expression was that of a fond lover but his fingers tightened around her slender wrist. "You are still very pretty, Jehane. Will you not work for me?"

"Never!"

With a prodigious wrench, she pulled free at last. Feodor seemed not to care and moved back to his own side again. "A shame. Your looks will not last forever."

"I can take care of myself, Feodor. I have never worked for anyone else."

"But you need a protector like any other whore."

She scowled. "I have Charlie for that."

"Of course. Your soldier boy. Always waving his sword and looking for trouble."

"He loves me."

Feodor nodded and murmured, "How sweet. And do you love him?"

"Yes, I do."

"I don't suppose you would want him to know that you sleep with other men."

"He sleeps with other women sometimes. So we are even on that score," Jehane answered honestly.

Feodor harrumphed. "Then I cannot use that against you."

"Why would you want to?"

"My dear Jehane, there will always be a battle between men and women. I find you a particularly interesting opponent."

"I am not exactly your enemy, Feodor," she said slowly.

"Nor are you my friend."

"No, but I had hoped—"

"You had assumed," he interrupted her, "that I would help you in the matter of this missing girl."

"Yes, that is true enough."

"But as I have said, I do not know her. So it seems that there is nothing we can do for each other."

Jehane drew herself up primly and wrapped her shawl even more tightly around her. "No. Tell the driver to head back to Soho."

*   *   *

A message was sent and was answered within two hours. It was done. Marko had arranged for a meeting with Georgina's stepfather, the earl of Cavendish.

The earl's residence was in Belgravia, not too far to walk from the neighborhood of St. James's. There were no clouds in the sky but the day had a gray aspect all the same, as if it had been somehow drained of life. The streets were quiet enough. Only a passing carriage or two rattled by, and the other men and women out upon errands of their own paid him no heed.

Marko came at last to the house and looked up at its narrow windows. There was something tall and forbidding about it, and the windows were narrow.

He had never met the earl, and wondered whether such a personage would even be polite to him. He had found out in advance that Mary, Georgina's mother, had retreated to the seclusion of the earl's country house. Hardly helpful.

He would have to agree with Severin that the girl's mother might well be jealous.

However, for his purposes, it was just as well that Mary would not appear. Men could talk frankly without a woman about.

The door was answered by a butler, who bowed and showed him into the study without delay. To get there, they passed through an immense, high-ceilinged room papered in red velvet and hung with masterpieces. The gilt furniture had been chosen not for comfort but to impress. It all looked very new and almost like a stage set.

Marko wondered if Mary Lennox had had a hand in the decorating of it. The gold-fringed draperies had a theatrical look.

The butler paused before a set of double doors carved from dark wood and rapped before entering.

"You may enter," said a male voice.

Marko followed the butler in, and nodded to the man as he bowed and withdrew.

The earl did not rise but gestured toward an armchair. "Good afternoon, Mr. Taruskin. You wanted to see me and I am glad that you are prompt. I know why, of course, but I would like to hear what you have to say about the matter of my missing stepdaughter."

Marko cast about for a suitably tactful reply. The conversation between him and Severin and her sister was not one he cared to repeat in every particular.

"A friend of Georgina's asked me to investigate—well, not a friend precisely, sir, but Georgina's teacher."

The earl gave him a thin smile. "You mean Severin."

"Yes."

"What can you tell me of her, Mr. Taruskin?"

"Ah—" Marko was taken aback. He had not expected to be questioned on the subject and he would have to be careful as to what he said. "She is a well-bred woman, to be sure, and well-educated."

The earl coughed into his hand. "I am not sure that the education she provided did Georgina good."

Marko was silent for several seconds. "I could not offer an opinion on that, sir," he said at last.

"I wouldn't expect you to. You are Severin's lover, are you not?"

Marko drew in a breath and decided to be honest. "I am."

"Thank you for telling the truth. I have had a difficult time getting anything resembling it from Mary. Sobs, hysteria—" —the earl waved a hand that bore a heavy signet ring—"it is all very tedious."

"Surely it is to be expected, sir. Georgina is her only child and her sudden disappearance must have been a tremendous shock to her mother."

"Wayward girls usually come back, in my experience," the earl said.

Marko was nonplussed. "And—do you have children of your own? If I may be so bold as to ask, sir."

"No, no. But I have lived long enough to know that passion is a fleeting thing. Georgina has fallen in love with a handsome soldier or some such nonsense. She will be back."

"How can you be so sure?"

The earl studied Marko for a long moment. "I have my sources. As do you."

"Ah." Marko felt he was being led by the nose. The earl was not a physically imposing man, nor was he kind, but he seemed to know more than he was telling.

Marko felt he had been presumptuous enough in arranging for this meeting without telling Severin—he could not give away something as innocent as meeting Georgina at the theater. What if the earl disapproved or blamed Severin? He would let the other man talk.

"May I offer you a glass of whisky?"

"No, thank you."

"Very well. Then you won't mind if I do, I'm sure." The earl rose and went to a mahogany sideboard. He poured himself a healthy drink from a crystal decanter and sat down again with the glass in his hand.

"Not at all, sir."

The earl sipped and his face grew a bit flushed. Marko glanced about the room, noting again the ostentatiousness of the décor. Even in this private room, it was deemed necessary to impress.

"I know something about your Pack, Taruskin, as you fellows call it," the earl said at last.

"Do you?" Marko was on his guard at once.

The earl raised a glass. "Drinking and whoring are man's great pastimes, are they not?"

"We are a social club, sir."

"Rather more than that." The earl's eyes, a mild blue, seemed suddenly sharp.

"Well, yes. Many of us are closely related."

"From Russia, isn't that right?"

"Originally. Some of our number were born in England."

"Which does not make them English," the earl observed shrewdly.

"Not English . . . not to the bone, no."

The earl downed the last of the whisky and set the glass down, licking his lips. "Exactly my point."

"I don't follow you, sir."

"That Severin is foreign or half-foreign and so are you. It is no wonder that Georgina has been—"

"I had nothing to do with the girl's disappearance. Nor did Severin."

"No?" The earl gave him a level look. "I was wondering if you were going to ask me for money if I wanted my stepdaughter back. You and your mistress might be conspiring together."

"Indeed not!" Marko half-rose, shocked by the remark, which did not seem to have been made in jest.

The earl only laughed, motioning him back down. "Such things happen. But your vehemence is convincing enough."

"I came here to ask your assistance in finding Georgina. That was all."

The earl sighed. "The matter is most troublesome. I had hoped to marry her off as soon as possible. But she will be as good as ruined if she is not found soon."

"Yes, sir."

"As a man of the world, I would have to say it seems suspicious to have you following her about."

"Then what would you have me do?" Marko was incensed. "Neither you nor her mother seem to have that much interest in finding the girl."

The earl shook his head. "I will be candid. Georgina is putting us to a good deal of trouble. But the scandal that would ensue would not reflect well upon us."

"She is the one at risk! Not you and not your wife."

"Indeed," the earl said. "Then I suppose you will have to do, eh?"

Marko tried to keep his head. "What do you have against me? It seems there is something, but you will not say it outright."

"Besides your being foreign?"

Marko gritted his teeth. He would not mind sinking them into the back of the earl's neck and giving his lordship a good shaking. But such wolfishness would not serve him well. "Yes."

The earl steepled his fingers. "It may be that I have misjudged you, Taruskin, but I do not like what I have heard about your so-called Pack."

"I cannot defend myself or my kinsmen without knowing what has been said about us."

"You may be a honorable man, for all I know," the earl went on. "But that is not true of all your relatives."

"What are you talking about?"

"Certain men of your clan or Pack or whatever it is you are have outside interests, you see," the earl said.

"Get to the point."

The earl stiffened and sat up. "You are insolent."

"You try my patience," Marko admitted. "But you cannot expect me to humbly take abuse." He could feel the fine hair on the back of his neck rise with his anger.

"Hmm. You are a man of spirit and I suspect you are a man of honor. That is good. But not all of you are."

"For the love of Wo—for the love of God, will you cease hinting and tell me what you mean, man?"

The earl laughed. "One of your relatives is a procurer. In plain English, a pimp."

"Who?"

"I am not sure, but I believe that the essential information is correct. Now you know why I thought you might be asking me for ransom."

"It is an insult and men have been challenged to duels for less."

The earl shook his head. "We are not equals and you cannot demand satisfaction from me. I have not besmirched your family honor, such as it is."

Marko was seething with anger. He could not very well argue and he had no idea how much the earl of Cavendish actually knew about the inner workings of the Pack. That he himself had been so oblivious was appalling. He would have to answer to Kyril for it if the earl's accusations were true.

"The fellow is quite enterprising. He provides excellent service. Fresh young girls, like my stepdaughter." The earl seemed almost not to care. "But I doubt that she has not fallen so low, not in so short a time. No, I believe, as I say, that she is simply having a fling. But it may be that this man—"

"The pimp, you mean."

"Yes, whoever he is, he may have news of her."

The earl fell silent. "Of course, she might well go upon the streets eventually if she is too ashamed to come home. I should hate to encounter her in the Covent Garden alleys someday."

"I will find out what I can," Marko said.

He took the long way back, scarcely wishing to enter his own home. Within it was a traitor or maybe more than one to the brotherhood of the Pack.

But the only person he saw upon entering was Pyotr.

"Hello, Marko."

Marko shot the other man a suspicious look, then immediately felt ashamed. Pyotr had been close to one of the murdered women, but that did not mean that he was guilty.

No, Pyotr was simple at heart, a low-ranking member of the Pack whose loyalty was unquestionable. His secret affair with a woman of the streets had been his answer to loneliness, nothing more.

Pyotr was neither dashing nor rich. Marko could not blame him for wanting someone to love.

"Pyotr, there is something I wish to discuss with you."

The other man nodded. "Is it about Adele?"

"She may have something to do with it."

He hung his head. "I brought her here. I should not have done it."

"Come." Marko steered Pyotr into his own sanctum, nodding to a silent servant or two as they passed.

He opened the doors to his study, making a quick survey of the room to ensure that there were no listeners. The earl's remarks had him on edge.

Pyotr looked around nervously and Marko realized that the other man had never been in the study. "Please sit down."

Pyotr picked the lowest chair, he noticed. Deferential to a fault.

"I have heard troubling rumors," he began. "Apparently things are not as they should be in this house, or even as they seem."

Pyotr fidgeted. "What do you mean, sir?"

The man's reply and manner were uncomfortably reminiscent of how he himself had felt when confronted by the earl, Marko thought, with chagrin. But he began. "Someone among us has broken the rules of our brotherhood. They may be unwritten, but they do have meaning."

"Indeed. I am proud to live by them."

Marko felt miserable. Since they were sworn to keep one another's secrets, he would break a rule himself if he asked Pyotr for information.

"Can you tell me if you know of anything that has happened here without my knowledge?"

Pyotr shifted uneasily in his chair. "You have not been much at home, Marko."

"No, I have not." His affair with Severin had consumed more time than he had thought. He could not be blamed for that, any more than he could blame Pyotr for falling in love with poor Adele. But Marko did blame himself for neglecting his role as leader in Kyril's absence.

"But as you say," Pyotr continued timidly, "there have been, ah, incidents."

"I will ask you no more about Adele. I know that her death was a great shock to you."

A tear ran from the corner of Pyotr's eye. "I never should have brought her here," he said.

"You had no other place to go," Marko said kindly. "Perhaps she did not."

Pyotr's simple kindness might have seemed like a godsend to a drab from the streets. If he had made his position in life seem more than it was to impress her, it was understandable.

Pyotr's room was below street level, near the kitchen. One could easily bring a woman to it and hide her away for several hours, before the cook got up and saw to breakfast.

"I thought I was rescuing her, you see," Pyotr said hesitantly. "What I had wasn't much, but she was nearly living on the streets."

"Who introduced you to her?" There was nothing for it but to ask the question.

"Why, I did that myself. I saw her walking by the river bank at Blackfriars, up and down and again one day, and it struck me that she had nowhere to go and nothing to do but walk until the sun went down, and she could creep away somewhere to sleep."

More likely to ply her trade, Marko thought with sadness.

"Anyway, I spoke to her and one thing led to another. You know how it is."

He nodded. "Yes, I do."

"Well, then. That is all there is to it."

Marko permitted himself a small frown. "So she was brought here?"

"I brought her here. I know I shouldn't have."

Marko rose and began to pace the room, his hands behind his back. "Did other men of the Pack bring women here as well?"

"I could not say, sir. My room is well below the others and so far from them all that I wouldn't know."

"Yes, that is so." Marko hated exploiting Pyotr's nervousness over his minor trangression to pry more information from him, but there was nothing else he could do. "But when you were not in your room—when you were drinking with the others, say—did you see or hear of anything untoward?"

"Denis would brag of his conquests, but they never came here."

"He is young and very handsome," Marko said. "It is to be expected. It sounds as if he obeyed the rules while he was under this roof."

Pyotr nodded thoughtfully. "He never gambled here either."

"Oh?" Marko raised an eyebrow. "I didn't know that he gambled."

"Yes, he loves all games of chance. He likes to brag about how much he loses. But he always says that Lady This or Lady That covers his bets."

And the lady was subsequently rewarded in bed, Marko thought. Denis, like all of them, relied upon the shared income of the Pack's carefully invested funds. Which would not cover gambling debts. Marko rather doubted that anyone covered for him. So Denis needed money but he was careful not to give the appearance of it. Marko made a mental note of that interesting fact.

"And then there is Feodor," Pyotr was saying. "He brought a few trollops here. I don't think he cared in the least for any of them."

Marko shook his head. Women did not find Feodor in the least attractive, as far as Marko knew.

"He is always in the coffeehouses, sir."

"Yes, I know. Coming up with half-baked schemes and hoping to attract investors, as usual. But he has no head for business."

Marko saw the surprised look on Pyotr's face and thought he should not have spoken so of his kinsman. Feodor was a distant cousin with rather less Pack blood than most of them. He could not help being less shrewd as well.

"If you say so," Pyotr replied.

Preoccupied, Marko turned to the window and looked out. He didn't see the street below, lost in thought. The matter of Georgina's disappearance and the miscreant within their ranks were not likely to be linked, as the earl had said.

The nobleman's condescending demeanor toward him still rankled. No, Marko would have to continue his search on his own. There was nothing for it but to keep looking.

"Thank you, Pyotr," he said, without turning around. "That will be all."

He heard the other man rise and leave the room, closing the double doors behind him.

On a street not very far away . . .

The girl they sought was working in a jeweler's shop. It was not on a street that any of the three frequented and was situated just outside each of the overlapping circles on Marko's map.

Georgina had already lost some of her bloom in the space of a week. Her sleep had been troubled and never more so than after her first night with Denis.

He had seemed so concerned, brought her drops from the chemist. The little vial was nearly empty. He had said he would get more.

She was groggy during the day and made mistakes. Tait was sometimes sharp with her. Georgina wanted to crawl home in shame but she could not bring herself to do it.

And then there was Denis. His infinitely gentle treatment of her was something she craved far more than the drops that made her fall into a dreamless sleep. Each night in his arms brought her more strange pleasure but he would never enter her body.

She lived in a limbo of pure pleasure and nameless fear in her rented room. Denis visited her often—she was never sure when he would. During the day she was terrified that someone she knew would enter the shop.

Georgina's life had been turned upside down. She had never imagined that the world could seem so strange and overwhelming and cold. Her previous life seemed to have happened to someone else. Now she was a nobody who worked in a shop and lived in a room, although she was allowed to try on pretty baubles now and then, which were shut away in the safe at the end of the day.

Along with her mother's jewelry. She asked Tait to unroll the silk cloth that held them now and then so she knew that all the pieces were still there. How she would ever bring it back and make amends, she could not even begin to think. Guilt consumed her every waking moment.

Her mother might have her tried as a thief for all she knew.

She took out a tray of rings to show a customer and rubbed her temples. She always had a headache now. The sleeping drops didn't seem to help at all.

The woman wasn't interested and Georgina put the tray back in the case when she left. She wanted to sit down but she knew Tait would not approve.

He had mentioned, though, something about her doing something else besides wait on fussy, complaining females who rarely bought anything. Georgina was not quite sure what it was. A hostess at a club of some kind. Serving drinks to men.

Denis had promised to go with her and introduce her to his friends there. She was ready for a change, she thought distractedly.

She locked the shop door and went to the back, looking over Paul Clavell's shoulder. He was painting an ivory miniature for a customer. At first she had thought it was work she could do, but he wasn't interested in teaching her.

Her natural dexterity seemed to have vanished along with everything else. The small brushes were hard to manage and her hands were clumsy. She looked down at them. They were shaking now.

If only she had Denis to rub them for her, and make love to her. She craved him more than anything. She would willingly be his slave if he asked.

12

"Circles within circles," Jehane said to her sister. "I feel like we are going in them, that is certain."

"We cannot stop now," Severin pleaded with her. "It is only the second day."

Their progress had been slow but that was because Jehane stopped to admire herself in the window of every shop they passed. Severin felt thoroughly annoyed with her.

"I must rest. We have investigated every milliner and dressmaker between here and Charing Cross."

"Do you call looking at your own reflection investigating? I do not."

Jehane ignored the barbed remark. "We have turned up nothing. As you said, Georgina has vanished."

"I refuse to give up. We can take tea and rest. Then I at least will begin again."

Jehane shrugged indifferently. "Suit yourself."

"Do you not care?"

"She is your pupil, not mine."

"That is true, Jehane, but even so—"

Her sister took her by the elbow the second she spotted a tea room. "You have a way of making me feel guilty."

"I didn't mean to."

"It doesn't matter. I suppose I ought to feel guilty once in a while, eh?"

"Jehane—"

Her sister was pushing open the door, making the little bell on it jangle wildly. "I would rather have stronger refreshment, but tea will do. The tables here are nice and wide. Let us spread out Marko's map and cross off where we have been."

"And then what?" said Severin as they entered. The tea room was dimly lit and she paused to let her eyes adjust.

"Then you can go one way and I will go another. We can cover twice the ground."

"Are you no longer afraid to be alone?" Severin asked as they took their seats.

Jehane waved her hand idly. "Should I be? It is broad daylight."

"But that doesn't mean you ought to ask dangerous questions alone."

"There is nothing dangerous about tea rooms and shops."

"You did mention circles of your acquaintance that I would not like, Jehane."

"So I did." Jehane smiled as the proprietoress came over and they gave her their order. "I will definitely be visiting those by myself."

"But—"

"You cannot forbid me," Jehane laughed. "All right, I will take someone."

"Who?" Severin asked.

"Ah—Charlie," Jehane answered, a little too quickly for Severin to believe her.

*   *   *

Several hours on, when it was dark but before the moon had risen, Jehane swaggered into a tavern, ignoring the catcalls of the men on the benches and in the booths. Keeping her cloak on, she went straight to the back and pushed open a curtain that closed off a small room.

"Hello, Feodor," she said to the man inside.

"Jehane—what an unexpected surprise."

"Is it? I don't think so. I know you have had my sister and me followed."

Feodor raised his eyebrows in stagey astonishment. "Indeed not."

"I saw the same little man behind us in every shop window."

"No doubt he was admiring your arse."

"He was following us. But I doubled back after I walked my sister home and followed him here."

Feodor craned his neck to look past her. Apparently he spotted the man, because he scowled. "A coincidence."

"I don't think so." She sank into the chair opposite him, picking absently at the horsehair that sprang from a tear in its upholstery.

"Hmm. May I buy you a drink?"

"I will have wine."

"Nothing stronger?"

"Not in your presence, no."

"Very well, Jehane." He folded his arms across his chest. "So you have found me here, although that is not difficult and proves nothing. This tavern is my headquarters. Everyone who knows me knows that."

Jehane accepted the glass of wine that a barkeep brought in on a tray. She took a sip, keeping her gaze on him, and set the glass down.

"You must still be looking for that girl."

"I have walked over half of London with Severin looking for her."

"What did you say her name was?"

"Georgina Lennox."

"Yes, that was it. With dark hair and green eyes? Hmm."

Jehane sighed and reached within the deep folds of her cloak, taking out a small bag that clinked. She threw it on the table between them.

"It goes against my principles to give a pimp money, but here you are."

Feodor eyed the bag, then picked it up. "How much?"

She named the sum in guineas.

"That does seem to jog my memory." He tucked the bag into a pocket of his own. "I think I have seen her."

"Take me to her then."

"And what will you do if I oblige you, Jehane?"

"Nothing for you, Feodor. The money is all you get."

"And what if I do not take you to her?"

She shrugged and the cloak came apart in front. Feodor stared hungrily at what he saw. "Then I will find her somehow. I will fuck anyone but you if I have to."

Her careless remark sparked a fire in his eyes that she did not see as she looked everywhere but at him.

"You are brazen, Jehane," he said at last. His voice was very soft.

"What of it?"

She rose and paced the room. He too stood up and grabbed her roughly by the shoulders, turning her to face him.

"Let me go, you pig!" she hissed. "There are fellows out there who would slit your throat if they thought it would please me."

"Call them in." His punishing grip on her shoulder lessened by one half when he placed a hand upon her throat. "If you can." But his fingers didn't squeeze and her breath didn't catch. All he did was stroke.

"So soft and smooth," he murmured. "Why do you wear no necklace? Has business been bad?"

"No."

"I hear that it has—that you keep to your apartments. Only Charlie is allowed in these days."

"You hear wrong."

Feodor grinned. "If you want him with you always, then you must ask him for his miniature and have it set in a locket. I know just the fellow for the job. Your young soldier would be happy to sleep forever between those tits."

Jehane twisted her head and sank her teeth into his hand. She drew blood but he seemed to enjoy it.

"Ah, but I drew first blood," he said triumphantly. "In a metaphorical way."

Free of him, Jehane stepped away, then realized that she had given him the sack of money. She raised her hand as if to slap him and he caught her wrist.

"Do you want your money back?" He placed her hand upon his body. "You can find it if you feel. Go lower."

Jehane snatched her hand back. "Take it then."

Feodor stood with his legs apart. His erection was obvious.

"Fighting excites me."

She turned to storm out, her cloak swirling about her.

"And do you know," he said conversationally. "It excites Miss Lennox as well. I find that she loves rough play. Do you want to see her? You will see nothing shocking. Her face is not bruised. Not yet."

Jehane stopped and gave him a searching look. "Where is she?"

"Not here, Jehane."

"Take me to her."

"Mind your manners. And say please."

"I will not."

Feodor permitted himself an exaggerated sigh.

"Oh, very well. She's only a short drive away. Presently residing in the bawdy house where you started out."

Jehane regarded him with horror. "That house—oh, God. Not there. That poor girl. I will go in and buy her freedom if I have to, but—damnation! No one knows me there now."

"No? Oh, yes. I believe you are right. The establishment is under new ownership."

She scowled fiercely at him, then looked out from the room to the men in the tavern. Not much time had elapsed but they seemed drunker than before. She would find no allies there.

"Take me to her," she repeated. "You can start a bawdy house of your own with the money in that bag."

Feodor drew it out and made a great show of undoing the drawstring. Then he poured the coins into his palm.

"Nice handful," he said. "All right, Jehane. I have no wish to quarrel with you. If you are done with your wine—"

"It tasted like poison."

He raised his eyebrows. "What dreadful things you accuse me of."

"You are capable of anything, Feodor."

"Thank you. It is gratifying to have your respect."

She shot him a furious look. "Where is your carriage? I will not stand here and bandy words with you."

"Waiting outside."

"Then I will meet you there."

Feodor nodded and watched her go. "Proud as ever, Jehane," he said under his breath when she reached the door that led to the street. His eyes glittered madly. "But you shall have your comeuppance. And soon. Very soon."

Severin pushed through the crowds upon the street, exhausted by her fruitless search.

She had described Georgina so often that she felt she could

see the girl in front of her, a shadow pleading for help. She could not shake the feeling that her student was in danger.

The hour had grown late and she had to sidestep men who'd had too much to drink in one tavern on their way to another. She caught a glimpse of red jackets and broad white belts, and sighed inwardly.

Oh no. A band of soldiers, making merry. She was sure to be jostled or fondled, and cursed at for not supporting king and country by not giving away a kiss.

The thought of an ale-drenched mustache forced against her lips sickened her. Stepping to the side, Severin looked down and dodged the oncoming row of military boots coming straight at her.

Too late. A strong hand seized her arm and she bumped into a red-coated chest. She looked up.

The soldier was heartbreakingly young and handsome. And he looked familiar. But where—

"Charlie," she breathed.

"That's me name," he said, laughing uproariously. "But how did ye know it?"

With a start, Severin remembered that she had only seen him asleep.

His companions looked her up and down, waiting for her answer and joking loudly among themselves.

"A guess, nothing more," she said. "Kindly let me pass."

Charlie didn't let go. "What d'you say, boys? Shall we let the lady pass?"

There was disagreement on that score. Severin looked around wildly for a gentleman who would come to her aid. A few of the better-dressed men avoided her eyes and walked swiftly on. No one would tangle with so many soldiers.

"Go on, then," Charlie said suddenly. "Sorry. Didn't mean to accost a lady."

Severin sighed with relief and hurried on, hearing their noisy laughter for another few minutes before she rounded the corner. She leaned against a wall, fighting a sense of panic. She was safe. Why was her heart racing so?

She put a hand over it to still its frantic beating and then the realization came to her.

Jehane had said she would go out tonight to some low place to continue to look for Georgina. With Charlie. But here he was.

Wherever she was, Jehane was alone.

And the only thing Severin could do was go back home and hope her sister would too.

The carriage ride proved uneventful, to Jehane's great relief, because they were in a part of London that was unfamiliar to her. Feodor was civil enough, for a man who was sulking about sex he wasn't going to get.

"Where are we going?" she asked. "This is not the way to the house where I learned my trade."

"Yes, it is. A roundabout way."

She looked out the window. The hubbub of the streets was reassuring. She could always scream for help or even jump out. They weren't going very fast.

Feodor communicated with the driver by sticking his head out and screaming himself. So it was not as if he were in league with the man and planned to kidnap her or worse.

The horse plodded on.

Feodor hummed.

Jehane grew restive and turned to him. "If you do not bring me to Georgina in five minutes, then I want to get out."

"How will you get home?"

"That bag of guineas is not all I brought with me," she said angrily, then wished she had kept her mouth shut.

But Feodor only raised an eyebrow. "We will soon be there."

She looked out the window again, not seeing his foot press a device on the floor. But she did sigh with relief when the carriage came to a jerking halt as the result of his surreptitious communication to the driver.

"This is not the place, Feodor!"

"I lied," he said calmly and stretched out a hand. "But you can get out if you like. Look, there she is."

Jehane looked frantically to where he was pointing. The light coming from inside the shop showed a girl in silhouette.

"Is that Georgina?"

"Yes."

She squinted. "I cannot make out her features."

"I thought you knew her."

"I have seen her—Severin is not in the habit of introducing her students to me."

"For obvious reasons." Feodor patted the bag of coins in his pocket. "Although you do make a very good living. Why don't you get out, Severin?"

"Because I am afraid you will drive off and leave me here," she said testily.

"But you said that you had kept some money in reserve."

"Well, yes," she muttered. With so many people about, she was not afraid that anything would happen.

No, a new fear had replaced it. That Georgina would see her, and cut and run.

Jehane well knew how skittish a runaway girl could be. And this would be—if it was her—Georgina's first glimpse of anyone who knew her family since her disappearance.

She was relieved to see that the girl was working in a shop. Why Feodor had misled her on that score, she didn't know. Getting his own back, she supposed.

"Do not drive off," Jehane said to Feodor. He only shrugged as she opened the door on her side and eased down to the street, going to one side of the shop window to look in.

The girl came to the window and Jehane saw her white hands hover over one necklace in a presentation box . . . and tremble. A flash of intuition told her Georgina was not well, even if she was working in the shop of her own free will. Still, it was better than the degradation of a common whorehouse, which could turn a girl into an unrecognizable creature in a matter of weeks. The hands withdrew, taking the box and appeared again. This time the girl they belonged to had to lean into the window and look down to see what she was about to pick up.

Jehane made a mental comparison of her young face to Severin's sketch. Turning into a doorway so that Feodor, who was still in the carriage, could not see what she was doing, she took a tiny notebook from the bag she carried and dashed off a note, folding it and writing a name and address on the outside. She glanced about for a likely boy and gave a melting look to the one who stopped ever so briefly to gaze back, beckoning him to her with the slightest possible motion of her hand, then whispering, "Deliver this for me—"—she slipped him the note—"and here is a shilling for your trouble. I have instructed the gentleman who is to receive it to give you a sovereign."

An artful dodger to the core, the boy concealed the folded note and the coin in his hand. "Yes, missus. Thank 'ee," he whispered back.

She watched him dash off as she came out of the doorway, nodding at Feodor, who threw her a curious look from the carriage. He did not need to know that she had summoned Marko.

"That is her," Jehane said as she clambered back in the carriage.

"You're quite sure?" Feodor asked mockingly.

"Yes."

"I do want you to get your money's worth."

"Take me home," Jehane said.

Feodor straightened. "Why? You are here. And there is the girl you say you are looking for."

"But she will not come to me. She will think I mean her harm."

"Can you read her mind? Right through the window?"

Jehane scowled at him. "Do you know how many girls like her I have seen?"

"No, I don't. How many did you help?"

She didn't answer that question. "I will get my sister and we will come back in our own carriage. Severin will be able to persuade her to come home."

"As you wish." He leaned out the window and instructed the driver to head for Soho.

He had interesting plans for Jehane. But he had to get her used to him first, lull her into letting down her constant guard. It would not be easy but it would be worth it.

Marko went through the things that Severin had brought the day before—the paltry evidence that Georgina even existed. The sketch of her. The scarf. The broken chain. He had no need of the sketch, but the scarf did interest him. The fine silk had the faintest possible smell—he could just detect it. Of course, attempting to follow a scent trail through a city as odiferous as London was next to impossible.

Next to impossible. But not completely so.

It had been a long time since he had done anything so wolfish, but he had to try.

Marko put the delicate material to his nose, memorizing the subtle traces of scent. He felt as if he were invading her privacy somehow.

But if Severin had thought it important enough to give to him, then he would make use of it as he thought best.

He could feel an older and deeper part of his brain come to life as he set the scarf to one side. He took the chain out of its little box and put it into his pocket.

Superstition. How very human of him. But he hoped very much to find her, connecting link to delicate link. Marko felt the fine hair down his back tingle and he knew he was in hunter mode.

The major d'omo came in, and handed a note to Marko. "The lad who brought it is waiting in the foyer, sir."

Marko unfolded it and read quickly, then dug in his pocket for a sovereign. "Give him this."

The man raised his eyebrows, obviously astonished by his master's generosity, but said nothing as he exited the room, leaving Marko alone again. He refolded the note and tucked it in the pocket the coin had come from.

Jehane had beaten him to it. Well, well. So one of the sisters had out-hunted him. He felt a little disconcerted but it was a good thing that Georgina had been found so swiftly.

The street he was on had the same mix of shops to be found anywhere in London. They were closing one by one, except for the taverns and the eating-houses. Jehane and Severin were nowhere to be found.

Men and women sauntered into one and then the other, satisfying their appetites for food and drink and companionship.

Marko began to feel that he ought to do the same. He stopped in front of a jeweler's or so he supposed from the empty display. Was it the one Jehane had meant? Her hastily written note had not gone into detail. He studied the headless necks attached to busts of black velvet, denuded of the jewelry they'd held, and presentation boxes that bore only the imprint of rings and bracelets.

A movement in the back of the shop caught his eye and for the merest second he thought he had seen Georgina. There was a girl, certainly, but the shadows at the back of the store were too deep to see her clearly.

She came forward. It was her.

Then a priggish fellow, tall and severe-looking with his chin sunk into a starched collar, glared at him and snapped down the blind over the window.

Even that short glimpse told him that the clerk was a strange one—there was something strange about the whole place, in fact. And what if Georgina was working there because she wanted to? Marko decided to stay where he was and wait for the women. Persuasion was preferable to force.

He bought a meat pie at a stall on the street, took a bite, and tossed the rest to a mongrel dog, who looked happy enough to get it.

Then he sat down in a doorway that looked like it hadn't been used for years.

The dog sat down by him, wagging its tail.

"Happy, little brother?" he asked it. He dodged a filthy, fur-faced kiss from the animal by turning away. And then he saw something just beyond the roofline of the shop. There was a skylight above the jeweler's store. He might get a very interesting view of what was inside from there.

He decided to wait. After another forty-five minutes, he was on the roof, breathing hard after his awkward climb.

The skylight had an iron framework set with almost opaque glass that distorted the shapes of two men walking about underneath him. What they were saying wasn't clear. So much for derring-do.

The clerk who'd pulled the window blind shut was undoubtedly still in the shop—so there was another man with him. Georgina was too.

Marko kept well back. It would be difficult for them to see him but it was not impossible. So. There were only two men, but what if one of them had a pistol? He could be a hero and storm the battlements—and then the girl might be hurt somehow.

He would do best to listen and watch for the moment. There was no telling what would happen next.

* * *

Tait went to the back of the jeweler's shop, walking with his head down, looking under the glass cases as if he were stalking a rodent. His eyes narrowed when he spotted a small stud that someone had dropped upon the carpet. He picked it up and twirled it between his fingers.

"Have you drawn the blind?" a voice called.

"Yes, Mr. Clavell. An hour ago. Did you not hear the snap?" He reached the work area where the older man sat.

"I found this," he said, showing the stud.

"Then put it in the safe and lock it up," Clavell said. He sat near Georgina, whose head drooped onto her folded arms. "I want to get home," Georgina muttered.

"Not yet. Is she sleeping?"

"Yes, I think so. I have been listening to her talk. She makes no sense."

"What does she have to say?"

"Nothing of interest. Have you heard from Denis? Has he found a taker for our prize jewel?" The old man's tone was nasty.

"I believe he has."

The discussion, even though it concerned her, didn't seem to register with Georgina one way or another. She raised her head and looked blankly at both men. They leered back. The shadows gouged their faces and lent them an air of menace.

"I want to go home," she said. She seemed about to cry.

"Denis will be along to take you to your room," Tait replied.

"No. I want to go to my real home." She tried to straighten but her head wobbled on her slender neck.

"You have given her too much," Clavell said in an undertone.

"Denis told me to have her ready. You wouldn't want her to scream, would you?"

"I should not have let you dose her, Tait."

The shop assistant threw him a look of scorn. "You would have poisoned her." He gave a nod toward Clavell's work bench. "Still tipping the fangs with that powder, I see."

The old man didn't answer. Georgina rose and made her way unsteadily toward a tattered chaise that leaked stuffing. She collapsed onto it, yawning.

"Good. She will sleep through her deflowering," Clavell said contemptuously.

"I suppose you wish it was you," Tait said.

"I cannot afford such tender fare," the old man replied.

"Nor can I," Tait sighed. "Alas, what she has can only be sold once."

"Unlike the jewelry we sell and send you out to steal back," Clavell said.

Tait emitted a creaky laugh. "Another good business," he said.

Clavell walked over and pulled back one of Georgina's eyelids using the gentle pressure of his thumb. "Hmm. I wonder when she will wake up. How much did you give her?"

"Two spoonfuls, mixed into her tea with sugar."

Clavell straightened and sighed. "She must not be eating much. It has gone to her head."

"Do you truly think she will stay that way?" Tait seemed a little anxious for the first time.

"We'll have to wait and see, won't we?" The jeweler returned to his bench, taking up another locket and fitting in a piece of ivory.

"I believe that Denis is meeting her purchaser even now," Tait said. "Should we make her more presentable?"

"You can if you like."

Tait began fussing with her collar and cuffs, smoothing down the folds of her gown. Georgina felt what he was doing and moaned. "I want to go home," she said again. "Please . . . let me go."

"There, there," Tait said soothingly.

"Listen to you," Clavell said. "You sound like her mother."

"I expect she does want her mother. Girls do."

Clavell shook his head. "Not one like this."

"You are hard-hearted."

"That is the way of the world, Mr. Tait. Ah, here is Denis, coming in from the shop next door."

The tall Russian entered via a partially concealed door in the wall, unlocking it for himself. "Well, well," he said. "How is our lovely little virgin?"

"I am afraid that Tait gave her too much," Clavell said. "Can't sell her if she dies. But he might want her. Tait strikes me as the sort of fellow who likes his women quiet."

"Shut up," Tait snarled.

Denis only shrugged. "He can't afford her. I can't either." He sat down next to Georgina.

"Where is she being delivered to?"

Denis snorted. "The best neighborhood in London. It is a good thing that she won't struggle. But there will be no trouble with the servants seeing her brought in. That's taken care of."

"It seems to me," Tait said carefully, "that I saw him outside this afternoon. He was with a lady in a carriage."

"What of it? He usually is. He doesn't like to walk."

"That doesn't explain the lady," Tait said. "She seemed interested in the shop."

"Of course. We sell jewelry."

"But what if she is a relation of our Miss Lennox?"

"Miss Lennox assured me that she has no relations, outside of her mother. And since she came into our shop with her mother's jewelry, I daresay she would rather not see Mrs. Lennox ever again."

"Well, I don't think the lady I saw could be Georgina's mother," Tait said. "She was much too young for that."

"There is your explanation. Himself, as you call him, has found another girl. Was she pretty, Mr. Tait?"

"Yes, very."

Denis stretched out next to Georgina on the chaise. "For purposes of blackmail, the prettier, the better. I could use a few new girls myself—my gaming debts are onerous and my creditors are pressing me in a most ungentlemanly way."

"Who will you prey upon this time? Anyone particular in mind?" Clavell asked.

"A politician or two. Someone who wishes to give the impression of public virtue."

"Don't they all," said Clavell. "Even that damned old ranter Fox and his whore Kitty settled down in domestic bliss eventually."

"Yes, well, politicians and whores have much in common. They promise satisfaction but only deliver enough to keep fools coming back for more."

"Hmph," Clavell said. "It surprises me, Denis, that you have never been sued for criminal conversation."

The man on the chaise laughed in a low voice. "I have bedded many a wife. Some husbands don't mind having someone else do the honors."

"Those of us who are old and ugly can only dream of such delights," Clavell said sourly.

"Tsk-tsk. I hear bitterness in your voice," Denis replied. "The poison you handle must be seeping into your system."

Clavell shook his head. "I am very careful with it. I only used it in Lucy's locket, you know."

"I wonder who found that."

"A thief, I suppose. He must be dead by now if he opened it and was pricked by one of the fangs," Clavell said. "Of course, it depends how deep the little wound goes."

"Let us hope he is. Especially if he saw her die—I cannot remember the punishment for robbing a corpse."

"Not hanging. Transportation, I should think," Clavell said.

"Hmm. I should hate to have someone like that remain alive," Denis replied.

"Denis, you never did tell us who killed Lucy," Tait said in a soft voice. "Or the other one—what was her name? Adele?"

"You don't need to know." Denis sat up halfway and looked down at Georgina. "It is a good thing the girl is unconscious. She should not hear us talk like this even if she is."

"Yes, there is no telling what she may remember," Clavell said. "But her mind is cloudy at the best of times. I suspect she will recollect very little."

Denis stroked her hair absently.

"You touch her like a lover," Tait said.

"I am, in a way."

"But—" Tait stopped talking when the tall Russian gave him a quelling look.

"She remains a virgin," Denis said. "Imagine that."

"How?" Tait asked.

"A gentleman never tells such things," Denis said, getting up. "And she will be too ashamed to ever reveal what I did to her. Come, one of you. Help me rouse our sleeping beauty."

"Not me. But good luck," Clavell said.

Georgina groaned and tears she could not control trickled down her cheeks.

"Do you have any smelling salts?" Denis asked. "Something to wave under her nose?"

The old man shook his head.

"Then you two may leave and go out and get dinner," Denis said. "I will rouse her in my own way."

They grumbled but Tait and Clavell obeyed, padlocking the back door and then having to unlock it when they went back for the money they'd forgotten, blaming each other under their breath.

Marko peered over the rooftop, looking down at their heads. The faint scent wafting from the doorway matched the one in his memory from the scarf. Again he caught a familiar whiff of packishness. But it didn't emanate from either Clavell or Paul, and he had not seen anyone else enter. He made his way down the wall to the street as awkwardly as he had gone up.

Marko was certain that Georgina was still somewhere inside. He shrank back into the doorway as Clavell and Tait headed away. They were talking intently in low voices and they didn't see him. Nor did they see the carriage that waited two doors down as they came out of the alley and turned the corner.

Marko's ears pricked up when he heard the passengers alight and walk to the door of the shop. They too conversed in low voices. Severin and Jehane had come at last. One of them tried the doorknob. He ran out from the alley with a finger to his lips. Severin stifled her gasp.

"What are you doing here?" she whispered.

"I followed my instincts," he replied simply. The sly Jehane might not have told her sister that she'd sent a note to him. He hated the idea of seeming less than a hero.

"Oh. Jehane explained that she saw Georgina but was afraid she might bolt. She said her hands were shaking terribly. Is she inside?" She tried to peer through the drawn blind.

"I believe so."

"Is she alone?" Severin asked.

Marko nodded. "At the moment, yes. I only saw two men and they have gone. We will have to act quickly if we are to bring her home without interference. Did you tell your driver to wait?"

"Yes. Were you able to get inside?" Jehane asked impatiently.

"No. There is a skylight, but I could not see much at all. And I could not hear the men very well until they left. Now—" Marko took both their hands and brought them around to the alley—"I need a hair pin to pick the lock."

Jehane handed him one and several dark tendrils tumbled down over her shoulders. Marko concentrated on the lock. Fiddling with its innards, he had it open in a minute and stepped inside the shop, moving noiselessly. Jehane and Severin were right behind him when he stopped, still in the shadows.

There was their quarry, on a chaise. With a third man. Marko swore silently. He'd have to fight the fellow, whose long, strong body held the girl captive. Something about him was very familiar. Marko paused, all his senses tingling.

The man stroked the woman's body, humming tunelessly as he pulled her skirt higher. His hand moved along her bare thigh and Marko heard her protest but weakly. "Want it, do you?" he said to her. "You shall have it, my girl."

Thunderstruck, Marko realized who the other man was. "Denis?" he said, aghast.

The tall man on the chaise whipped around, restraining Georgina with one arm. The leader and the cub of the Pack of St. James stared at each other in mutual shock.

Severin put a hand to her mouth. Jehane edged to Marko's side. "Damnation," she said softly, "I should have known."

"Georgina?" Severin asked. "Oh my God—it is her. Marko, do something."

Denis got to his feet and stood in front of the chaise. "Yes, Marko. Make a move." His voice was flat, but there was a strange fire in his eyes.

He had to stare the other man down, Marko knew. It was a leader's move, one that his eldest brother had practiced on his two younger brothers until he got it right. Kyril could do it so well they'd had to drop to their knees.

Marko took a deep breath and fastened his gaze on Denis, forcing him to look away, hoping he would look down . . . but it didn't work. The younger man took a step forward, looking at the frightened women instead of Marko and moving quickly.

Blast, Marko thought. The fine points of wolfishness might fail him, but street fighting would not. He landed a lightning-fast punch on Denis's jaw and the other man fell backward, grunting.

His head hit the carved frame of the chaise with a dull thud. Denis ended up on the floor in a sitting position, his head sagging forward onto his chest, a trickle of blood coming from his open mouth.

Georgina moaned and tried to move away from him, and Severin went to her, dashing past Marko. Jehane did too, whipping off a scarf and binding Denis's hands so swiftly that Marko did not see how she did it.

Denis looked at her, dazed, and then finally at Marko.

"You know what will happen, I think," Marko said.

"Exile," Denis managed to get the word out of his swollen mouth.

"Yes." Marko jerked the other man's neatly arranged ascot from around his neck and tossed it to Jehane. "Hobble his ankles. If he tries to stand, he will fall."

When she had done it—he did not want to think about how she had learned to tie a man in such effective restraints—he nodded toward Georgina, listening all the while for signs of the other men returning.

"Can you manage her between you?" he asked the sisters.

"Yes, I think so."

"Then make haste! The other two may come back at any minute."

Severin was already lifting Georgina to a sitting position.

"Bring her safely home and send a message to my house. Make sure it gets to Antosha." He looked around the shop's interior as if seeing it for the first time, banging open drawers until he found what he needed. Marko scrawled a hasty explanation for the Pack's secretary and gave it to Jehane as she too rushed to Georgina's side.

The sisters got the groggy girl up and half-dragged her until she managed to walk to the door, sobbing with shame and fear.

"Go!" he said.

Denis's partners in crime must have expected him to have his way with the unresisting girl, and take his pleasure for at least an hour. Marko worked Denis over for a while. The questioning process was rough, but he got the truth from him

Denis had needed money. He'd exploited the girl's attraction to him without acknowledging they'd met—easy enough to do, with the drugs he'd given her. The forced seduction of Georgina was a grievous sin, but he had not committed the worst sin of all: murder. Marko was satisfied with the answers he extracted.

When the manwolves charged with enforcing their laws arrived, he turned his humiliated prisoner over to them, knowing that daybreak would find Denis shackled in the hold of a ship bound for Siberia.

And good riddance, he thought.

Georgina cried in Severin's arms for hours. She explained . . . not everything, but enough. Jehane took her sister aside before she left and told her it was best that Georgina not remember much.

Later, alone with Marko, Severin stretched out upon her own chaise, pulling a blanket up under her chin that concealed nearly all of her. He could not blame her for wanting to hide.

Her improvised cocoon hid her well. It was odd to be so close to her again, less than a foot away, sitting in an armchair, and not go to her. He put the thought of their passionate lovemaking firmly out of his mind. Surely she was not thinking of it now. They had found Georgina more by luck than anything else, and there was no telling if that luck would hold. Denis was dealt with but his unknown companions might make more trouble yet—blackmail was a possibility, certainly. There was more than one way to ruin a young woman.

The ugly situation was complicated. Hardly the sort of circumstances under which he'd expected to see Severin again, but it couldn't be helped. If a woman in need asked for help, a gentleman was honor-bound to provide it.

Marko looked absently at his split knuckles, wanting to lick the trace of blood that seeped from them but realizing it would be a wolfish thing to do. He folded the hand that was less battered over the one he'd slammed into the cub's fine teeth.

He would not brag of it—he was filled with disgust for his kinsman's evil deeds. But the Pack itself was far more important than Denis, who would be banished from it forever. How to explain that to her, the Great Wolf only knew. He would let her bring it up if she wanted to. In the meantime, there had to be something safe they could talk about.

"It was kind of you to give Georgina your bed," he said at last.

"I don't think she was ready to face her mother. I was not surprised to find Georgina in a jewelry shop—Mary told me that she'd taken her jewels. She must have meant to sell them. I expect they are long gone and the money already spent."

"It is not as if we can go back and find out. That is an explanation that Georgina will have to make to her mother herself."

Severin nodded. "I cannot bring myself to tell Mary that her daughter is here until Georgina gives me permission, though. Mary will probably blame me for what happened, mark my words."

"That is unfortunate."

Severin drew the blanket more tightly around her. "It is the least of my worries, so long as we have Georgina safely back. I was beginning to think she was lost to us forever."

"Thank God she is not, and that she appears to be healthy." He didn't want to mention what he had smelled when they brought the half-conscious girl by him: opium. He supposed she had been given it in a tincture, taking drops from a bottle.

"Apparently she is still a virgin or so she said," Severin said thoughtfully. "But she is still feeling the effects of the laudanum she was given."

Marko nodded. So Severin knew. "May it bring forgetfulness then."

Severin cast him a long look. "But you and I and Jehane know much more—oh, Marko, what will you do? Denis is a relation of yours—nothing like you, certainly, but—"

Marko interrupted. "I apologize for his appalling actions. Denis has been taken away by my kinsmen and he will be exiled and severely punished for his misdeeds."

"And yet we may never know exactly what those were," Severin mused.

Marko's tone grew stern. "He will never set foot in England again. He was the procurer I was warned of—the one who uses the Pack of St. James as a front. I had my suspicions, of course."

"Why?"

Marko smiled slightly. "Would you rather not know who warned me that there was such a man among the Pack?"

"That was my next question," Severin admitted. "Of course, I could have asked Jehane, who would have found out if she doesn't already know."

Marko inclined his head in an acknowledging nod. "She took me aside when you were alone with Georgina, and she advised me that yet another man is involved—not the two who left the shop before you came, she is sure of that. I described them as best I could. One was old, and one was a young clerk. I saw him pull down the blind in front after I glimpsed Georgina."

"Indeed. I wonder who she thinks it is."

Marko shrugged. "She didn't say, only that she hopes to persuade him to betray Denis."

Severin gave him a worried look. "That will be a dirty bit of business if she does."

"As you have implied, she is not above it."

"Hmm," was all Severin said to that. "Well, then, who told you that there was a procurer in your midst?"

"No less a personage than Georgina's stepfather."

"The earl of Cavendish? Old Coyle?"

"Yes."

Severin pondered that, giving a slight shake of her head. "I suppose he ought to know. Did you go to see him then?"

"I did," Marko began. "I did not act swiftly enough and I cannot blame anyone besides myself for what has happened—"

"Not to Georgina, surely. The world is wicked. That is not your fault."

"No. However, the Pack cannot become a haven for those who prey upon the innocent. So much has happened on my watch and how little of it was known to me—I am deeply ashamed of that."

She was quiet for a while. "But you are not responsible for the wrongdoing of others."

"I am the leader of my kinsmen until my older brother Kyril returns from Russia."

"Hmm. And what if he decides to stay there?"

"Then I shall find a way to run away with you!" he burst out. "Semyon will have to return from Scotland and take over."

"Who is Semyon?"

"My younger brother. He can take over. I am not made for leadership, I fear, let alone heroics."

"You did very well tonight."

"I was told to make my way to the right place at the right time."

She cleared her throat. "You rescued Georgina. In my eyes, that makes you a hero."

"No. I did what needed to be done."

She let go of the blanket and reached out, touching him lightly on the top of his hand. "Your knuckles show it."

"I got a few answers out of Denis." He hesitated. "There is still much to be learned and—and other matters on my mind." How to speak of murder without frightening her further? "I suppose you have heard of the recent deaths of two young women, Severin. Unexplained deaths."

She nestled back into her cocoon, shuddering a little. "Yes. I read the papers."

"In both cases, there was a connection to—" He hesitated again. "Like Georgina, the victims both had a hidden connection to the Pack. But Denis is not guilty of murder, as far as I can tell. I still haven't gotten to the bottom of it."

"I see." She was thoughtful. "And tell me again why you call yourselves a Pack?"

"Ah," he hesitated. "It is our custom. That's all."

"Really?"

She gave him an amber-eyed look that Marko found most disconcerting. "Then I will not pry. But may I say . . . I am grateful for your help, Marko."

He waved away her praise. "I would do anything for you, Severin."

Their eyes met and an undercurrent of deep feeling flowed between them. He wanted to rise, to go to her and comfort her, but now was not the time.

Georgina went home in less than a week. Severin had a secret talk with the girl's mother and very little more was said. But she was no longer allowed to tutor her, and Mary Lennox would not say why.

13

A few days later...

Jehane met Feodor again at his favorite haunt. They were once again sequestered in the small curtained room in the back, looking rather warily at each other.

She had said little to Marko of her suspicions concerning his other kinsman—Marko had been horrified to find out that Denis was a whoremonger, and then preoccupied by deep concern for Severin and Georgina. Now, repelled by Feodor's sly expression, she wished she had taken Marko completely into her confidence.

Short of sleeping with Feodor, she could not think of a way to persuade him to reveal the precise nature and extent of his operations, or trick him into giving away the identities and whereabouts of his colleagues in what was probably a multiplicity of crimes. If he was not the murderer of Lucy and Adele, then he must know who had done them in.

But the bastard would never tell her unless there was something in it for him.

Feodor leaned back in his chair, arms folded across his chest. "So what is it you want from me?"

"A bit of information."

"Ask away." He put a leg up onto the table between them and crossed it with the other one, as if he were showing off the dirty soles of his boots. They were encrusted with mud and straw.

"Ugh. Did you just come from a stable?" she asked him, wrinkling her nose. "Your boots need cleaning."

He only laughed. "I will advise my valet accordingly."

"Oh?" She cocked a quizzical look at him. "You have a valet now, do you? You must be doing well, Feodor."

He nodded. "My business is on the verge of making a profit."

She lowered her cloak from about her bare shoulders, hoping to provoke him into staring at her the way he had before. "And what is the nature of your business? Are you quite on your own? If you don't mind my asking."

"I do mind. You and your haughty bitch of a sister are getting in my way."

She summoned up the self-control to keep from looking surprised. "Oh. Are you and Denis Somov partners in crime, then?"

"A blunt question."

Jehane could not deny that.

"And I won't answer it," Feodor said. "I understand that he bore the brunt of Marko's fury."

"I wouldn't know."

Feodor sat up straight. "The three of you conspired. My informants saw you and your sister hustle Georgina into a carriage and drive away, hell-bent on getting that girl back to her mother."

Jehane decided not to play innocent. Feodor wouldn't believe her if she did. "Who was not overjoyed to see her daughter, according to Severin," Jehane replied. "The lady shed a tear or two and then she said something about jewelry gone missing."

Feodor seemed unconcerned. "I know nothing about it."

Jehane shrugged, fighting her nervousness. "Then never mind. It is only jewelry. Severin asked me to help her and I did. She is my sister, after all. And you will not miss Georgina. There are thousands of silly girls like her in London, ripe for the picking."

"True."

She looked at him narrowly, annoyed by his casual tone. "Don't go looking for her again. Her stepfather is a powerful man who could cause you a good deal of trouble, Feodor."

He steepled his fingers. "May I ask you a question or two, Jehane?"

"Am I not here to talk?" She strove for a conversational tone. "Yes."

Feodor swung his legs off the table as he laughed loudly. "Are *you* quite on your own? What do you really want, Jehane? Have you decided you need a protector after all?"

"Certainly not."

"Then don't waste my time." He snapped his fingers in her face. The sharp pop disconcerted her and made her blink. "As much as I enjoy chatting with you, there are much more interesting things to do in the evening in London."

"Very well." She remained sitting. Feodor came around the table and stood in back of her. Ever so gently, he placed her cloak back on her shoulders.

"However," he said slowly, "if you desire purely physical company, I'm your man."

Jehane pressed her lips together. She supposed she could endure that much. Feodor had to be at the center of everything bad that happened, she was sure of it. But she could not prove it. Not yet.

She got into the hired carriage that Feodor summoned outside the tavern, not noticing the driver who sat upon the box. Hat brims pulled down low, greatcoat collars up, such men were as interchangeable as the broken-down nags in the reins they held.

Feodor clambered up after her, treating himself to a rude feel of her arse on the way. Jehane pressed herself against the side and glared at him when she sat. They rattled on in silence for some time.

She decided to have it out with him. Feodor would most likely cooperate with her, especially if he thought she would let him lift her skirts and get at what he wanted afterward.

"I was not quite truthful with you at first," she began.

"That was ever the case."

Jehane wanted to smack the smug look off his face, but she controlled her temper. "I have been considering your proposition that we go into business together," she said at last. "I just did not want to say so back there. The room is hardly secure and anyone who sidled by the curtain could hear."

"True enough." He sat up. "But they didn't. I pay the innkeeper to keep eavesdroppers away from my nook. He is not above using his fists."

She supposed that he did. "In any case, this is a more private place to talk."

"All right. Talk."

She took a deep breath and began. "After those women were murdered—Lucy and Adele—I received some letters. Threatening letters, my sister thought."

"Tell-tale tit, your tongue shall be slit. Was that one?"

"Yes." She looked at him narrowly. "Did you write them? You must have done so, if you know that."

"That is a rhyme that children recite. You can hear it every day upon the streets."

She turned her head to gaze out the window. He was right enough about that. She had tipped her hand a little.

"But I did write the letters to you," he said suddenly.

"Ah. I thought it was you. The handwriting was familiar."

"Was it?" He sighed. "I did try to disguise it. My dear Jehane, once upon a time I was in love with you and sent very different letters. Did you keep any of those?"

"No." A creeping sense of alarm made her shift uneasily on her seat.

"A shame."

"You were more naïve than Charlie then," she said with bravado. "I knew your feelings would change and in any case I didn't care for you. Besides, what kind of man falls in love with a whore?"

"You'd be surprised," he said calmly. "Even good men do. Our Pyotr rescued Adele and kept her in his cellar room to warm his lonely bed."

"That did not save her."

"No, but I know he didn't kill her." Feodor had moved almost imperceptibly closer.

"And how did you know that?"

Feodor smiled and patted her thigh through her dress. "The poor fellow wouldn't kill the only happiness he'd ever known, would he?"

Jehane eased his hand away. "Do not tell me more."

"There should be no secrets between us."

She turned toward him and her lips parted in a gasp of shock. There was a very strange look in his eyes: glittering and insubstantial.

"Have you not guessed, Jehane, that I still have feelings for you? That I have watched and waited for all these years?"

"N-no," she said, flustered.

He slipped a hand into his pocket and withdrew something smooth and small. A silver locket. He showed it to her, resting it on his palm. "I had this made for you."

"I don't want it."

His fingers closed over the locket. "You are capricious, Jehane, as well as inconstant."

"You could never afford me to be exclusively yours."

"Is that the only reason you sent me packing?"

Jehane felt nervous fear skittering up her spine. Whatever impulse had compelled her to seek him out had not been wise. "No. There were many reasons. Too many to list."

"Hmm. Whenever I tried to see you, or to approach you, I was spurned. I was too shabby. Too foreign. All I wanted to do was become successful and claim you for my own. As I believe I mentioned, it is only lately that I am able to anticipate profits. But the fee for Georgina, alas, will not be forthcoming."

Jehane shot him a murderous glare. "There. You might as well admit that you stole her away—"

"I had a hand in it. Are you going to alert the authorities? No, you shall not tell." He suddenly grabbed her by the throat. "You are nothing but a whore and a thief. You stole Georgina back."

She dragged at the breath she could take, in no way able to speak.

"You want to see me swing on a gallows, don't you, Jehane? You will never be safe unless I do."

"N-no," she choked out.

"We know too much about each other. I have had you followed for weeks," he continued in a voice tinged with lunatic rage. "You holed up when you learned of the murders and then you allied yourself with Marko. Fool!"

He wrapped a silk handkerchief around her wrists, letting go of her throat to pull the ends so tight the material cut into her skin.

She worked her throat. Her scream stalled in it—he'd pressed and squeezed so tightly that no sound came from her.

Feodor grabbed her hair and held her head steady as he

slipped something on a chain over it. She felt something smooth and cold and small slide between her breasts.

"A token of my affection," he murmured. "Now you are mine, Jehane. Marked as a wolf-mistress."

He forced a loathsome kiss upon her lips as he pulled her head back with the hair he held, thrusting his tongue down her throat and making her gag.

"Don't you like me?" he whispered into her ear when he broke it off.

All she could do was gasp and try to kick him. His long leg moved over hers and stilled her wild response. She saw him stamp his foot upon a lever set into the carriage floor and realized that the carriage was picking up speed in response to a silent signal. It was not an ordinary hired coach—it was his. And where he was taking her, she did not know.

"Has Jehane gone back to her own apartments?" Marko asked. "It seems to me that you have not mentioned her of late."

"She comes and goes as she pleases," Severin answered. "Now that the matter of Georgina has been resolved, I suppose she has gone back to her old ways."

Marko nodded. He understood her meaning well enough. Still, he was faintly troubled that the sisters had not spoken. Jehane's asides to him on the night when they'd found the missing girl had not been reassuring, but he had been preoccupied with Georgina and Severin.

"I have not been able to find the other two men I saw in the shop," he said at last.

Severin suppressed a shudder. "I think you can consider them gone. They would not have the nerve to show up on St. James's Street, would they?"

"They do not know who took Georgina. And Denis was spirited away and out of the country before he could inform his confederates." Marko scowled. "If I find them, there will be a bloody brawl, I promise you that."

"There must be no scandal. I promised Mary."

Marko could only nod. The need for discretion would trump everything. But he could not shake the lingering feeling that someone, somewhere, was waiting to do even worse.

He looked down at Severin, who was embroidering by the light coming in the window. She was charmingly domestic and self-contained. It was as if she could make the world in all its filth and squalor vanish somehow.

Still, she was vulnerable. He could not fight his protective feelings for her, which even extended to Jehane. Who would scorn them, of course, while secretly delighting in his attention, he suspected.

The sisters were devoted to each other, but he would do well not to provoke jealousy between them. He dropped a chaste kiss upon Severin's beautifully dressed hair. She murmured something when he did and then turned her face up to his for a kiss that wasn't chaste at all.

Her embroidery fell to the floor when he pulled her to her feet and went as far as she would let him. Nowhere near as far as he would have liked. Ultimately she pushed him away. Cursing himself for being a gentleman, he bowed to her wishes. But he wanted to howl with lust.

Marko eased his physical restlessness in the best way he knew how: by walking throughout London. What problems remained would have to be solved upon another day.

He had gone far indeed since leaving Severin to her quiet work—all the way to Hampstead Heath. There he sat upon a hill in the waning light of day and looked at London spread out below him. From here, its crooked streets and crowded lanes vanished, and the city seemed clean, with only the spires of churches and other great buildings to be seen. Just beyond was the curving silver ribbon of the river Thames.

Somewhere in all of it was Feodor.

His kinsman had to be up to no good—Denis gave much of the game away. Certain details remained unexplained, owing to the necessity of getting Denis shackled and promptly shipped off to Russia before he could escape and before any of his partners in crime came looking for him.

But finding Feodor was key to solving the mystery. Misbegotten bastard though he was, there were plenty of strumpets who would be willing to conceal him for a price. His sexual greediness might make catching him easy . . . or next to impossible.

Marko supposed he could ask Jehane for help, but something in him balked at the idea. She was too willing to put herself in harm's way. Besides, what if Feodor had a noblewoman for a lover? A word from the right lady to a biddable judge and Feodor would not spend an hour in gaol, but be escorted from the courtroom by a smirking bailiff.

Murder, however, was a hanging offense, unlike pimping. Marko still could not quite believe his kinsman was capable of cutting throats, and Denis had not said Feodor was guilty in so many words. Marko thought back to the other two men half-glimpsed in the shop, dodged before their return. Would it be worthwhile to go back there and continue the investigation? They had not seen him.

But surely Feodor would never return to the place, if he had ever been there. Marko pondered Jehane's involvement. From the start, she'd seemed not to care deeply about Georgina's plight, following her own principles, which were almost amoral, except for her attachment to her older sister.

The matter was puzzling. He looked again at London in the distance and decided to run all the way back.

He went down over the northwest roads for miles, then headed for a not too distant stand of trees, scarcely caring where he went, exhilarated by his exercise in the open air. The shadows had grown long. Then, out of the corner of his eye, he saw a black shape detach itself from the growing darkness and run toward him . . . then with him . . .

He knew who it was but he could scarcely believe it. In spectral form, his cousin had returned from the next world. "Lukian?" he gasped.

"Keep running," the shadow-wolf growled.

Side by side, keeping pace, the two Taruskins ran without saying more, in silent communication with every beat of their hearts. Struggling to comprehend it, Marko remembered his words to the Pack. *It is our fate to see our beloved dead as if they were alive.*

Then the great shadow leaped and rose into the air, vanishing, and Marko was alone again, breathless with astonishment. He slowed to a walk.

But the faint clopping of horses' hooves told him where he was eventually. Near Hyde Park. The breeze that tickled his nose had come over water, he knew that.

Still water, clear and cool. The Serpentine, of course. He hesitated, picking up something else in the air. Someone of the Pack was within a mile of him.

Lukian, of course. But the insubstantial vision was nowhere to be seen.

The trace of scent was male, certainly. And agitated, almost angry. He walked faster. The familiar smell grew stronger. There would be no rest for him until he tracked it to its source. Marko began to run and a few people turned around to stare.

It wasn't a gentlemanly run at all, but the long-legged, effortless lope of a wolf.

Still, he stayed in human form. And oh, he was handsome, or so a woman whispered to her companion as he went by them, intent on the hunt.

Well into the park after only a little while, Marko raced down the deserted lanes. He saw the tracks of carriage wheels in the dust. They had a sharp edge, unlike the blurred and half-erased tracks of other wheels that had rolled by earlier.

Recent.

The scent he pursued was stronger still. He caught a whiff of womanly sweat. No one but a manwolf could smell that, so subtle was it. But he knew it held fear.

Marko ran on.

Then he saw the carriage. Two indistinct figures alighted from it and the driver went on at a breakneck pace. Marko saw the carriage turn around a hundred yards ahead where there was enough room to do so and go even faster upon the return journey.

He heard the sound of a woman screaming. And growls. The dominant growl of a male, fully aroused.

But why was the female screaming?

The law of the Pack ensured that every female was willing. To force oneself upon a mate was unthinkable. The few wolves who had, overcome by lust and worse, had been chased off to die alone in the forest. Here, in the civilized precincts of London, it scarcely seemed possible that someone he had to know could be doing the unthinkable.

He was close enough to see that the woman and the man were struggling and then he caught a very familiar smell indeed.

Severin? Could it be she? But he only just left her—no, that had been hours ago.

He would tear out the throat of any man who hurt her.

Marko drew closer in a few giant bounds. It was not Severin.

It was Jehane. Her hair was down and flying free. She scratched at the face of—Marko could not see who it was at first—then he did.

Feodor.

But his cousin was a changed man.

His face distorted by rage and bloodlust, Feodor had Jehane by both arms. She kicked out but he parried with an upraised knee.

Marko launched himself at Feodor's back, feeling the transformation from man to wolf hit him in midair.

His clothes burst apart. His fangs sank into Feodor's neck. He heard his cousin howl . . . and too late, he heard the hooves of the carriage horse.

A sound like thunder. Rib-breaking, skull-cracking thunder.

The last thing he remembered was the sight of Jehane's face, screaming his name.

When he came to, he lay in tattered clothes upon the dust of the dark lane. Coughing, spitting out dirt and blood, he got to his feet again, beset by agonizing pain in his ribs.

He didn't dare touch them. More than one was broken. How long had he been unconscious? He had no way of knowing. He lifted his head and sniffed the air.

Feodor's smell was faint but that of Jehane was still very much present. And it still held fear . . . mortal fear. Had she survived?

Slowly, Marko squatted on his haunches, touching a hand to the ground, feeling for some trace of her.

A scrap of clothing.

Even a few pulled hairs.

Just not blood, he prayed. He couldn't smell any but his

own. Marko touched his hand to his throbbing head and it came away wet. The horse's iron hoof had left its mark.

But where was Jehane?

Marko looked around and saw the water of the Serpentine glimmering. The moon had risen. The surface was untroubled. Almost perfectly still.

He went toward it, going on blind instinct now.

Nearer, not far from the edge, he saw something under the water.

He walked more quickly, willing himself to get there in time. His footsteps sank into the soft turf and then he flung himself into the water full-length.

Like a woman trapped in a mirror, Jehane floated in it. Her face was on the wrong side of the looking-glass and no longer beautiful.

Feodor had done his worst.

Straining to stand, Marko pulled her up and into his arms. He staggered with her to the bank and laid her out full-length.

There was no one to see. Staying human was all he could do. Marko sat down by her, overwhelmed by silent grief. He might as well have torn out his own throat. Not a sound came from him.

He leaned over her body. Jehane's breast was still. Then he put his hand over her heart and felt something smooth and cold. He drew it forth: it was a locket. The closed case dripped water as he held it in his hand, still attached to the chain around her neck. He flicked it open and saw the head of a wolf in repoussé silver. The thing was identical to the one he had taken from the body of the first murdered woman. Feodor must have put it on her, taking a killer's pride in leaving his mark.

Marko dropped the locket when he saw Jehane's eyelids flutter and he leaned over her again, willing her to open them. For a fraction of a second, she did. He saw a pulse of life deep within her eyes. She was not dead yet. Dear Wolf, she could not die.

Marko howled. For Lukian. Only those who had gone beyond could keep the near-dead from entering the next world.

In another few moments, the great shadow-wolf landed beside Jehane and began to lick her face.

14

Severin could not even scream when he told her what had happened. Marko's words seemed to echo in her mind. Her sister could not be near death.

Not her laughing, vital, wicked, life-loving Jehane. The little child who had looked up to her, the young girl who had sought her counsel and, headstrong to a fault, ignored every word of it and gone down the wrong path, the fierce but loving sister she had loved in return might be forever lost to her.

"Why did you not warn me of your suspicions concerning Feodor?" she whispered brokenly.

"I had nothing more than suspicion to go on," he said. "Why he attacked her or what the nature of their relationship is, I still cannot say, Severin. Only when Jehane awakens will we know more."

"She might die!"

Severin fell to her knees and collapsed upon the floor in a near swoon. Marko knelt beside her. "I cannot ask you to forgive me for not protecting your sister and not preventing this," he whispered.

She wailed in a low voice that nearly broke his heart. The truth was cold comfort—and he still could not tell her the whole truth.

"I beat Denis to within an inch of his life," he went on. "Ah, but it was foolish of me to think that was enough, and that you and your sister and Georgina were safe. My dear Severin, do not give up hope. The Pack has powers that I am forbidden to explain—"

"Keep her alive."

"Whatever can be done for her will be done. And Feodor will be found and brought to justice."

"I hope to see him mount the stairs of the gallows." She would say no more.

Marko hesitated. "You must think of Jehane and not him. She was taken to my house—it was closer—you may see her in the morning."

"Bring her here."

"As you wish. But by the morrow. She should not be moved now." He reached out to stroke her back, but she curled away from him, her body taut with a silent shriek of anguish.

She felt her soul shatter at that instant. Something else took its place: a dark desire for vengeance against Feodor, should her sister not live. She went at Marko, consumed by fury. Clawing. Shrieking. He would pay. Someone had to. She could not wait for vengeance.

Her emotions overwhelmed her. That she might have to live the rest of her life without her sister could not be. It could not be. Severin would find her sister's assailant; he would pay for his crime in blood spilled ten times over. Her eyes widened as she saw a vision of it spreading from his head, scarlet suffused with a hellish black . . . and then she passed into blackness herself.

* * *

Marko carried her to her bedchamber and stayed by her well into the night, until a man and a maidservant came for him as arranged from the house near St. James's Square.

Hearing the soft knock before Severin's man could waken, he let them in. Marko knew that the best doctor among the Pack, Natalya, was with the badly injured woman, but he wished to see Jehane for himself before her sister awakened.

"Stay with her until I come back," he told the maidservant. "Her household does not awaken until after dawn."

"Yes, sir. The carriage is downstairs waiting for you," said the man who'd accompanied her.

He made his stealthy way out and dashed away in the carriage, hoping her own servants would not intrude until he could return.

"How does she?" Marko whispered, entering the secluded room in which Jehane lay. He winced at the sight of the bruises on her face.

"She is breathing peacefully," was all Natalya said. Married now, she wore her shining braids around her head like a Crown. A year had changed her from a girl to a woman—and what she'd seen tonight seemed to have made her older still. The sorrow in Natalya's eyes was for all women who had ever been hurt, he thought.

"I will keep vigil for a while," he said. "You must rest also."

Natalya nodded and rose. "I will stay within hearing. Call for me or ring the bell if you must. You have said there is need for great secrecy . . ." Her knowing eyes searched his.

"Yes," he said. "For now I can tell you no more."

He replaced her at Jehane's bedside. The clock ticked away the last hours of the night, and as Marko expected, the shadow of Lukian materialized in the room at four o'clock in the morning, the hour of the wolf, as the French saying had it. His cousin was in human form but dark and ghostly.

"Hello, Lukian."

His cousin nodded, and reached out a strong hand that Marko could see through all the same. Jehane's eyes were still closed but she stirred slightly when Lukian's hand caressed her brow. Marko drew in his breath when he saw the mark Lukian had left upon her forehead, a shimmering, insubstantial print of a wolf's paw. It slowly faded away . . . and so did the bruises on her face. Jehane's pale skin was flushed with a tinge of healthy color.

"She is a survivor, this one. Tough and strong. She will live," Lukian said softly.

Marko watched the pink flush fade to white again. "How do you know?"

"She must. Otherwise I will have to make her live," Lukian replied.

Marko only shook his head. "If she does not, you might as well kill me. Or Severin will."

"I understand," was all Lukian said in reply.

The cousins stood in mutual silence, observing the woman on the bed.

Marko spoke first. "Back in Hyde Park . . . you meant to bring me to Feodor, did you not?"

"Yes, Marko. I have been watching over you and all the Pack since the evil day when I lost my life on this earth."

"But why did you rise in the air and vanish? Could you not help me?"

Lukian sat in a chair. His clothes hung slack on his large but ghostly frame and his coat seemed to contain a hollow man. "I could not. I have no strength to do so. Nor could I be everywhere at once. But you happened to be in one of my haunts when I went looking for you."

"Do you mean Hampstead Heath?"

"Yes. One can see most of London from there. I often prowl the wild edge of it."

"How did you know that Feodor and Jehane—"

"I had been following him for some time. You had so much to explain to me this night when Jehane was brought here, and I could not tell you of it right away. He reeks, you know."

Marko shook his head. "I picked up nothing from him."

"No?" Lukian asked. "Perhaps certain senses are more alive in my dimension. I smelled lies, contempt, arrogance, and murderous intent."

"Only intent? Did he not kill the first two victims, Lukian?"

"I don't think so." Lukian wearily rubbed a hand across his spectral face.

"Then was it Denis Somov? The cub could not have lied to me—not under interrogation." He clenched his fists. His knuckles still hurt.

Lukian straightened in his chair and gave Marko a severe look. "You should have brought him to heel a long time ago."

With chagrin, Marko thought that he had utterly failed to do so. He had assumed, until the shocking sight of Denis pulling up the unconscious Georgina's skirts, that the tall cub was nothing more than a philanderer. "Yes, you are right. And I will never forgive myself."

Lukian frowned. "It is too late for such regrets."

"He received justice, as we reckon it."

"Was he unquestionably guilty?" Lukian asked.

"Yes. Caught in the act."

"Then he deserved what he got for breaking the sacred law of the Pack. We are sworn to protect the innocent."

"Georgina Lennox was that." Marko gave a heavy sigh. "She still is, physically, if not in spirit. But Severin thinks she will remember nothing of what happened to her."

"The girl is with her mother, then?" Lukian asked.

Marko nodded.

"That is as it should be. As I said, I could not be everywhere or I would have helped you find her."

"Where did you go, Lukian? How can you be still bound to this world?"

"The ties are not that strong, but they hold me. Habit, I suppose." He gave Marko a rueful, very slight smile. "I was ever a creature of habit, mostly bad. It took me a while to come back to earth, Marko."

Marko didn't meet his cousin's eyes, not wanting to remember the mortal battle with the Wolf Killer and his henchman Stasov. That day, as Stasov and Lukian sank into the Thames in an arc of fire that melted their skin, it seemed to all watching that Lukian had died to protect his brethren. Stasov's body had washed up. Lukian's, never.

Yet here he was.

Lukian smiled sadly at Marko. "I tumbled through a icy void that day," he said at last. "But I could not rise. The stars above hold our dead warriors, but I was not so honored. Perhaps I sinned too much in my life."

"No, Lukian—"

Lukian shrugged. "I did not value life while I had it. Now I do. But it was a long time before I was anything more than a shadow-wolf, driven by instincts. When I was able again to become as a man, I stole clothes to shroud myself and went about London by night."

"Did you never find rest?" Marko asked him.

"Sometimes. In a church."

Marko raised an astonished eyebrow at that remark.

"St. Mary-le-bone, of course." Lukian grinned. "It seemed appropriate for a former wolf. There were others like myself in the pews."

"What? From the Pack?"

"No. Shadow-people like me, scarcely able to hold up their clothes. They appeared in the late hours, not among the Sunday congregation. I heard them praying for strength as I did. And it was given me, but not in totality. I am not what I was, Marko."

"Still, I am glad beyond words to see you—"

They both fell silent as the woman on the bed stirred again and cried out faintly. Marko and Lukian rose and leaned over her.

Marko thought of something. "Lukian, can people who are not of the Pack see you as I do?"

"No," Lukian whispered. "She will remember nothing of my presence here."

His cousin's shadowy hand parted the opening of the gown Natalya had put on her, and they saw her breast rise and fall more strongly.

"Jehane is rallying." Lukian looked toward the window. "The sun is about to rise and its rays will help dispel the darkness that had her in its grip. Call Natalya in," he said. "I think other medicines may be needed now. I have done what I can."

"I must go back to Severin's house," Marko said suddenly. "She wants her sister brought to her soon. Do you think that it's wise?"

"You must, eventually." Lukian said thoughtfully. "They need each other. When I touched Jehane's forehead, I heard her soul whisper her sister's name."

By daybreak Marko had returned to Severin, carrying a bit of breakfast for her. He let himself in by the door he'd left unlocked, making no noise, and went swiftly to her. She pushed herself up from the bed and looked about, dazed. It seemed to Marko that the first wild grief had passed from her heart.

His face was the first thing her eyes focused on. He almost recoiled. He saw pure hate in them, hate born in a nightmare that still confused her.

Severin drew in a shaky breath. "Is Jehane alive?"

"Yes. Severin, allow me to help you. Please." He reached out a hand, half expecting her to strike it away.

But she didn't. Her natural gentleness was strong enough to subdue her rage, he thought with awe. She even let him lift her from the bed, seeming unsure of her body's ability to hold her up. He settled her into a chair.

"Wake up a little more. Then I will take you to your sister at once."

She let her head loll back and closed her eyes.

"You must eat something. A bite or two."

"All right." Her voice was as dull as her eyes.

He gave her what he'd brought with him: dark bread and cheese. She let him feed her a few morsels and then shook her head. "No more."

He looked about for something for her to drink. Yesterday's tea. It would do. He went to the tray and poured half the sugar-bowl into the teapot, swirling it around before pouring her a half cup.

"Here is tea. There is a good deal of sugar in it. Take a sip or two."

She drank the entire cupful and handed the cup back with a grimace as if it had been bitter poison she had to take and not sweet, strong tea. Then she let her head rest against the chair again.

"I should be with her. Tell me of how she passed the night."

"She is still not conscious, but there is hope."

Severin only nodded. Then she swallowed hard. Marko breathed a sigh of relief. The bit of breakfast had stayed down. She would need every particle of strength he could put into her.

Natalya rose from the bedside where she had been keeping vigil and came to greet Severin when Marko introduced them, giving him a sober look. Then she turned to Severin again.

"I am sorry to meet you under such circumstances, but there

is good news. Your sister will live. If not for Marko, she might not have made it here."

"I understand," Severin whispered.

"She is on the mend but she can take nothing by mouth," Natalya said. "My poultices will only do so much."

Severin looked at her sister, who lay still and serene. Her skin was pale but unmarked, and her lips pink enough. Her eyes were closed.

A doctor that someone had sent for, an Englishman, came into the room and murmured his name, and requested information that he needed. Severin gripped Marko's arm painfully hard as she identified the unconscious woman as her sister, Jehane. Like an automaton, she told him the date of Jehane's birth and their parents' names. Marko was surprised to hear that the sisters had different mothers, but he made no comment. When the inevitable question came as to other living relatives, Severin had answered in a broken whisper. "Only me."

When that was done, she retreated into a chair by her sister's bed. She pushed aside a bundle at her feet—something Natalya had needed to nurse her patient, Marko had thought. Then he realized it was Jehane's wet clothes.

He came over to her. "Let me take those away. Our maids can wash and dry them."

Severin looked away from Jehane and down at the bundle. She saw something and reached for it, then pulled out the locket Marko had found around Jehane's neck. It swung from its chain in midair. In the ensuing chaos he had forgotten it until that moment.

"What is this?" she said. "I have never seen Jehane wear it."

Marko hesitated. He had never told Severin of finding the first victim's body, nor of the poisoned locket around the dead woman's neck that he had hidden away. Now was not the time for such explanations.

Without waiting for him to answer, she slid a fingernail under the catch and opened it. Her eyes widened when she saw the face of the wolf. He was relieved to see that this one had no fangs—and glad when she snapped it shut, looking puzzled. She held it out to him and he took it from her cautiously.

"I—I have seen that locket before, Marko."

"What? Where?" He looked at Jehane and then at Severin. "Come. Let us not talk of it here."

She rose and pressed a kiss to her sister's forehead, smoothing her hair. Then she left the room and went with him to stand outside the door.

"In a jewelry shop. An old man was making one just like it."

"How very odd. What was the name of the establishment? Or his name?"

"I don't remember. But I did think then, when I saw the little face of the wolf, that there might be some connection to your—your Pack."

"Why?"

She bowed her head. "Jehane knew Feodor slightly. Those murders—you and I talked of them—"

"Yes, briefly."

"She summoned me when she first heard that women—women like her had been killed. She was afraid for herself, though she would not say exactly why. Among other things, she told me of the Pack." She fell silent for a little while. "And then, as the night wore on, we quarreled for some reason." She gave a troubled sigh. "I was upset and I went out to walk, frightened myself."

Again Marko asked, "Why?"

"I thought I was being followed. I dashed into a jeweler's shop and the old man working inside let me stay. It was there that I saw the locket."

"Not where we found Georgina, surely?"

"No. A different place."

"But there was an old man at the shop where we found her," Marko said. "I only got a glimpse of him—"

Severin shook her head. "I would recognize him if I saw him again. Do you know, I looked for the first place and could not find it. Let me see the locket you found on Jehane. Perhaps there is a silversmith's mark on it."

"No. I don't think so." Marko shook his head. "Back to the murders—"

"Yes," she said slowly. "When we brought Georgina home, you mentioned them. You thought there was a connection to the Pack, but not to Denis."

"I happened to find the first woman's body."

She gave a start. "The papers made no mention of that, Marko."

He nodded. "Their accounts of the crime were mostly sensational—I read them also. And I did not come forward, because I had no information to offer. It was by sheer chance that I found her dead. The scene was gruesome. I will not describe it. I was with a link-boy and no one else was about."

"Why did you not tell me—" She stopped herself. "Forgive me. Why would you?"

"I did what I could for her. She was never identified. Or claimed."

"But—" Severin thought back to what her sister had said. Jehane had known the victim's name. Lucy Pritchett. Should she tell him that?

"Above all, my concern was to protect the Pack," he was saying. "In such a case, suspicion might be directed at us."

Severin looked deeply into his eyes. He met her gaze with steadiness. She had to believe him. He had saved her sister's life.

"But the danger that I feared was within my own house," Marko went on. "Feodor had to have been the killer." Puzzled, he thought of Lukian's saying the opposite. "I believe he will kill again."

"We must find him. And the old man. If only Jehane had told me the entire truth from the beginning—" Tears welled in her amber eyes as she looked up at him. "We are all in danger. Oh, Marko—"

He reached out to her and held her in his arms.

"We will get to the bottom of this somehow. But we will do nothing until your sister is stronger. I will protect you both."

He looked over her shoulder and saw Lukian standing in back of her, with a wolfish look in his eyes.

May I speak mind to mind, cousin?

Marko nodded, kissing Severin's hair.

Take her home. I will continue the investigation on my own.

Marko shot Lukian a questioning look, but there was nothing he could say.

He brought Severin back to her house when it was decided among the three of them—Marko, Severin, and Natalya—not to move Jehane. He'd reassured her that her sister would be well-guarded night and day, and that Feodor would be torn to pieces should he set a filthy paw within a mile of St. James's Square.

Leaving her sister only with great reluctance, Severin thought that Marko too was feeling the strain—she had heard him talking to himself in the halls of the house on St. James's Street now and then, as pale as if he had seen a ghost.

Her disordered mind sometimes made her think she heard two men talking when she knew only Marko was about. It didn't matter. Nothing mattered but making Jehane well and strong again.

And Natalya was seeing to that. Severin instinctively trusted the young woman whose poultices and herbs, Marko said, were the difference between life and death for her sister. On her own,

Natalya provided a flask of herb liquor for Marko to administer to Severin.

"She will need this," Natalya whispered to Marko. "Give her just a little at a time."

Still distraught, Severin accepted the drink in the small glass that Marko handed her. It was curiously smooth going down. She assumed it was to help her sleep. Well and good. She needed to, and she was in her bed, in her loose nightgown.

He soothed her and caressed her until she drifted off. The first sound she heard when she opened her eyes was the soft sound of the piano in the next room.

Marko—it must be him—was playing a melody that sounded like a song from long ago, something that had first been sung in a wild land far away. Never set down in written notes but plucked from ancient instruments that no longer existed.

The chords were not at all like Hadyn or Bach, the music she was used to. Not churchly or solemn. A wild sound but tempered with yearning and emotion. The strange music eased her heart a little. Just a little.

Severin closed her eyes and felt tears as hot as blood course down her face. She had not been able to keep her sister from harm—she could not help being consumed by a guilt that was greater than her fear. Jehane had nearly become a victim, if not a wholly innocent one. Yet she was grateful that her sister was alive.

In a little while Marko ceased his melancholy music-making and came to her. Severin got up and went into his arms. Her disordered thoughts churned wildly in her brain, but her body was still, almost limp. Lost in his own sad thoughts, he sang, under his breath, the same ancient melody which he had played, and then stopped.

Severin raised her head to look him in the face. And then she kissed him, craving his tenderness. His ardent response seemed an affirmation of life itself.

When his lips lifted from hers, he gently touched her cheek. "When this is over, Severin—"

She fought a rush of passionate feeling for him. "Will it ever be? I never knew there was so much ugliness in the world."

"Yes," he sighed wearily. "I too have seen enough of it."

"I know I cannot, yet all I want to do is run away and hide—"

Marko gave her a smile. "Here we are. We will make our own world, then. Just you and me."

His lips brushed hers again with infinite gentleness, and she felt a stirring in her soul that permeated her body. Severin arched her back and pressed her breast to his, wanting to feel his steady heart beat and his very masculine warmth. In better times, she had craved his sensual strength. Now, at the worst moment of her life, she needed it. Needed him. All of him.

He held her more tightly and they kissed long and lovingly, swaying together like creatures caught in a storm. Naked under her nightgown, she felt every inch of his body, especially the long, muscular thigh that pushed hers apart.

Half-sobbing, Severin kissed him frantically, riding his thigh while she clutched his shoulders, wanting release and forgetfulness . . .

Only a few minutes later, they were both naked, and he was above her, his sad eyes on hers, his hand wiping away the tears that flowed.

"Are you sure?" he whispered.

"Yes, y-yes," she said in a broken voice. "I must have you, Marko. Give me all of you—"—she slid her hands down his back to hold his taut hips—"all your strength, everything, all—" She cried out when he entered her with one deep stroke and stayed there without moving, still looking into her eyes.

She began to move under him, willing his body to give hers

solace, making a silent demand for him to penetrate her with the utmost ardor and chase away the coldness that threatened to consume her. He could not be still for long with such stimulation.

Marko began to thrust and each time he did, she cried for more. He hushed her with kisses, slid a hand under her damp nape to free her tangled, sweat-damp hair. His other hand slid under her bottom and he spread his fingers so widely that he nearly encompassed both her buttocks, holding her strongly against each deep downward stroke he gave her.

Severin cried out and he captured the wild sound with his mouth, not letting go from first pulse to last, not coming himself . . .

When it was over, he kissed away the last of the tears on her eyelashes and cheeks, and smoothed her hair from her temples.

"What about you . . ." she whispered.

"In good time," he whispered back.

15

They made love through the night, lying in each other's arms in the moonlight, recapturing the heedless bliss of their first sexual encounters. If they had known then of all that was to happen, they might have waited—she was glad now, if she could be glad about anything, that they had acted so swiftly on their desire. It was as he said, she thought dreamily. They could make a world of their own.

She fell asleep completely enfolded by his body, then woke just before dawn, restless again. There was nothing to do but wait until the sun came up and let him sleep. She eased out of his embrace and got up, putting on the same loose gown. She wanted to walk but she could not go out upon the street. Severin quietly mounted the stairs, balancing a candlestick in her hand.

By its flickering light, the upstairs rooms that opened into other rooms gave the effect of moving through different worlds and back in time. Each was ornamented in a riot of design, with geometric tiles in mosaics or painted vines and flowers. Her feet sank noiselessly into the thick carpets her mother favored.

Giselle, French-born but steeped in the customs of Constantinople, had added touches of blue everywhere to keep off the evil eye.

Severin had to wonder if her younger sister would have been safe if she'd lived here with her. Even from the grave, the protective intent of their mother still surrounded both of them somehow. When Natalya gave the word, Severin would bring her sister here to heal. And then, with Marko's help, she would find Feodor and see that justice was done.

The danger that still awaited them shattered her peaceful mood the moment she thought of it. She sank upon a low stool padded with rich velvet and wept. At least her mother, off somewhere in a heaven of her own, would never know that one of her daughters had nearly met a violent death.

But there was hope and Severin could not cry forever. Her tears were wasted—they did not relieve her feelings of foreboding. She dashed them away as she rose and began to wander, heading for the room at the end of all the rooms, her mother's sanctuary. She stopped at a portrait of the three of them done only months before her mother's death, sketched in pencil on canvas on a happy day that she remembered well, finished at leisure in the painter's atelier. Still, the likenesses were excellent.

Little had changed here. Even the old chessboard was set up as if players would soon move the pieces, the ivory and ebony chessmen waiting patiently in double rows. She reached out a hand and moved a pawn up two spaces, just to alter the symmetry.

Things never touched might as well be dead, she thought miserably.

It seemed to her as she moved about that the room was suffused with her mother's presence. Severin needed to be here, enfolded in a realm that seemed in some ways enchanted to her now.

Here, two little girls had had their hair carefully combed and braided by their mother. Giselle sang to them in French and told them the fairy tales of Perrault, which she knew by heart, and taught them all she knew of beauty.

She'd watched over them as if they were more precious than her own life. The move to England had upset her daughters' health. She nursed them through their childhood illnesses, mixing potions from Ruksana's herbs and oils brought from Tashkent. She'd hovered over Severin and Jehane until they were well again and scampering about. They had whiled away hours reading their books on the carpets, playing hide-and-seek, and dominoes, and chess with these very pieces when they were older.

She and Jehane, so close in age, had rarely quarreled then. Her mother reproved them when they did, telling them that all through life they would have only each other. Severin was only beginning to realize how alone her mother had been in her beautiful cage.

Severin wondered if she herself would ever marry. No matter what, no woman was safe somehow. A sister was indeed a great blessing.

The long hours of waiting made her pensive as well as restless. For whatever reason, Jehane had put herself in harm's way to help rescue Georgina. She'd known more than she'd been telling—Severin had suspected that—but even so, Jehane had risked much.

She had never been able to judge Jehane for what she did. Whoredom could be defined as the other side of respectable marriage: male desire ruled each realm.

To think that she, Severin, had instructed young girls to mince their steps and their words to catch a husband, had taught women how to adorn themselves with trumpery things that proclaimed wealth and social position given to them by men and taken away just as easily. She had essentially disguised herself in cast-off finery and moved through the fashionable world like a ghost. Unseen, truly—except by Marko.

She remembered her purpose in coming upstairs and went to a small inlaid cabinet, pulling on the tassel that opened the narrow doors. Inside it, ranked on shelves, were tiny bottles and flat jars that held medicines and potions. Some were nearly empty, the contents evaporated. Some still held liquid or unguents. Severin opened a familiar one and sniffed.

Attar of rose. Jehane's favorite scent.

So her sister had missed the only mother she had ever known. Jehane never spoke of Giselle, but something of her pervaded Jehane's life. Severin set the bottle of perfume aside.

She took out the others one by one, trying to decipher the flowing copperplate script on those that had labels. Her mother had been instructed by nuns and her handwriting was very fine. Her maid, Ruksana, in her brief lifetime, had taught her mistress how to make what was inside each bottle, some for sickness, some to preserve health.

One Severin remembered caused a delicious languor to spread through the body. She'd had it on occasion. She uncapped it and shook a drop onto her fingertip, licking it, hoping it would calm her nervous agitation. In a few moments, a pleasant warmth stole through her limbs and she relaxed almost imperceptibly. So it still worked. She supposed that the whole bottle would bring a restful death.

Ointment for beautiful eyes, said a label in French. *To keep men faithful,* said another. That jar held pills, to be dropped into the drink of one's lord and master, Severin supposed. It seemed unthinkable that a man might actually take them of his own volition.

A cure for lovesickness. The bottle of liquid was full. Had her mother not needed it or not known what was in it? Severin could only wonder. It might hold poison, she thought cynically.

She felt tears well up in her eyes again and this time she let them flow. Long-hidden emotions rushed through her, overwhelming her. If only Marko would wake up and find her . . . and comfort her. No, she thought sadly, forcing the thought away. Then, as if her mother's voice had spoken in her mind, she heard wise words. *No one can live without love.*

That was a truth she could not ignore.

Then, as if she had summoned him, she turned to see Marko standing in the doorway of the room.

He was clad in breeches and his untied shirt, exuding a sensual, manly warmth. Despite her unsettled mood, she smiled at him.

"There you are," he said. He yawned, looking around. "I heard your footsteps above me when I woke up. I hope I am not intruding."

"No."

"I have never been in this part of your house."

"You are welcome here," she said. Marko, big, solid, and strong, seemed to belong in this feminine sanctuary all the same.

He glanced at the painting on the wall and went over to peer at it. She came closer, providing him light enough to see. "Lovely," he said. "So that is your mother. But not—"

"Not Jehane's. I know you heard me tell the physician of that. But my mother raised us as sisters in every way."

"What was her name?"

"Giselle. She was French."

"And what of your father?"

"Oh, he was English to the bone. But unconventional."

"What did he do?"

Severin allowed herself to smile. "Do you know, we have never had a conversation like this."

"No, we have not. But we must. I fear you will assume the worst of me, now that two of my relatives have proved to be scoundrels and worse."

"I have already told you that you are not to blame for the faults of others," she said softly.

"So you did." He sighed. "A while ago. Enough time for me to worry."

Severin patted him on the back. "He was a dealer in silk. We lived in Samarkand and Tashkent."

"Exotic indeed."

"We were far away from what you would call civilization."

"I see." An odd smile quirked his lips.

"Although I don't suppose you are perfectly conventional yourself," Severin said.

"No, I am not. Nor do I wish to be."

"Your family is Russian." She was turning the subject of the conversation around to him. She wondered if he would notice it.

"Yes, originally. We come from the far north of Russia. There are still Taruskins in Archangel. It is a port on the White Sea," he added when she gave him a polite but baffled look. "My oldest brother is there now with his wife."

"Oh."

"Their new son is with them," he added.

Was that a trace of wistfulness in his voice? She could not be sure.

"They made me an uncle soon enough after their marriage."

"Ah."

Marko unlaced his fingers and sat back, resting a hand on his thigh. "Alex will be walking before I see him again."

Severin only nodded. He seemed so happy when he talked about his family. She envied him for having such a big one.

"And are there others?"

"Sisters and brothers, you mean?"

"Yes," Severin said.

"I have a younger brother—I believe I may have mentioned him. Rather wild, but he means well. He's in Scotland now."

"And your parents?" Her little trick was working well enough. She had successfully distracted him.

"Both dead."

Severin pressed her lips together. "We are alike in that way, then."

"I think we are alike in many ways. Severin," he said gravely.

"That is neither here nor there." She got quickly to her feet, uncomfortable with the thoughts he raised.

"You did not finish telling me of your family," he said. "But perhaps I have overstayed my welcome. I will go if you wish me to. Shall I send a carriage to fetch you later? I am sure you will want to see Jehane."

He rose also and crossed to her, looking down into her eyes.

Severin could not look away. There was deep feeling in his gaze and even without holding her, he radiated strength that she still needed badly.

Marko reached out a hand and lightly clasped her shoulder. She did not recoil. He bent down and pressed a chaste kiss to her lips, then straightened as if he would indeed leave.

"Don't go," she whispered. "I will show you more. I cannot seem to stay still . . ." She let the sentence trail off without finishing it.

"I understand," he said.

She opened the connecting door to the rest of the upstairs and waited for him to say something.

He drew in his breath. "How interesting it all is." He looked about, taking in the details of the ornate tilework and carved wood. The low sofas and ottomans were even more richly upholstered than where they had just been. "And how exotic." He looked at her. "This is a hidden side of you."

She led him on and they came at last to her mother's final retreat.

Severin turned around to see that Marko had spotted another painting of the three of them. "Ah. Here you are again," he said.

"Yes. As babies."

He studied the painting thoughtfully. "You and Jehane looked like twins at this age—" He broke off. "Forgive me. She is younger, of course. I should not have said that."

"We sometimes thought of ourselves that way, though." Severin's voice was tinged with renewed sadness.

"You were safe in your mother's lap. As you are now," he said.

"What do you mean?"

Marko turned his gaze to her again. "The instant you walked into this room, your expression changed."

"Oh? I would not have known that."

He nodded. "Your eyes glowed, as if you felt happy for a moment."

"I do feel comfortable here, it is true. It was a sanctuary for us all."

Marko was quiet for a moment, still looking around at the vases and objets d'art in the room. "Everything is chosen with such care."

"My mother loved beautiful things. But she never invited anyone here."

"Do you mind if I ask why three such lovely women felt the need to hide away?"

Severin hesitated. "We were very different. And we were shunned for it. Jehane turned her back on society altogether and I am only tolerated by it."

"I imagine so."

She invited him to sit on a low divan and he did, more upright than he needed to be. Severin perched on the matching ottoman, looking up at him.

Marko was silent.

"Among other things, Jehane was illegitimate," she said at last. "My father never did marry her mother."

"Was your mother, ah, still alive then?" Marko asked.

"Yes." Severin twisted her hands in her lap. "You already know that Jehane is my half-sister, but not that she is the daughter of my mother's Persian servant, Ruksana. There—I have said it."

He regarded her with curiosity. "The way you say that is rather strange, Severin."

She drew in a deep breath and her next words came out all in a rush. "He bought Ruksana on a journey to Persia. She was a slave, not a servant. And he fancied himself a pasha. There is no law against an Englishman doing as he pleases when he is not in his own land."

To his credit, Marko did not look shocked.

Severin did not find it surprising in the least. "So we learned to behave properly. We never did quite look like English roses, though."

Marko smiled slightly. "No. But you and your sister are far more beautiful—you are roses from a very different sort of garden. An oasis, perhaps."

"How romantic of you to say so."

He reclined a little, resting on one elbow. "It is true."

She shifted on her low seat, feeling too near him somehow. The relaxed pose of his body made her remember him in a very different way, and she chided herself silently for letting so sensual a thought arise.

"So. Have I scared you off?"

"Not in the least. I have a confession of my own to make."

She looked at him with mild astonishment. "You do?"

He nodded. "It is a tale that goes very well with candlelight."

Severin listened with amazement when he told her who he really was.

Born under a blue sun that never sets. Riders on the back of the ice wind. He told her the legend of his ancient race whose blood mingled ages ago with that of Russian wolves.

A spiraling trace of smoke rose from the candle when he was done.

"There. That is my story."

"It is beyond belief. Yet—"—she gave him a sly look—"I did think you were extraordinarily wild in bed. Now I know why."

"Speaking of that . . ."

"Yes," she said immediately.

16

Lukian's voice shattered his dream.

Get up! And come away!

Marko sat bolt upright. Severin was sprawled peacefully across the other half of the bed, having wriggled out of his embrace. He looked out the window from where he was, seeing the deepening blue of the sky. They had slept away an entire day—not surprising, after making love the way they had.

Damn you, Marko! Come!

He got up and looked down to the street. There stood Lukian, ghostly but steadfast, waving frantically. He had spoken mind to mind—Marko was grateful he had not howled or yelled instead.

Marko gathered up his clothes and boots, dressing as quickly as he could. He ran down the stairs, nodding without speaking to an astonished chambermaid on her way up. It was a good thing that Severin's household was not in the least conventional. The girl closed her mouth and kept it shut.

He exited by the front door and raced after Lukian, whose

large shadow was already far down the street, drawing near him with the effort of a sexually exhausted man.

"What is it? Has Jehane—"

"Sitting up and taking nourishment."

"Good, but—"

"No time for explanations, cousin!" Lukian ran on. "I found them at last!"

"Do you mean—"

"Feodor—and an old man—trying to drag a safe from a shop—" Lukian paused to let a horse and carriage get across the street, and named the place he'd seen them. "Where you said—" And off he dashed again.

"Yes, yes!" Marko kept pace. They reached the neighborhood where they had found Georgina after several minutes more. People in the street stared at Marko, running with half-undone clothes and seemingly talking to himself. Then they shook their heads and moved on after he was gone.

Lukian stopped short of the shop, and motioned to Marko to do the same. "There they are."

He looked over Lukian's insubstantial but very broad shoulder and saw Feodor inside the window. Feodor was arguing with a much older man, and neither noticed that they were being watched.

"Shall we, cousin?" Lukian asked, turning around.

"I would swear you had come back to life!" Marko exclaimed.

"Perhaps I have."

They charged into the shop, startling the two men they had watched. The safe they had been quarreling over lay on its side, its door locked.

"What are you doing here?" Feodor snarled.

Marko looked at him levelly. "You will find out."

The other man gave a disapproving cluck. "Feodor, there is only one of him and two of us, even though I am old."

Feodor strained his eyes enough to see Lukian, a menacing shadow that increased in size by the second. "No, he isn't alone." He looked toward the door in the wall that led from the shop next door, but the wall grew black as Lukian moved instantly to cover it.

Puzzled, the old man squinted at it. "My eyes, my eyes. What is going on?"

Marko could not decide which man to take first—and Lukian had said that Feodor was not guilty of murder. Beating him soundly as he had Denis would have been fair punishment for what Feodor had done to Jehane, but he could not kill him until he was sure of his crime. Marko settled for a look that promised death, pinning Feodor to the spot where he stood. His older brother would have been proud of him, but inside Marko shook with fear. "Talk," was all he said.

"Go to hell," Feodor snarled. Marko increased the intensity of his fixed stare—by the Wolf, his gift was stronger than he'd thought. Far stronger. Feodor's eyes bulged.

"Garh." Feodor was unable to talk. So it worked. The old man stared until Marko's look pinned him too. Feodor dropped to his knees, clutching his head in agony.

"Then you talk, old man," Marko said. "What is your name?"

The other man looked uneasily at Marko and then at Lukian's giant shadow on the wall. "What is that? It looks like a wolf—"

"Never mind. Tell me your name and what you do."

"Paul," the old man said. "Paul Clavell. I am a silversmith."

"Ah. You make lockets, I suppose." Marko widened his eyes and watched him flinch.

"Yes. There is no harm in that, surely." The old man glanced at Feodor.

Wait. Marko heard Lukian say the single word but no one else did. *I will try to enter his mind.*

"Ahh," Clavell said, rubbing his forehead. "Something afflicts me—I must—I must—" He groaned and collapsed into a chair.

There. I have done it. Lukian's shadow moved from the wall to fall over the man in the chair.

"What have you done?" Clavell hissed. "The pain is unbearable!" He began to rock in the chair until Marko's hand on his shoulder held him still.

"Tell me what I want to know. It will stop when I say so," Marko said. With a mingled feeling of dread and exultation, he realized that he might know all within minutes. How to hold these two until help could be summoned was another question. He would have to think fast and act faster.

"Were you and Feodor pimps? Did you lure Georgina into your shop?"

"Y-yes," Clavell said.

"And did you kill the girls that did not cooperate?"

"No. Not by myself."

What did that mean? Perhaps the old man was not capable of murder on his own. Marko noticed how his hands shook now. He cast a quick glance at Feodor, still moaning with agony and helpless for the moment. "Did you make the locket that I found on Jehane?"

He was silent. Then the shadow falling over him grew blacker and Clavell cried out. "Yes!"

"And did you make the one that was found on the murdered girl?"

"Lucy . . . yes, I did. But how did you know—"

Marko realized he had given himself away and cursed himself for a fool. "And what of the poison in it?"

"Put in at the lady's request," Clavell said through gritted teeth. "Although Lucy Pritchett was no lady."

"It is not your place to judge her or anyone, old man," Marko growled. "And I expect you or Feodor sent me the poisoned letter."

"I know nothing of that."

"Never mind. Quickly now, tell me—who was the woman I saw in the street on the night of her murder?"

Despite the pain he was in, the old man cast him a narrow look. "Were you there?"

Marko wanted to shake him senseless. But he could not take back what he'd inadvertently revealed.

Find out more, Lukian screamed silently. *Give me a reason to hurt them both*. Marko nodded.

"Who was she?" he asked the old man again. Clavell writhed in the chair when Lukian tightened his grip on his mind.

"Adele Darrieux," Clavell gasped. "Lucy's half-sister."

Lucy's sister . . . and Pyotr's lover. Adele Darrieux was the sad little whore Pyotr had rescued and brought to the house on St. James's Square. Marko's mind whirled.

"She—she wanted a locket too. I made one for her. And one—"—the old man looked at Feodor, by now nearly unconscious—"one for Jehane," he finished.

Marko scarcely knew what to think. How and when Severin's sister had become involved in this repugnant scheme, he could not imagine.

"Feodor found out that Lucy had talked. We arranged to meet her in the street late at night—he held her arms and I—I made the cut on her neck. When I concentrate, I am precise. I saw no reason to mar her beauty." He held up his hands to show Marko what he meant. They were not shaking now.

Lukian's shadow became darker still and more concentrated. It was as if he had truly entered the old man's mind.

"Tell me more of Jehane," Marko insisted.

"She!" he cried. "She wanted nothing to do with us!"

Feodor groaned something that sounded like an agreement.

"Then why—" Marko began.

Bring the other one under control, cousin!

Lukian's warning came too late. Feodor scrambled to his

feet, maddened and strengthened by the pain that had held him. Without Marko's direct gaze, he had gained enough strength to run for the door.

Clavell, momentarily free of Lukian's shadow, stood and shoved his chair against Marko's knees. He buckled and fell backward, cracking his head against a glass case. Through fading vision, he saw the shards fly up and about, points of dangerous light, and then everything went black.

He came to a little later, with Lukian crouched beside him, still a shadow but in human form. He was mopping away blood from Marko's face with a handkerchief.

We will find them, was all he said. *They are guilty.*

Marko wanted to cry. He had hoped to save Severin and Jehane once and for all. Now the chase would begin again.

He was at the Baltic docks, where the ships came and went from northern seas. Within an hour of the struggle at the shop, he'd stationed men there to watch night and day, and make sure that neither Feodor nor Paul Clavell left the country. It had been days. He had not seen Severin in that time, had insisted that she stay home with her sister despite her protests.

Their allied agents checked the hold of each departing vessel, and members of the Pack prowled through the innermost recesses. So far, they had found nothing. His agitation increased and he had begun to suffer from insomnia that nothing could cure. The guilty men would escape or they would strike again, Marko was sure of it.

He watched a rat run nimbly up a hawser and into a ship. If Feodor or Paul Clavell did flee the country as stowaways, they would have to live on such flesh, he thought. Raw. It would make a fitting meal for such despicable men.

The wind picked up and . . . there it was. The scent of fear and anger. Male.

Marko looked about him. Which direction had it come from? Mingled with it was the smell of lumber, wet and mossy, left in heaps upon the dock as unclaimed cargo.

He rose and went toward the rough logs, which were uncut, long as trees but limbless.

He saw nothing, but then the pile was twice as high as his head and a hundred feet long. He would have to walk around it or climb it or both. Marko put a booted foot on a low log to test its stability. It was the longest of the lot and had to weigh a ton.

The bark still clung to it but moss filled in the crevices. Its slippery surface was more of a problem. He bent down to brace himself and made his way up to the top little by little.

The wind nearly knocked him off his feet. But it carried the scent that was imprinted on his brain forever—the scent of a killer.

Feodor was here somewhere. And Clavell was undoubtedly with him. He had not expected to find them easily and he could not readily summon help. Damnation.

He felt unequal to the task, alone as he was. The flatness of the London docklands made the sky seem infinitely vast. He could see across the Thames to the giant pools where the East Indiamen ships disgorged cargoes of tea and spices and exotic goods. But he dropped his gaze to his immediate environs, sweeping the quays and warehouses crowded with men, looking for the two.

Then Marko saw them. He crouched down. Paul and Feodor were dressed as Russian sailors, their faces concealed by scruffy beards that had been dyed. They attracted no notice in the jostling throng waiting to board a ship bound for the Pack's motherland. It was being swung around by its shouting, scurrying crew. Marko went down the way he had come and pushed through the crowd, trying not to attract too much attention.

Feodor was taller than most—he did not lose sight of him.

Then Marko saw his cousin turn to survey the crowd and noticed that his nostrils flared. He had been scented in turn.

Marko met Feodor's terrified look at him, and continued to press forward. They would not kill him among a watching crowd. The lawlessness of the docks did not extend to murder in broad daylight. But his progress was blocked by a sweating gang of sailors coming through with wheelbarrows of provisions from the chandler's. They forced their way through the throng, and Feodor and Paul seized their chance. They stooped down and, as if they had dissolved into the air, vanished from his sight.

Marko pushed harder, ignoring the sailors' curses and ran to the very edge of the dock. He looked desperately at the ship and the brawny seaman who stood by waiting to lower the gangplank. They could not have gone on board so quickly, not without him seeing.

Then he heard a gigantic groan—it was not human, but the groaning of giant timbers bumped and battered. His sensitive ears picked up the faintest indrawn breath and looked down.

Feodor was clinging to the pilings that stood upright along the water side of the dock, in between two massive logs and just above the water. No one saw him but Marko. The pilings were splintered but steadfast, rubbing against each other as they absorbed the tremendous force of the ship being moved along the dock.

Paul Clavell was in the water, swimming. The old man at least attracted the attention of the crew, who threw him a rope he didn't seem to want to catch. He struck out feebly for the opposite side of the dock. Marko didn't care if he drowned—Clavell deserved worse. His only thought was for Feodor. The man had shown Jehane no mercy. If he were to be crushed by the oncoming ship, Marko would not reach out a hand to save him or utter a single word or cry.

A minute ticked by, then another. Feodor gazed up at him,

his eyes blazing with hatred. "I cannot swim," he growled. He looked toward where his partner in crime had been in the water. Clavell had gone under, and the sailors on the ship called for help. One jumped in and dove repeatedly, but came up shouting that the man in the water was gone.

"Then you must meet your fate."

Marko straightened. With a speed he would not have thought possible, the ship shifted sideways toward the dock and slammed against the pilings. The giant timbers groaned and sighed, as if they had swallowed something vile.

They had. Feodor was crushed in his hiding place, but no one save Marko knew of the ignoble death of the man hidden between them.

A week later the men of the Pack returned to the dock to retrieve what was left of Feodor. The rats had got there first, and there must have been hundreds of them. There were nothing but gnawed bones to bury.

Marko wrote again to Kyril, making a separate page with the details of the deaths, which he would seal and fold inside the rest of the letter. His elder brother could decide whether and when to show the gruesome account to Vivienne. There had been no mention of the incident in the newspapers—men died often on the docks and common sailors, as Feodor and Clavell had pretended to be, warranted no notice.

He reread his missive, concentrating on the last page.

The decision to send our cousin Denis Somov into exile was made before this happened—I consider myself again satisfied that Denis was not guilty of murder. The letter that went with him to Russia, which you have by now, gave an account of a crime nearly as shocking. For the sake of that young lady's reputation, I did not mention her name and will not do so now. She is doing well, or so I hear, but her mother keeps her at home. Neither I nor Severin are permitted to call upon her, as her mother assigns part of the blame for her daughter's near-ruin to us. But no one knows of the matter—only the shop's clerk, a Mr. Tait, is at large, and he struck me as a craven sort, unlikely to ever show his face again.

As far as Denis, I assume that our men brought him to you before the journey inland to Siberia and permanent exile, so you have judged him for yourself.

My dear brother . . . to be a leader under such circumstances was a test which in some ways I failed, at least at the beginning. I cannot blame Severin—I had fallen in love with her on the night I saw her. It took Braykbone's warning and his edict to stay away from women before I remembered the solemn responsibility you had charged me with. Forgive me, Kyril. I wanted to do better . . .

There was more. He refused to edit the emotional words of apology or deny his own shortcomings. Kyril would judge him too.

Several weeks later, the second letter arrived in Russia. Kyril unfolded it, setting aside the sealed page inserted within and reading the other pages without comment. It was as Marko had said: Denis Somov had come through Archangel and gone with the guards assigned to him to the frozen wastes where he would live out his days alone.

Kyril longed to be back in London, and to reassure Marko that he had done the best he could with no brothers of the closest blood to help. Kyril was not sure that he could have acquitted himself as well as Marko had done on his own. He handed the letter to Vivienne at last.

She read each page carefully, looking up with tears in her eyes at one point. "So Lukian survived," she said.

"In a way."

Vivienne looked down at the sleeping baby in the cradle beside her. "You have another uncle, little one. Ghostly, but an uncle all the same."

"Ah, my dear—" said Kyril, breaking into a sad smile. "It is a strange world that we of the Pack live in. Between one realm and the next."

Vivienne rose and went to him. "I would not have it any other way, my dear husband."

He pulled her on his lap and kissed her very thoroughly, caressing her thighs while he did through the folds of her dress. "I love you more than ever, you know," he murmured into her ear.

"Hmm," she said. "I think we may soon have another wedding to celebrate. When I held the letter, I could see Severin. I believe Marko truly does love her."

"Like us? Forever after?"

"You will have to ask him that, Kyril."

He stroked her back. "Go Pack. We must return to London."

Vivienne threw her arms around his neck and hugged him hard. "Nothing would make me happier."

EPILOGUE

Marko was not sure if the point was worth making, but he would have to, sooner or later. "How can you want me? I am a man adrift. I have lost faith in the blood bond of the Pack."

"It still means something, Marko. Surely it does."

"Not to those who corrupted it."

"But you are not like them and you never will be. You are brave and loyal and—"

"Flawed."

"Perhaps. So are we all."

"I suppose you are right, Severin. Some more than others, certainly. Denis and Feodor were fully blooded members of the Pack, but they strayed far from its law."

She continued to walk with him through the physick garden, taking one path and then another. "It is tactful of you not to mention Jehane. She still has not explained everything about her involvement in the matter."

He shook his head. "She had the bad luck to know Feodor— and she was not quite as wary as she should have been. In the end, she did everything she could."

"I suppose so." Severin heaved a sigh. "And now she is off to the continent with her colonel."

"What happened to Charlie?"

Severin smiled slightly. "Oh dear. He introduced Jehane to the colonel, who commands Charlie's regiment."

"I see. Well, your sister lives her life on her own terms."

"She always has," Severin said thoughtfully.

Marko stopped and looked down at a plant, frowning. "What is that doing here?"

"It is some kind of herb."

"It is wolf's-bane, my dear."

Severin looked at it a little more closely. "Does it work to repel men like you?"

"Indeed," he said indignantly. "Why would you want to?"

"I am only teasing, Marko. I do not like you in such a gloomy mood," she laughed. "But I promise you that I will not plant it in our garden."

"Are you planning one?" He looked down at her fondly. "It is hard to imagine you grubbing in the dirt with a trowel and getting muddy."

"But the flowers will be worth it."

"I hope so. Well, I had better see to my investments. Levshin and Antosha are tutoring me in the dullest aspect of leadership: accounting. If gardening becomes your new passion, I expect that the prices of tulip bulbs will rise."

"You do indulge me, Marko," she said happily.

"I want to. And I am glad that you are thinking of growing things and blooming plants. There has been enough death about us to last me for a long lifetime."

He brought her to a halt and enfolded her in his arms. Severin looked up at him with joy in her eyes. It was a measured joy—she had been through too much to feel otherwise and her time of healing was not over.

"I was going to ask," he began, "if you would want . . . hmm. I am not quite sure how to say this."

"Just say it."

He nodded. "I will. But may I kiss you first?"

"Of course." She turned her face up to his and he put his hands over her cheeks to position her correctly, trying to avoid the sides of her bonnet.

"Damned inconvenient," he murmured. "Why must you wear this enormous thing?"

"It is a blustery day," Severin said primly. Then she smiled. "At least it will provide a little privacy."

"I suppose so." He gazed into her amber eyes and brushed her cheek lovingly with his thumb. "But I think that people passing by will assume that I am kissing you."

She put her hand to the bow and yanked out the knot, swinging the bonnet by its ribbons. Her hair fell down and was tossed by the breeze. "I don't care if they see."

Marko laughed and drew her back against him. "Very good."

He gave her a tender kiss that warmed her down to her booted toes.

"Well done, Marko," she said when he was finished. He looked very pleased with himself. "Now what was it you were having so much trouble saying?"

"Oh." He straightened his lapels, which she had been clutching during the kiss. "Yes. Back to that. I was wondering if you wanted to spend that long lifetime I was talking about . . ." He trailed off and gave her a speculative look.

"Yes?"

"Well, with me." He straightened himself up very tall as Severin gazed at him, dumbstruck.

"Are you asking me to marry you, Marko?"

"I am."

He stood there waiting and she stood there drinking him in.

The collar of his overcoat was flipped up against the cold and his hair was tousled in the breeze. He glowed with ruddy masculine health and handsomeness. She could not quite believe that such a man was hers to have and to hold.

"If you say yes, you will make me the happiest man on earth."

The sweetness of the look in his eyes was enough to shout her answer. But she didn't.

"Please say yes," he added nervously.

"Oh, Marko," she whispered. She looked at him with loving wonder. "When have I ever said no to you?"

"Often! Is that a yes? For God's sake, woman, just say the word!"

"Yes!" she shouted, flinging her bonnet away on the breeze.

The story continues.
Here's a sensual advance look
at Noelle Mack's WICKED: THE PACK OF ST. JAMES,
coming in March 2009 from Brava.

Masterful, seductive, and very much in demand, Semyon Taruskin does not deny his reputation as a lover. But one woman alone has enchanted him: the seemingly innocent and bewitching Angelica Harrow. He would risk his own life to protect hers, for Angelica lives in fear of one who betrayed her, a notorious rake who has disappeared under mysterious circumstances. Was the man murdered? Or transformed into a different—and far more malevolent—entity?

For her love, Semyon will reveal his supernatural powers in a lethal battle for dominance of London's private hells. The last man standing shall claim Angelica—and Semyon's passion for Angelica is proof that the wildest blood runs hottest . . .

"Angelica . . . come to me." Semyon scarcely dared to touch her, although the woman he desired so hotly was not two feet away. She had taken down her hair and stood so still that her raven tresses seemed to be made of black glass, tumbling between her shoulders in a motionless waterfall that heightened the whiteness of her extraordinary skin. The gown she wore bared nearly all of her bosom. He had glimpsed that much under her cloak when he'd waylaid her leaving the ball.

To which he had not been invited.

She had permitted him a brief conversation, then given her hand to the strapping footman who helped her into her sedan chair. Effectively and rather rudely dismissing Semyon. He had not followed her then. No, he had taken pains to arrive at her Belgravia address at least an hour later, where he had persuaded her manservant to bring up his card to her and waited upon the topmost stair for her answer like any lovesick swain. But Semyon had not been entirely surprised when the servant bade him enter five minutes later. He had given her the utmost in physical pleasure on their one night together; she would naturally understand that he wished to do so again.

Would she turn around, he might glance downward and see her pretty nipples in the tiny frill that adorned her decolletage.

"No," she whispered at last.

Semyon gave a slight start. He had almost forgotten that he'd asked her to come to him. Admiring her fine figure and the way her gown narrowed at her waist, then fell in sensuous folds over her womanly bottom was making his cock hard and his mind soft. Since she wasn't looking, he adjusted his stiffened member discreetly inside the soft leather breeches that kept it pressed back. He cleared his throat. "Are you still angry?"

She made no reply.

Undoubtedly she was, Semyon thought with a sigh. Well. Then he would have to break through the odd reserve that had sprung up between them in the last several days, and attempt to placate her. He closed the distance between them with one stride and reached out, just touching the rounded, sweetly warm flesh of her upper arms.

Flesh that another man had lately touched, because another man had been dancing with her.

Not him.

The thought troubled him, but he stroked and soothed her all the same. Then he felt Angelica tremble, a feeling that seemed to him to have arisen deep within her body.

Ah. So what he was doing was having an effect. Excellent. He had the very great advantage of being completely alone with her.

Whoever she had been dancing with was far away. Semyon hoped the damned fellow had been jostled by clumsy couples on the crowded floor and compelled to fend off other men, bowing before her for the privilege of holding Angelica's gloved hand and stepping through a few measures, before being pushed aside by yet more men.

The ball had been given by Angelica's best friend, the dissolute Lady Brodie, a Scots noblewoman with a reputation for being wild. It was strange that he, Semyon, should have been excluded from the Brodie mansion in Mayfair. But then, her ladyship had been irked that her interest in him had not been rewarded in kind.

Indeed, from the moment Semyon had seen Angelica, he'd not wanted any other woman.

Her trembling increased. He moved his caressing hands from her arms to her waist, clasping her lightly. Then he smoothed her gown over the sensual curves of her hips . . . then her bottom. Then he lifted the material but only by an inch or two. Just enough to see that she had slipped off her shoes before he arrived upstairs and wore only stockings on her pretty feet.

Her white heels were visible and so was the delicate, decorative clocking on the ankles of her stockings. Semyon was not sure where to begin. And then, suddenly, Angelica turned around, seizing her gown in her own hands and pulling it from his grasp. Slowly, with due regard for his state of arousal, she lifted it much higher than he would have dared . . .